The Foster Daughter

ALSO BY SONYA BATEMAN

STANDALONES
He Came Back For My Daughter
The Husband Killer
The Realtor
The Foster Daughter

THE
FOSTER
DAUGHTER

SONYA BATEMAN

Joffe Books, London
www.joffebooks.com

First published in Great Britain in 2024

Cover art by Nick Castle

ISBN: 978-1-83526-790-5

To Andrew and Josh, for putting up with me every time I said "I swear I'm almost done with this" . . . when I was definitely not almost done with this. I love you so much more than I can say.

PROLOGUE

Five years ago

I don't know how I'm still alive.

The last thing I remember is being in my hotel room at the conference in Philly, answering my phone that shouldn't have been ringing at one in the morning. Hearing something . . . impossible.

Now, I'm shoving my car into a non-parking space in the tiny lot at Upstate Emergency Room in downtown Syracuse. It's been three hours and change, though the drive here should have taken almost four.

I can't remember a single second between that nightmarish phone call and now.

Somehow, I managed to bring my purse. It's the only thing in the car with me — no suitcases, no work material, none of the equipment from my presentation. Everything is still at the hotel three hundred miles away, and I couldn't care less.

I grab my purse strap and propel myself out of the car, sprinting for the ER entrance. My limbs are screaming; my head is shrieking like a brass band. My eyes are on fire. The

1

only thing keeping me on my feet is the desperate hope that there's been some kind of monstrous misunderstanding. One big fuck-up of a mistake. It *has* to be a mistake.

The automatic doors seem to take forever to open. When there's enough space, I dash through and nearly collide with a second set of doors that don't move at all. I'm looking around wildly for a button or an intercom, about to start banging on the glass, when a tinny voice says, "Ma'am, I need to see some ID."

I whirl toward the sound to find a security guard in a navy-blue uniform behind a sheet of Plexiglas to my right. Her face is impassive, the expression of a woman who's seen hundreds of frantic people trying to get through those doors and will not break the rules for any of them.

"Please. My name is Katrina Martin." I scramble for my purse, my hands shaking as I try to unzip it. My heart thrums, pounding out *hurry-hurry-hurry*, as if my speed will change anything. "My daughter—"

I can't finish the sentence. I won't believe it. I *won't*.

The security guard's features relax, but only a fraction. "ID, please."

"Okay. Okay." I finally yank the zipper open and fumble around for my wallet. Instead of trying to fish my license from behind the plastic pocket, I flip the bifold open and shove it awkwardly into the scoop tray under the barrier. "Please," I say. "They told me . . . I just drove all the way here from Philadelphia. It was for work. I've never left her overnight before. Somebody got it wrong, didn't they? She's only five years old. Where is she?"

Something in the woman's face changes then. An unbearably heavy flash of sympathy that strikes me in the chest like a lightning bolt.

Suddenly, I can't breathe.

The second set of doors opens, and I stumble through them without bothering to retrieve my wallet. Several sharp gasps of air come in, but they won't go out. Around the corner, behind the guard booth, a handful of people in the waiting area stare at me. One of them is a uniformed police officer.

The security guard emerges from the back of the booth and nods, and the officer starts toward me. "Mrs. Martin?"

It's real. Oh, God, this is really happening.

I'm getting dizzy, on the verge of passing out. I have to breathe. I close my eyes and pound my chest. Once, twice, a third time. Finally, the air rushes from my lungs. I wobble on my feet, panting as I force my eyes open.

The officer is in front of me now, pity mingling with concern in his gaze. "Ma'am, do you need medical attention?"

I shake my head hard. "My daughter," I say. "Where . . . ?"

A distant part of me keeps trying to return to the phone call, to the questions that still have no answers. Questions about Tyler, about Lynette. Where are they? How could this happen? *What* happened?

"Mrs. Martin, I need you to come with me," the officer says.

There's a bronze nameplate on his pocket. It says VERITAS. *Truth.* That means truth, doesn't it? His name is Truth. Officer Truth.

I don't want it to be. I am desperate for none of this to be true.

"Please take me to my daughter," I whisper.

After a beat, he says, "Come with me, ma'am."

He doesn't say he will. I'm cognizant enough to realize that, at least.

A hand settles gently on my elbow. The officer doesn't say anything more, but somehow, my feet respond to the careful encouragement, and I'm walking. First beside him as we cross the waiting room, then behind him after we reach a heavy door that buzzes and unlocks when he stops in front of it.

Beyond the locked entrance is a dimly lit hallway with doors on either side. Most of them are closed, though I can see one partway open, down on the right. A cone of soft yellow light spills from the angled doorway like a spotlight.

Is my daughter in there? I want to ask, but not a word passes my lips. There's an eerie stillness inside me, an empty calm like the eye of a hurricane, because the part of me that knows this is not a nightmare or a mistake is overtaking the part that insists on denying reality.

It's a frozen, suspended moment, and I want to stop. To stay in this tiny cushion of time where I know I can't go back, but I also don't want to go forward. The other side of the storm waits ahead, and it will be so much worse than the one I've fought through to get here.

Yet I'm still walking behind the officer, my feet following the directions my heart wants to refuse. We pass the open door, and though I don't glimpse anything inside the room, I hear someone weeping in there — great, wrenching sobs and moans that teem with the anguish of loss.

This is where they take you when the worst happens.

The thought makes my breath hitch hard, and I shudder and clench my teeth. I'm not sure why I'm trying so hard to hold it together. Don't I have every right to fall apart?

No! the desperately delusional part of my mind screams. *They're wrong. They have to be wrong!*

A massive swell of some cold emotion far worse than anxiety balloons within me, and as I did in the frantic drive up here, I blank out but apparently continue to operate. Because I'm suddenly somewhere else. A small waiting room, maybe, though the furniture looks far more comfortable than the plastic or vinyl chairs that waiting areas usually provide.

Officer Truth is in here with me. So are two other officers and a man seated in one of the chairs, slumped so far forward that his head hangs past his knees. I can't see his face, but I know him instantly.

"Tyler?" The word emerges like a plea, begging my husband to tell me it's not true. Yet there's another emotion behind it, barely discernible in my plaintive tone. A hot knife of anger slides through my overtaxed brain.

4

This thing, this *impossible* thing, happened on *his* watch.

I'd worried about myriad things, leaving Tyler overnight with Marisol for the first time. He was a good dad, and there was nothing he wouldn't do for our daughter — there were just a lot of things he *didn't* do regularly. So, I'd suspected that he'd feed her nothing but fast food. That he'd let her stay up way past her bedtime and watch movies she shouldn't be watching. That she wouldn't have a bath or brush her teeth all weekend. That her hair would be a tangled disaster when I got home.

Nowhere on my list of concerns was that my healthy, well-behaved, careful, beautiful five-year-old daughter might be . . .

"Tyler!" I startle myself with a hoarse shout as I jerk toward him. "What happened?"

The knife in my brain cuts deeper as he slowly raises his head. He wasn't even the one who called me. The police did. I had to hear this news from a complete stranger who wouldn't give me any details over the phone when I was three hundred miles from home.

My husband finally looks at me. His eyes are swollen and shockingly red. Beyond the deep pink of excessive crying, almost crimson. Like blood. He can barely meet my gaze as he struggles to keep those eyes open. His face is puffy, and a runner of drool hangs from the corner of his mouth.

"Kat?" he slurs, then blinks several times. "I dunno. I dunno what . . . happened."

Oh, my God. Is he fucking *drunk*?

My rage is instant and complete. Everything seems to turn as red as Tyler's eyes, and I'm so close to lunging at him that I actually jerk forward an inch or so, then stop short.

His hands are hanging between his legs, elbows propped on his knees.

There are handcuffs on his wrists.

Why is he handcuffed?

I whirl toward the officer who brought me into this room. "*Where is my daughter?*" I hiss at him. "Somebody tell me what the hell happened. Right now."

". . . need to see her. Let go of me! *Mom!*"

Running footsteps accompany the voice from the hallway beyond the open door. In the space of a heartbeat, I experience the purest, most achingly beautiful joy I've ever felt in my life, followed by a cruel plunge into the worst stomach-clenching horror.

That's not Marisol's voice.

Lynette bursts into the room, somehow looking more miserable than Tyler. My seventeen-year-old foster daughter's cheeks are streaked with black from her makeup, and it looks like she's yanked some of her own hair out. Strands of it are still twisted around the fingers of her left hand, and what appears to be one of her gel nails is tangled in the locks near her ear. The skin beneath her eyes and around her nose is bright red and inflamed. There's a bruise on her forehead.

And I hate her. I hate her for being alive when my *real* daughter is . . . not.

The feeling only lasts for a split second before guilt flames through me, flushing my body all the way to my scalp. I'm sickened that the thought even occurred to me, and I almost blurt an apology. Considering the way I grew up, I should absolutely know better.

But before I can react at all, Lynette grabs my arm with both hands and starts pulling me toward the door with a ferocity I've never seen her display. I stumble and nearly fall before I take a few steps toward her to correct myself.

Something about her behavior terrifies me in ways I can't define, though it's not her I'm afraid of. I feel my world shattering, all the light and color going out of it, and I know that nothing will ever be good again. I will be irrevocably changed for the worse. Plunged into eternal darkness.

When Lynette finally speaks, she confirms my fears.

"Get away from him!" she shrieks, her wild gaze darting from me to Tyler. "Mom, he killed her. *He murdered Marisol!*"

CHAPTER 1

Present day

My daughter is screaming.

The sound wakes me — or at least, I think it does. I can't move, can't breathe, can't see a thing. An echo of that scream, the frantic, wordless, high-pitched cry for help, lingers in my ears. Or maybe it's in my mind, because it couldn't have been my daughter.

Am I awake?

As soon as the thought crosses my mind, I know what's happening. I haven't had an episode in years, but it's back with a vengeance.

Hello, darkness, my old friend.

My brain races to remember the steps. *Breathe.* That's the first one. For an instant, I don't think I can. Panic swells as I envision never taking another breath again, wonder how long I can live without oxygen. My heart races with fear.

I can feel my heart. That means I can breathe.

Air rushes into my lungs in a tearing gasp, almost before I realize I'm inhaling. I seize the tiny thread of control and force myself to exhale slowly. Then again. Bit by bit, the thunder of my heart calms, and terror unravels until I'm floating in a sea of nothing.

Move.

I need an anchor, a reminder that I am a physical being capable of controlling my body. I push my thoughts outward, imagining them racing through my veins, lighting them up in the dark. They glow crimson, like the blood that fills them. And I follow the branching path to a finger, the right index. *This is mine*, I tell myself. *I will point at the ceiling.*

I feel a twitch, distant and untethered. But I remember to breathe. I try again, and again, until the pathway races green from my fingertip to my brain. And I am pointing.

Another finger twitches, then a third. I wiggle them. My hand clenches weakly, and I feel the sheet beneath me as it brushes my palm.

Finally, a fist.

Green light floods my body, and I collapse into a sprawl, panting as my muscles unlock and my vision begins to sharpen. Yet the panic lingers, waiting to overtake me again, because something is still not right. I'm not where I should be.

This is not my bedroom.

Before the haze can envelop me again, I force myself to be logical. To reason with my brain. *It's sleep paralysis,* I tell myself firmly. *Nothing is happening to you. Just wake up.* But the anxiety keeps growing.

Then, I remember the countdown my therapist taught me.

Five things you can see.

I see fabric. Puffy blue fabric at the corner of my eye that might be a cushion. I see . . . carpeting? Yes, a dark-striped runner on a hardwood floor. Hardwood floor: that's three things.

Wait. I don't have hardwood. Do I? But the carpet runner is so familiar.

Two more things to see. My hand dangling, my fingertips less than a foot from the floor. A wooden leg that belongs to a coffee table. It's a living room, and I'm lying on a couch. But it's not my couch. Not my living room. And yet it is.

I am home. Not the home where I live, but the home where I grew up. And for reasons I can't pinpoint in my murky state, the realization spikes me with fresh fear.

I can't deal with that now.

Four things you can feel.

The plump arm cushion of my parents' living room sofa, comfortable enough to act as a pillow — the blue fabric I saw. Damp sweat along my back from being pressed against the couch, and across my skull from the nightmares I thought I'd left behind and my efforts to regain control. The breeze from the ceiling fan above, shivering my scalp as the sweat cools.

The butterflies in my stomach, a frenzy of motion as I anticipate remembering the awful reason I'm here. My mind rebels against the idea.

Fabric, carpet, hardwood, hand, leg.

Cushion, sweat, breeze, butterflies.

Three things you can hear.

I hear a faint, rhythmic squeaking as the ceiling fan dips at a certain point with every rotation. It's familiar, comforting. I used to fall asleep out here to that sound. My dad kept claiming he wanted to fix it, but I told him—

No. I'm not going there yet. Two more things.

I hear *shush, shush, shush* as if it's being whispered from inside my skull. It's my heart beating in my ears, slowing while I recognize my surroundings even as the anticipation of total recall makes it pound harder. I hear *tick, tick, tick* from the grandfather clock in the dining room.

Fabric, carpet, hardwood, hand, leg.

Cushion, sweat, breeze, butterflies.

Squeak-shush-tick.

Two things you can smell.

A faint, sour odor from my damp armpit. The whisper of fabric softener from the clothes I just washed.

One thing you can taste.

9

Acid rising up my throat at the idea of waking up. Of facing a reality I don't want to accept.

Again.

As I finish the countdown, the anxiety dissipates like someone is turning down its dimmer knob. Deep, aching sorrow and guilt take its place. The feeling is so similar to what I experienced after Marisol that for a moment, I'm back in that hospital room, with Lynette screaming and yanking me away from my handcuffed husband.

Ex-husband. The one thing I did right in the past five years was initiate divorce proceedings before that sick son of a bitch who'd fooled me into thinking he was human set foot in his first courtroom.

Tyler Martin was another pressing issue I'd have to deal with soon. When I heard what was going on with him a few weeks ago, I discovered the true meaning of *apoplectic*. It's one of those emotions you can't really understand until you've experienced it. But then something else happened — something far more important than the shit stain I married.

And now, here I am. Dealing with the fallout after I failed yet another person I loved.

I groan and shiver as I shift onto my back and stare at the ceiling fan above the couch. I really shouldn't have fallen asleep. It was already after seven when I laid down, hoping to put a movie on and forget for a little while. Now, darkness presses against the outside of the windows, and the soft glow of the end table lamp doesn't reach beyond the dead eye of the television I never turned on.

My phone rests on the coffee table. I snag it, check the time, and groan again. It's almost eleven. There's no way I'm getting a decent night's sleep tonight.

Especially in this eerily silent house that used to be so full of life.

I stand and slip my phone in my pocket, then cross the room to turn the overhead light on. As the glow floods every corner of the room, my attention is drawn to the wall on the far side, the one with the fireplace in it. The one I've avoided looking directly at since I got here.

But suddenly, I can't look away from it. All those faces. All those names.

All twenty-seven of my brothers and sisters.

My parents always knew they wanted multiple children. They planned to have their own, but after I was born, Mom couldn't get pregnant again no matter what they tried. It only took one long, drawn-out, and failed fertility attempt for her to decide she didn't want to go through that again. So instead, they decided to become foster parents.

They planned so much, right from the beginning. They would take in older kids, ten and up, the ones who had far less of a chance at permanent placements or adoptions. They would pay everyone equal attention, make sure no one felt the 'bio kid' was getting special treatment. Whoever was here would be family.

That's why they created the Hearth Wall.

Everyone who stayed in this house, including me and my parents, went onto the wall. For each person, there was a sheet of paper with their full name at the top, then a Polaroid picture of them. Beneath the picture was a mini-profile. *Call Me, Likes, Dislikes,* and *Fun Fact.* Finally, there was a painted handprint under each paper in a rainbow of colors, since each child got to pick what color they wanted to use.

I made mine green. I was six when I filled out my little profile, a few days before the first foster arrived. So, it read:

Katrina Gray
Call Me: Kat
Likes: My camera
Dislikes: Sausage (yuck!)
Fun Fact: I wish I had wings

Little-girl me didn't really understand the Fun Fact category.

There are so many faces up there. Whether you stayed for years or only a few days, you always got to join the Hearth

Wall. Become part of the family. I'm so proud of my mom and dad. They did so much good in the world.

I've dropped the ball on their legacy.

On the wall after my parents and me is the first foster who moved in with us. Michelle DiMarco. She was fifteen when she arrived, eighteen when she left. I remember my six-year-old self being in awe of this teenager, this loud, brash, opinionated woman-child with her dyed hair and tight clothes, her expressive brown eyes and all the makeup she wore. I was fascinated when she showed me her bras — she had a dozen, all pretty and lacy in so many colors.

I didn't understand at the time that she'd been forced to grow up fast. She was a kid who seemed like an adult to me.

I read the profile she'd filled out carefully in fancy bubble letters.

Michelle DiMarco
Call Me: Mickey
Likes: World peace
Dislikes: Fakers
Fun Fact: I can do a split

Her handprint is an electric purple, only slightly faded with age.

My gaze skims the wall, taking in photos and scrawled words that whisper through the years and target my heart. There's Jackson Green, the first boy who stayed with us after three girls came in and one left. He wanted to be called Crusher or Ranger, though we ended up calling him Jax. He liked 'middy-evil weapons' and disliked 'sleeping,' and his fun fact was that he trained dragons in secret. Kind of a weird kid, but I remember enjoying the stories he told.

I keep going, looking at them all. A few I only vaguely remember or don't recall at all, but we had several short, temporary stays. As I get toward the end, the most recent, I remember a lot more. Alina Cruz, likes books, dislikes splinters. Drew

Seaborn, likes smiling and playing outside, dislikes snow and really big snakes.

Naomi Young. Her Call Me line says *Don't*. Likes is blank. Next to Dislikes, she wrote: *You*.

And her Fun Fact? *I hate this house*.

My mother called Naomi a 'challenge.' Most of the time, I called her the enemy, because she had it out for me and everyone else from day one.

I shiver involuntarily and move on to the last profile. Evelyn Wells, call me Evie, likes Taco Tuesdays, dislikes having cold feet. For her Fun Fact, she wrote 'I'm too ugly to love.'

Evelyn struggled with so many things. My parents kind of bent the rules about equal treatment when she arrived, because she really did need extra attention, but none of us minded. We all felt bad for Evie. All of us except Naomi, of course.

She arrived the year before I graduated high school, and she was already doing a lot better when I left for college. Whenever I checked in at home, my parents told me she was continuing to improve.

Which was why it came as a shock when she ran away at fifteen.

Evie pulling a runner was the beginning of the end of an era. Within two weeks of her disappearance, we lost Mom for good, and the remaining fosters were removed from the care of my grief-stricken father. And then there were two.

Now, there's only me.

Two days ago, beloved local meteorologist and minor celebrity Joe Gray gave his last weather report. At 9:03 a.m., during his fourth on-the-hour weather spot, hundreds or maybe thousands of viewers — including me — watched my father collapse and die on live television.

Yesterday, I nearly gave myself alcohol poisoning in an attempt to summon the courage to leave my house in North Syracuse. What had been *our* house, the place where my daughter once existed. The place I'd barely set foot outside since I lost her.

This morning, I made the half-hour drive to Fulton, my childhood hometown, and walked into my parents' house for the first time since Marisol's funeral. Where I promptly collapsed and cried for what felt like hours.

Of all the many people I've failed in my life, I let my father down the most.

I drag my attention away from the Hearth Wall and head out of the living room, through the dining room to the kitchen. There, I grab a bottle of beer from the fridge out of the six-pack I bought earlier and settle at the kitchen table with it. I tell myself there won't be a repeat of yesterday's booze fest. I'm only hoping that a little alcohol will help me sleep after such a long, unexpected nap.

I've already decided to crash in my childhood bedroom while I'm here. The foster bedrooms will only make me feel worse, and I can't bear to set foot in my parents' room.

With the beer cracked, I grab my phone and tap the Facebook icon. There's something I should do before I try to go to bed. I swipe to my groups and open the Fulton Grays page.

Though I've turned myself into a recluse over the past five years, at least I managed this.

I started the group about six months after my daughter's death — my daughter's *murder* — when I realized I'd barely spoken more than four or five words to an actual person since my last agonizing court appearance in Tyler's trial. I worked from home, interacting with clients through email. I had groceries and the occasional DoorDash delivered. I texted with my dad rather than calling him. And even then, I didn't see that changing in the near future. Every day was a dark day, a struggle to find a reason to get out of bed.

Yet part of me knew I needed some form of human interaction. I still couldn't tolerate being with physical people, but there was Facebook.

I started by finding and reaching out to Mickey DiMarco, my first foster sister, who by then was in her early forties to my mid-thirties and still seemed as brash and larger-than-life as the wild teenager I knew. Chatting with her, catching up with her life, was an unexpected balm to my splintered soul.

So I looked for more foster siblings online and created a group where we could all stay in touch. There were twenty-two members total, including me . . . and Dad, who'd loved the idea and participated frequently. We'd even managed to find Evie Wells, the runaway — living in Florida and doing well after some troubled years.

I'd managed to post to the group about Dad after I forced myself to make the necessary arrangements. To let them know the when and where of the services. Now, I have to respond to what I know will be a slew of heartbreaking condolences.

My post has seventeen care reactions and thirty-eight comments.

I'm not sure I can bring myself to respond to them all, or if I'm even capable of doing anything beyond tapping the little heart. Still, I open the comment thread and start reading.

The first response is from Evie.

Evelyn Wells: *No, not Daddy Joe!!! Kat, I'm so, so sorry. I can't even get up there right now, it's too short notice to take time off. I wish I could hug you!*

There's a reply to her from Mickey: *Oh, honey, same. Sending hugs down to you, too.* The two of them never met — over the fourteen years my parents fostered kids, Mickey was the first in and Evie was the last — but they've become online buddies through the group.

Mickey's comment on the main post is next.

Mickey Dee: *I just can't believe it. I was watching when he fell, and it still doesn't seem real. Kat, honey, I love you. This SUCKS.*

My eyes sting, and I let the tears fall as I skim more comments from my foster siblings.

Blake Mulder: *God, how awful. He was a great man. Rest in peace, Mr. G. I'll try to make the funeral if I can.*

Mary P. Lovell: *My heart is breaking. All my love to you, Kat.*

Jackson Green: *So sorry for your loss.*

Nevaeh Davidson: *I was watching! Crying so hard RN. He was the best foster dad. Love you guys so much.*

Alina Cruz: *I don't even have words. How could this happen?! He was in better shape than me! Kat, you know I'll be there. I'm so damn sorry.*

I have to stop reading after Alina's comment when a harsh sob steals my breath. She's right — Dad was in excellent health. He'd even been dating a significantly younger woman for the past four years or so. I'd felt guiltily relieved when he told me about Clara Crawford, because in my grief-warped mind, if he had someone to spend time with, that meant I was kind of off the hook for quality interactions.

I always told myself I'd have plenty of time to spend with Dad. Like maybe when he retired.

But now, "too late" had arrived with unyielding finality.

I'd been a terrible, selfish daughter, and I could never apologize for my behavior.

Shivering, I scroll back to the top of the comments. I can't take reading any more tonight. I'll slap a heart on everything and try again to face my epic failures in the morning.

As my finger hovers over the react button on Evie's comment, my phone pings with a notification. A new message on my Facebook business page. I've already announced that I'm taking some personal time and closed comments on all my posts there, but this is a direct message. I want to ignore it, but I decide to reply to whoever it is once and say I'm not available until at least next week. Especially if it's a new client inquiry.

I tap to open the message, and my blood runs cold.

Daddy Dearest: *Your father was not the man you think he was, Katrina. I know what he did. Soon, you will, too.*

"What the *fuck*!" I gasp and drop my phone on the table like it's a snake trying to bite. The horrific words remain, impassively shrouded behind the glass.

Is this some kind of sick joke? It has to be. Some anonymous asshole hiding behind a screen who saw the news and just likes to watch the world burn, trying to prod me for a reaction. It's not hard to find me online, nor the fact that meteorologist Joe Gray is my father, and my business page is public.

My first instinct is to block and report the disgusting little troll, but I decide not to. The more bullshit he spouts, the easier it will be to get someone in authority to take action. Instead, I screenshot the message, then close the app.

Now I'm furious, and I let myself feel it as I return the untouched beer to the fridge and head upstairs to bed. The anger is easier than the complex, painful knot of grief that will resurface when I'm spent.

And I've got plenty of anger to go around.

CHAPTER 2

It feels like I've only been asleep for about five minutes when I hear the screams.

This time, I know I'm not dreaming.

Awareness floods me instantly, and I bolt upright in bed. A little girl is shrieking in fear. It sounds like it's coming from directly outside.

I throw off the blanket, stumble to the window, and yank the curtains back.

Moonlight reveals the spacious back yard my childhood bedroom overlooks, though the view has changed drastically. Gone are the swing set, the sandbox, the picnic table and propane grill, the small aboveground pool. The signs of a happy family with happy children.

Now, the six-foot chain-link fence encloses a flagstone patio with a few Adirondack loungers and Dad's tool shed in the far-right corner, instead of the far left where it used to be. An empty expanse of perfect grass spreads between them. Dense, neatly trimmed holly bushes grow along the back fence, nearly reaching the top.

As I stare, alert for anything to explain what I heard, I catch a flash of movement. Something pale beneath the thick, dark greenery next to the shed. There's a space of stillness, silence, in which even the old house seems to hold its breath.

Suddenly, the bushes rustle and jerk violently in the place where I saw the pale flicker.

The scream comes again, this time broken and breathless, each segment pushed out like a woman in labor — *aaaaah-aaaaah-aaaaah-aaaaaaaahhh!* Yet it's clearly a child, the eerie sound made more disturbing by the muffled quality through the glass.

And a foot kicks out from beneath the hedge. Tiny, dirt-smudged, heartbreaking.

I stop thinking. I whirl away from the window and race across the room, grabbing my bathrobe before I yank the door open. As I race down the stairs, shoving my arms into the robe, I realize the back yard floodlight should have come on. It was on a motion sensor.

On the first floor, I whip around the banister and beeline for the back door. Through the living room, the den, the dining room. Into the kitchen, where I slow long enough to grab the flashlight Dad always keeps plugged in above the counter next to the coffee pot for emergencies.

I have a vague recollection of leaving my sneakers by the back door earlier today. But I don't see them there now, and I'm not going all the way back upstairs to grab a pair. I fling the door open and rush outside barefoot.

As I cross the patio, thumbing the flashlight on, something crunches beneath me. Bright pain slashes my foot, and I stumble and nearly fall. I bite back a scream and pan the beam back over the flagstones. Shattered glass, sprinkled and splashed with my blood. The floodlight bulb. It looks like it fell whole from the fixture, metal screw end and all.

How is that possible?

"Aaaah-aaaah-aaaah-*aaaaahhh!*" The cry sounds again, raspy but bright in the cool night air. The holly bushes rustle and jerk.

I wince and crouch, trying to pull the glass from my foot. "I'm coming, sweetheart," I call out, turning the flashlight toward the hedgerow.

The sound and motion stop abruptly.

My heart sinks. The kid must be terrified, and I don't blame her. "It's okay," I say soothingly. "I'm going to help you. Don't be scared."

There's no response. Not even a whisper.

Hurriedly, I pick out the two biggest shards from my flesh. Several small pieces are still embedded in my foot, but I can't worry about that now. I need to get to the girl. I have to save her. Save my daughter . . .

No. Not my daughter.

I squeeze my eyes shut briefly, pushing the images away, and lunge to my feet. As I limp as quickly as possible across the yard, directing my way with the light, the holly bush shivers. A soft whimper unfolds.

"It's going to be all right," I tell the child, keeping my voice gentle.

She doesn't respond or acknowledge me.

Finally, I reach the hedge and drop to my knees. "Okay, sweetheart," I say. "What happened? Are you stuck in there?" It's a pointless question, really. There's less than a foot of space between the ground and the thick wall of vegetation. She must've wedged herself in somehow.

I lean down and direct the flashlight under the bush.

Another breathy cry bursts from the small figure, coming in rapid bursts that stretch into an undulating, glottal wail. She starts thrashing again. I see her feet kicking out.

"Easy, easy," I soothe. "I'm going to get you out—"

The child's foot rams into my jaw, cutting me off with a startled yelp. Starbursts fill my vision. I hear the thump against my bone like a single drumbeat struck in the center of my brain.

She's still screaming. Mewling, really. Still jerking like a fish caught on a line.

I shift my head out of kicking range, then reach out and grab the nearest ankle. Not hard, but firmly enough to stop the leg from moving. My heart lurches at how cold her skin is. God, how long was she out here before I heard her? "I'm here to help you, okay? Please, try to hold still."

No words reply, but she falls silent and stops moving.

"Right. Here we go," I murmur. With my free hand, I bring the flashlight under the hedge and start inching toward the girl. I manage to get my head into the space and try to look up at her. I can't see much beyond that she's wearing something yellow. She's pinned between multiple stiff branches — it almost looks like she was trying to swim up through the hedge.

There's no way I can pull her out of there. She'll have to be cut out.

I exhale, long and slow. "Okay, sweetie. It's going to take a while, but we'll get you out of this nasty bush. Can you tell me your name?"

She doesn't respond.

"My name is Katrina. Kat," I tell her. "Maybe you can tell me yours when you're not stuck anymore. You must be uncomfortable, right?"

Nothing. She's probably too terrified to speak.

I bite my lip. I don't want to leave her alone, but I have to find something to get her out. At least the shed is right there, and the pruning shears should be inside it. The only problem is that it's locked, and the padlock key is inside the house.

At least, I hope it is.

"Listen, I'm going to grab a . . . tool to help us," I say, not wanting to use the word 'scissors' in case it scares her more. "I'll be right back for you."

Still, she says nothing. I hope she at least understands what I'm doing.

I ease myself back, pulling my head out first, then the flashlight. I give her ankle a gentle, reassuring squeeze before I let go and struggle upright. "I'll just be a minute."

I turn and start back toward the house, trying to ignore the pain in my foot. My jaw is still throbbing from the kick, and I'm pretty sure I'll have a sizable bruise there. But I need to help this child before I help myself.

Before I've taken more than a few steps away, the girl starts keening again.

"It's okay," I call back. "I promise I'm not leaving you there."

The sound doesn't stop. If anything, it gets louder.

My heart twinges, but I have to keep going.

I hustle as fast as possible back to the house, skirting the shattered bulb on the patio. Thankfully, the shed key is still where my father kept it for as long as I can remember — hanging from a nail in the wall, too high for kids to reach, beside Mom's framed Holly Hobby print that reads *No matter where I serve my guests, it seems they like my kitchen best.* I grab it and limp-rush back toward the shed.

The girl is sobbing now, the quiet sound more heartbreaking than her screams.

Though it doesn't seem to make a difference, I keep talking to her in a calming tone, explaining what I'm doing as I open the shed, find the pruning shears on the neat pegboard of Dad's tools, and start carefully snipping branches away. She seems to settle somewhat while the flashlight is on her. I have no idea how long it takes, but after what feels like hours of cutting and shifting, I'm finally able to see her.

And my chest tightens until I can't breathe.

Light-brown hair, terrified blue eyes pooled with tears. A pale-yellow pajama set with silver glitter stars. Four or five years old.

Marisol.

Before the panic and horror can set in, I force myself to look at her, to *really* look. Her hair is dark blonde, or maybe light brown. Her eyes are a paler blue. The heart-shaped face is similar, but the bone structure is different. She is not my daughter. She can't be.

She's a hurt, scared child, and she needs my help.

"Okay. We're almost done," I say, reaching for the biggest branch that's trapping her arm — the last impediment to movement. Her wide-eyed gaze remains on my face as I test the branch and determine she's likely to fall if I cut it without bracing her. "Can you put this arm around my neck?" I ask, nodding to her free arm.

She simply keeps staring at me.

Maybe she's in shock.

I take her hand and carefully position her arm around my neck. Before I can ask if she's able to hold on, her grip tightens without prompting, and I feel the smallest sense of relief. She's not talking, but at least she understands me.

She whimpers a few times while I slice through the last branch. When it snaps, her weight thumps against me. I drop the shears and hold her with both arms, backing away from the gaping, ragged hole in the hedge where she'd been trapped.

"We did it!" I smile as the child's face tips up toward me. It's smudged with dirt and tear-stained tracks, scratched and bleeding in several places. "Now, let's get you inside and check you over. Then we'll figure out where you belong."

She stares at me, silent and unblinking. Then, she wiggles in my arms as she tries to turn back toward the hedge.

A frown tugs at my lips. "What are you . . ." I trail off and look past her. There's something else in the bushes, caught above the divot I carved to get her out. The flashlight I left on the ground picks up snatches of dull white and orange, a faint shiny green.

I shift the girl to my hip and plunge a hand in, heedless of the scratching branches, until I feel something soft. It takes me a few minutes to extract the object. A stuffed calico cat with green jeweled button eyes. Worn but clearly well-loved, hand-stitched in a few places where it must have torn.

The girl lets out a wordless cry and reaches for the toy with one hand, the other still firmly clasped around my neck.

I hand it to her. She crushes it against her chest, then leans into me. Sobs rack her body.

Holding back a shiver, I turn and carry her back toward the house. She was trying to get to her toy, which she wouldn't have been able to reach from outside the hedge.

And it couldn't have gotten that deep into the bush on its own. Someone must have shoved the stuffed animal in there. Most likely the same someone who removed the floodlight bulb and broke it.

Whatever happened to this girl, it wasn't an accident.

CHAPTER 3

The girl still hasn't said a word.

She's sitting at the kitchen table, the bedraggled stuffed cat tucked under her arm and a plate of untouched Oreos in front of her. I looked her over when we came inside, and what I've seen doesn't tell a pretty story. She's scratched and banged up from her encounter with the hedge, but that's not all.

There are dark, possibly finger-shaped bruises around both her wrists.

With her not talking, I have no way to tell who she is or where she belongs. I'm certainly not going to start banging on doors at four in the morning. She needs medical attention, in case she's injured in a way I can't see, and I'll have to turn her over to the police.

I considered calling 911 right away and having them deal with this. But even the mere thought made me ashamed of myself — because it was selfish. For an instant, I wanted her to be someone else's problem, because she looks so much like Marisol that it hurts.

I can't do it, though. I won't turn her over to a fresh batch of strangers until I absolutely have to.

For now, I need to make a few quick preparations, then bring her to the emergency room. Fulton doesn't have a hospital, and the urgent care center isn't open yet. We'll have to drive to Oswego, about fifteen minutes away.

I tell her this as I'm hunting through the drawers for something to wrap my foot. She doesn't react one way or another, only stares at me with those big, watery, pale-blue eyes.

Finally, I find a kitchen towel and secure it in place with a couple of rubber bands. It still stings like hell, and I'll have to get it looked at because I can feel fragments of glass in there. Good thing we're going to the ER. I'm also glad it's my left foot, so I can still drive.

"Okay." I move in front of the girl and smile. "I'm going to grab a pillow and blanket for you, then we'll bundle into the car and go see a doctor who can help you. It looks like you're not hungry right now, and that's fine. Would you like something to drink?"

She's watching me, but she doesn't even try to speak.

"Tell you what. I'll get you a glass of milk, and you can drink it if you want to. Okay?"

Nothing.

I manage not to sigh as I walk past her toward the cabinet that holds the glasses. I'm sure it's not her fault that she isn't talking. She doesn't seem belligerent, angry, or uncooperative — just scared. Again, I think she must be in shock.

Opening the cabinet is another tiny blow to my system in a time that's been full of those. I haven't looked around the house much since I got here. I couldn't bring myself to. Still, I've noticed so many changes, from big ones like the back yard to small ones like this cabinet. It used to be filled with a bright, eclectic assortment of child-safe cups, fun chunky mugs, and plastic tumblers that would last through the rigors of multiple daily uses.

All that remain on the shelves are matching sets of glassware and coffee cups.

I would have known these things if I'd come home to see Dad at any point within the last five years.

My hand trembles as I reach for a glass, then change my mind and grab a mug. At least it has a handle, so it should be easier for the child to drink from. I know she's not a toddler and she can probably handle a big glass, but I want to keep things as simple as possible.

As I turn back toward the table, the mug slips from my shaking hand and shatters on the tile floor.

"Oh, I'm so sorry!" I say automatically, knowing the sound must have startled the girl. "Don't worry. I just dropped . . ."

I trail off and stare at the figure sitting at the kitchen table, her back to me. She hasn't moved at all.

But she *must* have heard the cup break.

"Hello?" I call toward her in a louder-than-normal voice. "Sweetheart, can you hear me?"

There's no reaction.

After a few seconds of internal debate, I raise my hands and clap them loudly, three times in rapid succession, my gaze fixed on the girl.

She doesn't flinch or turn.

Oh, no. Is she deaf?

Quickly, I grab the broom and dustpan from the nearby cupboard and sweep up the mess. The last thing either of us needs is more sharp objects embedded in feet. I lean the broom against the wall and carry the dustpan past her, toward the trash can beside the stove.

She watches me walk by, her expression slightly curious.

She has no idea what happened just now.

After I dispose of the mess, I pull out a chair and sit facing her. "Can you hear me at all, sweetie?" I ask, knowing the question is ridiculously stupid if she can't. I have to try, though.

Again, she watches me but says nothing.

I don't know sign language, and I have no idea if she does. She's so young, at the age where she'd probably just start

27

kindergarten in the fall a few months from now. But maybe we can communicate a few things if I try from the assumption that she can't hear anything.

"Okay." I inhale deeply, then release a slow breath. Keeping the girl's gaze, I cover my ears with both hands and shake my head, then point at her and assume a questioning expression.

She blinks, squints at me, then slowly nods.

I desperately hope that means she understood what I was trying to say and has answered with a yes.

"Great! We're getting somewhere," I say brightly. Then I point between me and her a few times and pantomime a steering wheel. "We're going to see a doctor," I announce, despite being almost positive now that she can't hear the words.

Her eyes flare wide, and she tries to reach across the table toward me with her free hand.

"What? What's wrong, sweetie?" I take her grasping hand, and she squeezes me as hard as she can and shakes her head.

Suddenly, I think I know what she's trying to say.

"I won't leave you," I tell her, pointing between us again. I lift her hand in mine and cover it with my other one. "We're both going. Together."

I'm not sure if she fully understands, but she offers a reluctant nod.

I try not to think about how we're finally getting somewhere. Because I know what will happen when we get to the emergency room. The police will get involved, and a social worker, and she'll be taken away from me. They'll either find the girl's parents or place her in temporary care. Judging by those bruises and the fact that she was somehow in my yard alone in the middle of the night, I'm guessing it will be the latter.

She's not going to like that. And I'm starting to think I won't, either.

* * *

28

There's almost no one in the emergency room when we arrive, and we only wait for about ten minutes before we're whisked into a room. Two nurses have come and gone, asking a flurry of questions while they settle the girl in the bed and me in a chair beside her with my foot propped on a stool. They've brought a juice box, crackers, and fruit snacks for the girl. For me, they offered coffee and ice water, which I accepted, and an array of granola bars, which I declined.

Even if I was hungry, I don't think I could eat anything.

We've also seen the doctor on call already. He entered not long after the nurses, looked us both over to make sure nothing immediate needed attention. After a few quick checks and more questions about the girl, not many of which I could answer, he said a nurse would be in to take care of my foot and that he had to order some tests for the child. He also mentioned he'd notify the police and the caseworker currently assigned to the hospital. So we have that to look forward to.

At least it's quiet for now.

A thick, pale-green curtain is drawn across the entrance to the room, and the lights are dimmed to encourage as much relaxation as possible. Unfortunately, I'm no stranger to this place. It's been years, but I've visited Oswego Hospital several times. As a patient, and as a family member of a patient.

The last time I was in a hospital . . .

I can't think about the last time right now. If I do, I'll never make it through this.

The little girl appears to have about as much appetite as me. She barely glances at the snacks, but she sips at the juice box, still clutching her cat as she gazes around the room with mild curiosity. She seems slightly more relaxed.

I'm not sure I can do the same.

As I'm trying to think of more ways to engage her, maybe by finding out whether she's been taught to read and write, the curtain whisks back halfway and a figure steps into the room. Male with a shock of orange hair, average height and build, dressed in a sweater and khakis. He's carrying a clipboard, and there's a lanyard around his neck with an ID badge, though it's twisted so the blank white back shows.

Before my taxed brain can recognize that there's something familiar about him, he stops and grins. "Kat Gray," he announces. "This is *not* how I wanted to bump into you again, but I'll take it."

I blink, trying to process him. Finally, something clicks in my head, and I experience the first trickle of happiness I've felt over the past few terrible weeks. "Oh, God. Drew," I reply, instinctively starting to get up for a hug before I remember my foot.

My brother looks fantastic.

He doesn't hesitate to cross the room, lean down, and hug me with one arm. When he steps back, his beaming expression dims. "I'm so sorry about Dad," he says. "That's lame, right? Honestly, I don't even know what to say."

"Thank you." I'm touched that he still calls the man Dad. A lot of the foster kids never progressed beyond 'Mr. and Mrs. Gray' or their first names. Mostly because several only stayed for a few weeks or months. Drew Seaborn is one of a handful who stayed long-term or had permanent placements.

He's also the only long-timer I haven't been able to find on Facebook.

And now I feel even guiltier because I haven't tried harder to find him. Drew, Alina, and Evie were the last fosters living at the house after I graduated high school and through most of my first year of college, until Evie ran off and things dominoed from there. I'd been close to them all, but I never found out what happened to Drew.

I had no idea he'd become a social worker or was ever interested in the field, though I shouldn't be surprised. He was always the first to welcome new arrivals, to help put the fosters at ease, even the ones we knew wouldn't be staying long.

I can see that part of him shining through as he turns his considerable charm to the little girl, who's been watching us warily. "Well, hello there," he greets her when she's looking at him, then he points to her stuffed cat. "That's a very nice kitty you have there. What's her name?"

The instant he points, she whimpers and tries to shove back on the bed, clutching her toy even harder.

Drew immediately lowers his arm. "Oh, don't worry. I won't take her. I have my very own kitty," he says. "Would you like to see her?"

The girl says nothing, and she doesn't relax.

"All right. Maybe in a minute." Drew turns to me, the congenial expression still fixed on his face. "Dr. Lourdes gave me the broad strokes about how you found her," he says. "Told me you think she might be deaf, and he agrees that's likely. Do you think you'd be okay to tell me more? I know you have no idea who she is, but anything might help."

I glance at the girl and smile, and she gives me a little smile in return. "Sure," I tell him, relieved that he's all business right now, instead of trying to catch up with me. "What would you like to know?"

"Hold on, let me grab a chair. I'll be right back."

Drew ducks out of the room. I watch him go, remembering the boy he used to be. He was fifteen when I left for college, seventeen when I had to come back unexpectedly. By then, he'd been with us for almost eleven years. He made friends with everyone, adults and kids alike, almost instantly.

Well, everyone except Naomi, though not for a lack of trying. Naomi never liked anyone.

Briefly, I wonder where Naomi is now, what she's doing. Not that I'd have kept up with her. She always seemed to hate me the most, and that was saying something, given the vitriol she poured out constantly.

It's not long before Drew returns with a rolling office chair. He leaves it next to me, then drags a wheeled side table from the corner of the room — one that looks intended to extend over a bed — and does something to lower the height so he can use it seated. His easy, efficient preparations say this isn't the first time he's done this kind of meeting in a hospital room.

The girl in the bed watches him bustle around, then finally relaxes when he takes a seat on the opposite side of me. She must've decided he's not going to take her toy away.

Drew lets out a long exhale and places his clipboard on the table. "I'm sorry we have to do this now," he says. "This can't be an easy time for you. I'll try to move things along as fast as possible, but . . . you know how the system is."

"It's okay. Take your time." I manage a smile, but my struggle is more exhaustion and grief than any desire to get this over with. I'm already feeling protective of the girl, and not just because she looks like my daughter. Because I *do* know how the system is. I know it doesn't always work the way it should.

And I don't want this child going from bad to worse.

Drew asks me exactly what happened, occasionally prodding for details but mostly listening to me talk. He takes notes as I explain. When I finish, his expression is contorted in sympathy. "Poor kid," he says quietly with a glance at the little girl, who's tracing the black patches on the stuffed calico with a finger. "She definitely has a strong attachment to that toy."

"Yes, and I'm pretty sure someone used that to hurt her." Now that the panic has eased a little, anger toward whoever abused this child is taking its place. "It's hard to picture without having been there, but it was clear whoever did this deliberately arranged it so she'd get stuck in that hedge."

"Oh, I can see it. I remember those holly bushes." Drew frowns, starts to turn a page on his clipboard, then stops and pulls out his phone. It's vibrating with a call. "Excuse me a second."

He stands and walks away a few steps to answer in a low voice. After a few brief words, he says, "Okay, I'll be right out." He ends the call and pockets his phone. "The police are here," he explains. "I need to talk to them, get things moving on that end. I'll be back soon."

I'm about to reply with something inane when the curtain pulls back further and one of the nurses from earlier wheels in a cart full of fluids, bandages, and sharp implements. I'm guessing that's for me. "Now, let's get you fixed up," she announces, giving me a smile that seems far too cheerful this early in the morning. Or this late, depending on how you look at it.

Drew ducks out of the room, and I brace myself for more unpleasantness.

CHAPTER 4

Three hours later, long after my glass-free foot is cleaned, wrapped, and settled into a constant throb, the last of the girl's test results come back. Her wounds are thankfully superficial, and she's slightly dehydrated but not malnourished. The doctor believes her hearing loss is permanent congenital deafness, not due to injury. She's cleared to be discharged.

The only problem is, she has nowhere to be discharged to.

The two officers who were here checked the missing persons database and didn't find anything close to a match. They're going to start a door-to-door check through the neighborhood in an hour or so, when most people will be up and around. They're also posting a notice on Fulton's community Facebook page, which is apparently pretty active.

I'm honestly not sure any of that is going to work. It doesn't seem like she wandered away and got lost. But I know they have to follow procedure.

In the meantime, the girl has no one — and Drew just gave me more bad news.

"We don't have any open foster placements in the entire county right now." He finishes the message he's tapping into his phone, sends it, and slides the device in his pocket, frowning as he glances at the child. She's curled up with her stuffed cat and fallen into a fitful sleep. "None of the dedicated homes have available beds, either. But . . ."

I raise an eyebrow when he doesn't finish the sentence. "But?"

He whooshes out a sigh. "I don't know. I really hate to ask, considering . . . everything. But it looks like *you're* in the system for Onondaga County. I had no idea you'd registered as a foster parent." The look he gives me holds a flash of accusation, but it's sadness instead of malice. He pauses and swallows. "Anyway, you're showing as available. Under Katrina Martin."

A shiver of sick fury runs down my spine. Not at Drew, but at the mere mention of that name. I hate that my ex-husband still has that kind of power over me, especially since he's no longer where he's supposed to be. And that's the worst part. The deepest cut.

I push it down and focus on what Drew is saying — or rather, what he's not saying.

He wants me to keep her.

"Oh, God. I don't . . ." Even as I start to protest, part of me knows I'm going to say yes. Dad's funeral is in two days — well, technically it's tomorrow now — I've barely had time to breathe, and I don't even know if I'm going to stay in town. But I can't abandon this girl.

Drew shakes his head slowly. "I know. I'm so sorry to even suggest it, but there's literally nothing available," he says. "Hopefully, it won't be for long. I'll keep pushing for an opening, but we'll probably find where she belongs soon. This is likely a non-custodial parent case. Which means the custodial parent won't hesitate to contact the police, and we'll have her home by lunchtime."

Something in me eases at that. Drew's theory makes a lot more sense than the idea that this child was deliberately abandoned. Custody battles can really bring out the ugly in people, and they happen all the time.

"Okay," I tell him. "What do you need from my end?"

He flashes a hesitant smile. "You'll do it?"

"Yeah." I glance at the sleeping child, the way she clings to the stuffed cat like she'll drown without it. "I want to help her."

"That's what we like to hear." Drew beams.

He extracts a slim packet of paperwork from his clipboard, then asks for my license so he can take a photo and change my name in the files. My parents' house was removed from the system after all the trouble when I was in college, first with Evelyn, then my mom's unexpected death, but Drew says it's easier to renew an address than to add a new one. I won't even have to go to the county DSS office for this.

I can just take her home.

"So," Drew says carefully while I'm reading lists and checking boxes. "You were doing foster care?"

I bite back the urge to snap at him. Though we haven't been in touch, he must know about my ex-husband. About my daughter.

She wasn't the only one I lost, either.

But I know these things, and my refusal to talk to anyone about them, are what kept me isolated for so long. What kept me from spending time with my father until it was too late. Now that I have a chance to reconnect, I can't make the same mistake with my siblings. At least, the ones who don't hate me.

"I was," I finally reply. "I had to stop, after . . ." I trail off and give him a pleading look. I can't talk about Marisol. Not yet.

Thankfully, he seems to understand my unspoken request. "Well, I'm glad you did, even if it wasn't for long. Every willing foster helps. Thank you for doing that."

I don't feel like I deserve gratitude, especially considering the way it all ended. A nearly unbearable wave of guilt threatens to swallow me, and I have to close my eyes until it passes. "I'm just happy I can help out now," I murmur, forcing a smile. "But look at you! Hardest job in the system. I'm the one who should be thanking you."

He gives a self-effacing chuckle. One hand goes to the back of his neck, but the flush creeps around it anyway. He's always been a bright-red blusher, with his fair skin and freckles. I remember seeing him a few times so red that his face practically matched his hair.

"Well, you know," he says. "The place I was in before you guys . . . it wasn't great. Mom and Dad more than made up for it, though. I wanted to do everything I could to keep other kids away from situations like that. So, here I am. I've only had the job for about a year, but I love it."

Part of me wants to ask him what happened after that disastrous spring, when they made him leave. Drew was six months from aging out and being able to choose where he lived. After they decided Dad couldn't foster parent solo, they forced Drew back into care somewhere else. No one would tell us where or with whom.

But now isn't the time to dredge up more painful memories. We have enough of those on our plate already.

I finish the packet, and Drew flips through the pages, scanning and nodding. "Looks great," he says, securing the paperwork on his overstuffed clipboard. "Like I said, there's a good chance we'll find where she belongs soon. If not, I'll have to do a quick home visit. That can wait until . . . after, though."

He means after the funeral. After I bury my father next to my mother in the same cemetery that holds my daughter.

After I'm the only member of my family who's still above the ground.

"I appreciate that," I tell him.

"Least I can do."

We hug, and he glances at the sleeping girl in the hospital bed after we pull apart. "We'll have to call her something until we find out what her name is," he says. "And I should make a note of it, just to have a common frame of reference. Do you want to go with the traditional Jane Doe, or something else?"

I don't want her saddled with the most anonymous name possible, even if it's only for a few days. It feels callous and lazy. I think for a few moments, then say, "What about Holly?"

Almost immediately, I want to take it back. Does that sound cruel because I found her stuck in a holly bush? I was actually thinking of the Holly Hobby print in the kitchen, but it could mean both.

"I love it. Holly it is." Drew makes a note on his clipboard. "I'll go find Dr. Lourdes so he can discharge you both, and you can go home and get some rest."

After he leaves the room, I try to quell a sudden burst of sizzling nerves. Am I truly ready for this? It's been five years since I lost my daughter. Time is supposed to heal all wounds, but the slashes across my heart still feel raw and gaping. And this child, Holly, really does look so much like Marisol.

But I've already agreed, and I'm not going to give up on her the way I gave up in the past. I won't let the pain stop me this time.

I'm going to take her home.

CHAPTER 5

Holly is still asleep when I get back to the house around 8:30 in the morning. I carry her inside and settle her on the living room couch, so I can be there when she wakes up. Even exhausted as I am, there's no way I'm getting back to sleep anytime soon.

I head into the kitchen, looking back to make sure I can see the back of the couch through the dining room. After I start a pot of coffee, I open the fridge and stare into it. Food wasn't a priority for me when I came in yesterday, so I haven't really taken stock of the kitchen. There isn't much here. I'll have to go grocery shopping sooner than I thought, especially considering my unexpected guest.

Egg whites, skim milk, and wilted vegetables won't hold much appeal for a five-year-old.

The evidence of my father's healthy lifestyle sends a twist through me. Once again, I find myself wondering how he ended up dead. He was only fifty-eight and in excellent health as far as I knew. He never smoked, wasn't a heavy drinker, and exercised regularly. I knew he was still in good shape, at least physically.

I may not have seen him in person for five years, but I watched him every weekday morning. Until the last one.

They told me it was a catastrophic stroke. He was gone before the ambulance got there. It was eerily similar to my mother — sudden, unexpected death. For her, it was a brain aneurysm. Twelve years ago. Right here in this kitchen. She was alone in the house, and she dropped dead. My father found her, thankfully before any of the foster kids got home from school. It happened only a few days after Evelyn went missing.

Only a day before I'd planned to come home from college and help with the search.

I wince and close my eyes, trying to push the memories back into the box marked PAST. They never stayed there for long. Time had a way of eroding the locks with every new mistake, every fresh regret.

But at least for now, I have something else to focus on.

I give up on the fridge and find some whole-grain bread, then make myself some toast. By the time it pops up, there's enough coffee brewed for a cup. With breakfast in hand, I head back to the living room and settle into the armchair.

Though I'm not looking forward to it, I need to check Facebook. I open the app and let out a relieved breath to find no new DMs. Hopefully, that means Daddy Dearest was a one-off slimeball who's not going to bother me unless I engage with him.

However, there are new posts and comments in the Fulton Grays group.

When I open the page, I'm overwhelmed with photo collages, heartfelt tributes, and a new flood of comments. There are even two new requests to join the group. One is from Drew, whose Facebook name is apparently Droo Zoo. The other is Clara Crawford.

My dad's girlfriend.

It still feels so bizarre to think those words.

I approve Drew immediately but hesitate over Clara. It's not that I dislike her — quite the opposite. Though I never came here to Fulton, my dad insisted on seeing me in person a few times a year. My birthday, his birthday, Christmas, that sort of thing. He arranged it so he dropped by at least every month or so. Just to check on me, he'd say, if it wasn't a holiday. He would come to my place in Syracuse, and he wouldn't take no for an answer.

Not that I'd ever have refused to let him come in, though there were a few times I wanted to. Times when I'd had especially bad nights or bad weeks, when I wasn't sleeping, when I hadn't bothered to clean anything or shower or even change my clothes for a few days.

And soon after he started seeing Clara, she would come with him to visit.

I was incredibly surprised the first time he brought her over, but I didn't mind. Clara was a nurse, somewhere in her forties — I never asked her age — which made her at least a decade younger than Dad, but the gap didn't seem to matter. At least to them. She was a nice lady, quick to smile, happy to be helpful, but with a no-nonsense manner, like a school teacher who knew you didn't really need the bathroom when you asked for a hall pass. And she clearly cared for my father.

Unfortunately, those monthly-ish visits were my only contact with her. I had no idea how serious she and Dad had been, whether I should have included her in planning the arrangements, what the protocol was for her at the services. I'd only briefly considered her over the past few days, and with no easy way to get in touch, I'd decided not to. I couldn't take the strain of trying.

As far as her joining the Facebook group, technically, she didn't qualify. But I felt bad that she was yet another victim of my years-long human avoidance campaign. From what I'd seen, we probably would've gotten along great if I tried. And she would probably appreciate all these tributes to Dad.

I hesitated for another minute, then tapped to accept her. Finally, I went through and reacted with a heart to every new post and all the comments on mine. I tried to avoid reading or looking at most of them, but by the time I finished, I'd seen enough to bring me to tears again.

Then, just as I'm closing the app, my phone rings.

I jerk, even though I'm looking right at it when the screen starts flashing. At first, I don't recognize the caller, and I'm briefly convinced that Daddy Dearest creep from Facebook has somehow gotten my cell number.

Then I remember what I started doing before my already constricted world imploded further, and I answer the call.

"Ms. Gray, good morning." Gerri Baker sounds crisp and professional, the same way she's sounded the three previous times I talked to her. "Please allow me to extend my condolences on your father."

"Of course. Thank you," I say slowly, not sure how I'm supposed to respond to that. She delivers the oddly phrased sympathy as smoothly and evenly as fresh asphalt, without a hint of feeling or a fleck of intonation.

I suppose lawyers have the emotion educated right out of them while they're in law school, much like doctors and accountants.

"I have an update on your case," Gerri continues. "I'm afraid the courts won't allow us to file an appeal against commuting Tyler Martin's sentence. He'd already been processed and released, pursuant to public reports of his exoneration, and we have no new evidence to present."

"What? He's *out*?"

"Yes, he was released from the Jamesville Correctional Facility three weeks ago. A judge granted a gag order to keep the media from revealing the status and terms of his release until he could be safely relocated." Gerri trots this news out with no hint of inflection, as if she hasn't just lobbed a grenade into my already fractured life.

I'm so incensed, I can't even sputter. I'd looked for a lawyer the instant I heard the insane news that the court somehow decided Tyler was wrongly convicted. Innocent. He'd served less than five years of a life sentence, and now he was free? Out in the world?

"He *murdered* my daughter!" I finally shout, then glance at the little girl sleeping on the couch before I remember she's deaf. She doesn't stir. I blow out a frustrated breath through my nostrils and lower my voice. "He shouldn't be out," I say. "He's a killer."

"Apparently, there is evidence proving he's not." Gerri sighs. For the first time, a sliver of emotion enters her voice as she says, "Listen, I'm not going to charge you for this. I really am sorry."

Sorry doesn't put that bastard back behind bars, does it? I manage not to say that out loud. Gerri Baker is not the arbiter of America's broken justice system. She's only a lawyer. "Thank you," I manage. "I appreciate that."

We end the call, and I toss my phone on the coffee table in disgust. I can't believe this is happening. *How* did he pull this off? He's not innocent.

He planned it. He *admitted* it.

I'm going to be sick.

I close my eyes and exhale, trying to rid my mind of Tyler Martin. He doesn't deserve one more second of my time.

I have to at least try to relax if I'm not getting any more sleep today. Almost without thinking, I grab the remotes from the end table beside the chair and turn on the television. The cable box is already on. It's set to DNC News — the channel where my father worked. And they happen to be reporting the weather.

My stomach clenches, and I fumble for the cable remote. Yet my brain insists on recognizing that the woman cheerfully delivering the weather forecast — as if the man who had this job yesterday didn't drop dead where she's standing — looks familiar.

A banner appears along the bottom of the screen with her name. *Marcia Matthews, Weather.* And finally, it clicks.

That's not right. Marcia is the morning news co-anchor with Bryon Halloway.

". . . team with what's happening in your neighborhood today. Bryon?"

I blink as Marcia finishes the weather and the camera switches to the news desk. A man and a woman are seated behind it, broad smiles for the audience. There's Bryon in his usual seat on the right. And on the left . . .

"Good morning, Central New York. If you're just joining us, this is Bryon Halloway for DNC News, with my brand-new co-anchor—"

"Naomi Young," I blurt aloud, while Bryon says it.

My foster sister. The one who hated us all. Especially me. The only foster my dad tried to get rid of — though my mom wouldn't let him.

What is she doing *there*?

"Thank you, Bryon." Naomi's blinding white smile stretches. Her rich, dark-brown hair hangs in loose waves past her shoulders, streaked with blonde highlights. Her amber eyes gleam from a golden tanned, heart-shaped face with perfect cheekbones. "And thank you, Marcia. Speaking of the weather, we'd like to take a moment here at the top of the hour to acknowledge one of our own."

Her face rearranges itself into a somber expression, and I want to punch it through the screen. But I'm too stunned to move. I can't even press a button to change the channel.

Bryon takes over, his features equally sorrowful. "DNC News's longtime morning weatherman, Joe Gray, recently passed away after a short illness." At least he winces slightly as he reads 'short illness' from the teleprompter. That's a terrible way to phrase 'died during a live broadcast,' and I imagine a copywriter at the news station is about to lose their job. "This afternoon, we'll rerun our tribute to Joe, right after the noon news broadcast."

The camera moves to Marcia. For an instant, I think I catch her in a glare directed at Naomi, but it's gone fast. "That's right, Bryon," Marcia says. "Joe was a champion in the community, and he will be sorely missed. I've got some big shoes to fill."

"We'll all miss Joe," Naomi says as the news desk appears again, and Bryon offers a grave nod beside her. Naomi straightens and folds her hands over a small stack of papers on the surface in front of her, then continues without missing a beat.

"In one of today's top stories, a local man wrongly convicted of homicide, who was exonerated and released last month, will be making a string of appearances in the area to promote his upcoming new book."

Oh, God. I can't breathe.

Bryon smoothly picks up the patter. "Thirty-four-year-old Tyler Martin, previously serving a life sentence for the murder of his daughter, five-year-old Marisol Martin, has written a book about the ordeal he suffered while serving almost five years for a crime he didn't commit. Penned while he was imprisoned, the new book, *A Father's Nightmare: The Tyler Martin Story*, hits bookstores and retailers this Friday. In a comment at yesterday's press conference, Mr. Martin said—"

The television snaps off as I force myself to regain control and mash the button.

I don't fucking believe this. He's not only getting away with it, but the son of a bitch somehow managed to write a book? And get it published? He's profiting from murdering my daughter. And according to at least one lawyer, there's nothing I can do about it.

A fresh shiver runs down my spine, and I lean my head back and clench my fists until the nails dig into my palms. This is too much. Tyler being freed, losing my dad, and suddenly becoming the primary caretaker for a little girl with special needs who I know nothing about. All after spending five years as a virtual hermit, actively avoiding close relationships. Do I even know how to care for a child after so long?

But I know I'm just making excuses. Still trying to crawl back into my shell, when I promised myself I'd really try this time. Because despite my self-imposed isolation, I actually don't want to spend the rest of my life alone.

I shake my head and focus on what I need to do today. Step one should probably be to make sure Holly and I don't go hungry. Honestly, the last thing I want to do is slog through a crowded grocery store, and I'm certain my new charge won't enjoy the experience, either. She's been through enough today.

Fortunately, I have a better solution in mind.

I jog upstairs to my old bedroom, where I dumped the small pile of luggage I brought in yesterday, and grab my laptop bag. Back in the living room, I plug it in next to the chair and set it up on the side table.

Online shopping and delivery services have been my savior over the past several years. I've invested in annual memberships to my most frequent retailers and services, including Amazon, Instacart, and Walmart, mostly for the free delivery. All of which are available here in Fulton, too.

My best bet is the local Walmart. I open the website and check the available delivery times. The next open slot isn't until 6 to 7 p.m. I consider paying an extra ten dollars for express delivery, but then remember there's a curbside pickup option. That one has available slots within the next few hours.

I can handle that. We won't have to get out of the car, and it might be nice to go for a drive that doesn't end at the emergency room.

So, I start placing the order, searching the dusty recesses of my mind for what five-year-olds like to eat.

CHAPTER 6

The Journal

I can't believe I'm stuck with this so-called "family."

This isn't my first time in foster care, but all the other times were temporary. This time, they're saying I'm in the system for good, or at least until I turn eighteen.

I don't think I'm going to last for that long.

The mom is one of those insufferably nice, chipper people that you just know has to be fake. Nobody's that happy. The dad wasn't even here when the social worker dropped me off like a stained shirt at the dry cleaner's — one she has no intention of coming back for after I'm all cleaned up. It hasn't even been a whole day since that happened, and I already hate it here.

But I can't leave. I can't run away, or even act out and get sent somewhere else.

It's not allowed.

Right now is the first minute alone I've had all day. These people want me to Talk About Myself and Get to Know Them, so they can Include Me in the Family. I hear the capitalization in these phrases they trot out like they're reading them from some kind of foster parent manual. Chapter One: Trick Your Foster Kid into Thinking You're Nice.

I don't know how many chapters they have to go until they start the Treat Your Foster Kid Like Shit (Except When the Social Worker Visits) section, but I know they'll get there. Everyone gets there eventually.

That's one of the reasons I'm writing this journal. Social workers and therapists keep telling me to give people a chance, that not everyone is going to act like I'm worthless trash, but they're wrong. No one is nice, no one is selfless. No one really loves foster kids the way parents love their actual kids. Or at least the way parents are supposed to.

Another reason I'm keeping the journal is . . . well, I can't say that one. I'm not supposed to tell.

You'd be surprised at all the things I'm not supposed to tell.

Anyway, I'm stuck here for a while. I may have to stay, but I don't have to like it. And I already know that I won't. The only thing I have going for me is that, at least for now, there's something I hate more outside this stupid foster house than inside it.

If I ever see my actual mother again, I think I'll kill her.

CHAPTER 7

If it wasn't illegal and potentially dangerous, I'd have buckled Holly into the front seat. I worry about her riding in the back, out of my sight. For now, she's behind the passenger seat, so I can at least glance back and see her.

I included a booster seat with the grocery order I'm picking up, though. So on the way home, I'll switch off the passenger airbag and have her up front.

The drive from my parents' house to Walmart is less than ten minutes. I'm passing Lake Neatahwanta now, and the afternoon sun winks off the surface in bright spangles. And there's the 'big kids' playground near the shore. It has a steeply angled climbing net and a complicated set of geometric monkey bars, and a few benches off to the side, set on a patch of sand with a wood-beam border.

A pang of nostalgia hits me hard at the sight. I'd almost forgotten it was here, even though it was a major part of my childhood — especially high school, oddly enough. There's an age requirement on the place. I think it's thirteen and up. I used to come here with Alina, then Drew joined us when he was old enough.

Aside from a handful of short-timers who didn't stay with us for more than a few months, that was the family for most of the time I was in high school. Me, Alina, and Drew, then Evie, who was too young to come with us, and Naomi, who was too bitter. Going there made us feel so grown up, being able to play where the little kids couldn't. Of course, Naomi relentlessly dragged us for thinking that hanging out at a playground made us more adult, no matter how old you had to be to get in.

It didn't matter to us, though. We still went. Afterward, if we had money, we'd head up the road to Mr. Mike's for chili cheese fries and pink salad, then eat our haul on the end of the pier that juts out into the lake. The thirty-minute walk never felt that long back then, even in the depths of summer when the sweat stuck our shirts to our backs and pooled at our waistbands, and our faces flushed as red as Christmas lights.

I can't share this place with Holly, but I remember there's another playground a few blocks from the house. One more suited to smaller kids, with traditional swing sets, slides, and jungle gyms, plus a mini water park where you could push a button and turn on a multitude of sprinkler and shower fixtures for ten minutes at a time. We all loved that place, too — even as we got older. Maybe I can take her there, if they don't find her parents soon.

As good as it feels to reminisce, the memories are tinged with sorrow and guilt. I shouldn't have stayed away for so long. Hell, I shouldn't have let that bastard Tyler talk me into moving to Syracuse, where he grew up, to raise our daughter. *My* daughter. He has no right to claim he was her father. Back then, he kept pointing out that the drive was short, less than half an hour, and we'd come to visit all the time.

But it wasn't long before that half-hour drive started to feel longer. First, it was the extra time it took to pack up a baby and all her things. That evolved into increasingly heated battles to make Tyler agree to go in the first place. And if I wanted to go without him, he'd complain that we didn't have enough time as a family when he wasn't working. Finally, after Marisol hit eighteen months, we started adding foster kids to the mix, and it became almost impossible for me to handle that kind of outing alone.

I should have said screw it and gone anyway, even without Tyler, but I was so tired. Constantly prodding him, fighting with him, even coaxing Marisol into enthusiasm for the drive after listening to her father whine about how hard it all was . . . it drained me. I'd all but given up trying.

Then that bastard murdered my daughter, and I didn't want to go anywhere. See anyone.

I spent too long wallowing in my personal nightmare, and it nearly consumed me.

"We're almost there," I call out as we pass the plaza with Tractor Supply and Dunkin, then I huff and cringe inwardly. *She can't hear you, idiot.* I think about looking back to give Holly a reassuring smile, but I don't want to take my eyes off the road. Instead, I glance in the rearview mirror to check on her.

She's sitting up, staring out the side window. One small hand rests on the filthy stuffed cat that's perched on the seat beside her. At least she's wearing clean clothes now. My parents always maintained a sizable stash of kids' clothes in a range of sizes, neatly stored in the attic, and it was still up there.

I'm hoping I can slip that toy through the washer and dryer tonight while she's asleep. Right now, though, I don't want to take it away from her. Especially since I can't explain what I want to do with it.

I also hope I can find some way to breach our communication barrier. She doesn't seem able to read or write, but maybe we can work on simple gestures or something.

Anything would be better than the nothing we have now.

We're approaching a traffic light. Just in time, I remember the Walmart sign is impossible to see from this side because of the trees in front of it and pull into the left lane so I can make the turn. The grocery pickup is around the back of the massive, sprawling gray building. I make another left before the parking lot and drive around on the access road.

No other cars are parked and waiting for curbside, so I pull into the "1" slot closest to the employee door and check in with the app, noting that I am driving a silver Ford Taurus. I turn off the engine, pop the trunk, and turn in my seat to smile at Holly.

She's watching me, and she offers the tiniest smile in return.

Some of my anxiety eases. I wish I could tell her why we're here, but I'm pretty sure she'll be able to figure it out soon. I hope I've bought at least some food she likes. Maybe next time, I can show her the website and see if she'll point to something she might want.

If there is a next time, I remind myself. She could be going home at any minute. Someone out there might be frantic with terror right now, racing to find their little girl.

Or they could be lying in a blacked-out stupor, unaware their child is missing.

Or they might be dead. Heart attack. Home accident. Murder.

Or they abandoned her on purpose. In my parents' back yard.

"Stop catastrophizing," I mutter to myself. There's no point in trying to guess what happened, and it's probably nothing that shocking. Few things are ever as dramatic as we imagine them to be. All I can do is wait for the police and social services to figure it out.

In the meantime, I'm going to take care of her the best I can.

Movement at the corner of my eye catches my attention, and I look toward the employee door. It's opening, and a wheeled trolley stacked with blue plastic bins is emerging. I turn back to Holly and hold up one finger, not sure if she understands that I'll just be a minute. She doesn't react. But I'm sure she'll realize I'm not leaving her.

I open the door and start getting out of the car, planning to help store the loose items they'll bring out in the bags in my trunk. I need to grab the booster seat and set it up, too.

As I'm standing, I catch sight of the person pushing the cart out — and I freeze, unable to stop staring.

Lynette?

Oh, God, it *is* her.

She was sixteen the last time I saw her, which means she's twenty-one now, but she still looks so young. So vulnerable. The guilt I've felt ever since then swells up, closing my throat and stinging my eyes. She's the reason I don't deserve Drew's or anyone's gratitude for my 'services' as a foster parent.

I failed her so badly in the end.

I can't believe she's here. Not that it's a stretch to consider she's moved from Syracuse to Fulton, but to be *here*, working at this store when circumstances bring me to the same place?

Maybe it's a sign. The universe giving me the chance to apologize, even though I don't deserve her forgiveness.

She's still propping the door open with the cart when she sees me. She stops in place, too. Her eyes widen, and her mouth falls open. She stays like that for a long moment. But as I take a step toward her, she closes her mouth. Her jaw clenches. Even from here, I can see her knuckles turning white as she grips the trolley handle. Her glare cuts into me.

Then, she backs up, pulling the cart inside with her. The heavy steel door slams shut.

My heart shatters. Part of me wants to run after her and beg her to let me apologize, but I can't. Even if I didn't have Holly with me, I wouldn't. It's not fair for me to expect anything from her after what I did.

A small sound from inside the car reaches me. I turn and look into the back seat. Holly is stretching her arms toward me, her hands opening and closing.

Does she want me to pick her up?

A flutter of happy anticipation fills my chest. I circle the car, open her door, and bend to unbuckle her seat belt. As soon as the restraint retracts, she curls her little arms around my neck. I straighten with her, and she rests her head on my shoulder.

After a morning filled with people who are disappointed in me, this soothes my soul.

I stand near the open trunk with her, watching the employee door. The last thing I'm going to do is be upset with Lynette, but I do need the groceries. I'm thinking about opening the app to see if there's a number I can call when the door opens, and the same cart emerges. Only this time, a different person is pushing it.

The blonde woman appears to be a few years older than Lynette. She also looks supremely annoyed. I'm not sure if it's because she's doing this instead of her coworker, or because Lynette told her who-knows-what about me, and I'm not going to ask for clarification.

She trudges toward the car and stops beside the trunk on the opposite side. Her features brighten when she sees Holly, who's watching her warily. "Good morning," she tells me, then her voice takes on a higher pitch as she addresses the little girl. "Hi, sweetie. Is all this food for you?"

Holly squirms and buries her face in my shoulder.

"Aw, she's shy. That's okay," the young woman says.

I'm relieved I don't have to explain that she's deaf, so I don't contradict her.

The blonde extracts the booster seat I ordered from behind the bins and holds it out toward me. "You want the rest of this in the bags?" she asks, with a nod at the trunk.

"Yes, please." I take the seat with my free hand. "Thank you."

She makes a noncommittal sound and opens the first plastic tote.

I carry Holly to the front and open the passenger side door. I'll get her settled into her seat, then help bag the items. This woman works with Lynette, and I have no idea how well they know each other, but I get the sense she's cool toward me because she either saw Lynette's reaction or my former foster daughter mentioned something about me. Whatever the reason, I won't pry.

At this point, I only want to take my groceries and go home.

By the time I get Holly buckled in and retrieve her cat from the back seat, the blonde is finished loading the trunk. She slams it shut, and she's walking away before I can reach her to say thanks. "Have a good day," she calls without turning around.

"Thanks, you too," I lob after her, but she doesn't acknowledge me.

Lynette definitely must have said something.

I climb back into the driver's seat with a sigh, then bow my head and close my eyes. I want to run in there, track her down, and beg her forgiveness. I want to tell her that I meant what I said. That I had the adoption papers ready for us to fill out together. I'd even planned a mini-vacation weekend for us to celebrate as a family. But then the unthinkable happened, and I could think of nothing but making Tyler Martin pay for what he'd done.

By the time I realized what I was doing to Lynette, they'd taken her away.

And I was so broken that I didn't fight to get her back.

With a heavy heart, I start the engine and disengage the passenger side airbag. At least I have someone else's welfare to consider, for however long that lasts, to distract me from my failures as a mother, and a daughter, and a sister.

I only hope I don't fail Holly, too.

CHAPTER 8

Either Holly really enjoys mac and cheese or she was starving, because she finished an entire bowl of the mushy, clumpy mess I made for dinner. Apparently, my box meal skills have languished. I was going to try giving her something else after I took a bite and found it tasted like cheesy wallpaper paste, but she'd already started inhaling hers.

Next time, I'm getting the shells and cheese with the premixed sauce, and I won't cook the pasta for so long.

The day has been surprisingly calm since we got back from Walmart. Holly follows me like a shadow, but it's not like I'm doing anything she can't be around. She doesn't seem to get agitated about anything unless I leave her alone for too long.

We had a late breakfast of cereal — fruit loops for her, raisin bran for me — then an early lunch of microwave meals. She had chicken nuggets and dinosaur fries; I had sweet and sour chicken over rice. I know they're not the healthiest choices, but she's been through a lot. I'm not ready to push a diet of lean meats and vegetables on her yet.

After lunch, we settled on the couch for a while, and I arranged my laptop on the coffee table to catch up on emails for current clients.

I work as a freelance video editor. Clients send me raw footage and tell me what they're looking for, and I create a professional finished product with background music, text overlays, jump-cuts, and visual effects. Wedding and anniversary montages, birthday videos, commercials, online video advertisements, and a surprisingly large number of custom jobs that don't fit into a neat category. I've even done Insta and TikTok reels, though I prefer to avoid the super-short jobs.

Though I've closed my Facebook page to new activity and rearranged my projects to give me at least a week off, in freelance work, there are always a few loose ends hanging around. I turned on Cartoon Network for Holly while I answered questions and performed quick fixes or change requests. She'd seemed, if not engaged, at least mildly interested in whatever show was on.

Now, we're back in the living room after cleaning up from my less-than-gourmet dinner attempt. My plan is to put the cartoons back on and spend a little time researching how to communicate with deaf children. Then, I want to bring Holly up to the attic and try to encourage her to pick out some clothes she likes, hopefully using whatever tips I find online.

But after we're settled and I open my laptop, I head to Facebook and check on the group page first. I remember that I haven't looked since I added Clara, and I wonder if anyone will have an issue with that.

A quick scan shows that Clara hasn't made any comments or posts, but she's added a heart reaction to all the tribute posts for Dad. I don't see anyone objecting to her presence, but I do see that Evie tagged me in a post.

Hey @Kat Gray, how are you holding up? I'm still so sorry that I can't get up there, but I want to send an arrangement for the funeral. Daddy Joe liked chrysanthemums, right?

A memory strikes me with such sudden clarity that tears instantly well in my eyes and stream down my cheeks. It was soon after Mickey came to stay with us, while she was still the only foster kid. She'd arrived in the middle of the school year and had a bad day — high school kids could be awful shits, no matter the generation.

I was sitting at the kitchen table with her while we both did homework, trying to cheer her up, when I had the brilliant idea to give her a present — as a six-year-old girl, I still thought presents solved everything. So I'd rushed into the back yard and picked her a pretty blue flower from my mom's garden. To match her hair. At the time, I didn't know it was a chrysanthemum.

When I presented it to her, she blinked as she took it. "Thanks. Um, what is it?"

"A flower?" I'd said. "I dunno."

"Oh, look at that! It's Chris Ant the Mum."

My father's voice boomed cheerily from the kitchen doorway as he walked in. He'd already clocked that Mickey was upset, but she didn't respond to the lame joke he tried to cheer her up with. He hadn't pushed her to explain anything, either.

My parents never pushed. After I became a mother, I developed a new sense of awe that they'd managed to have so much patience, because my supply ran short a lot more often than I wanted to admit.

When he said that, we both looked at him with wrinkled brows. "It's what?" Mickey said with the tiniest hint of spark in her glum tone.

"Chris Ant the Mum." Dad grinned, strolled over to the table, and filched a piece of paper from the stack I was using to practice spelling. Then, he pointed to the pencil in my hand. "May I borrow your scribbler, madam?"

I giggled and handed it over.

He walked past the table to the island counter, made a dramatic face at us, then turned and hunched over, scratching something on the paper. When he turned back, he held up a cartoonish but passable drawing of an ant wearing a hat with a flower stuck in it, and a smaller ant holding a balloon. "See?" he said, pointing to the bigger ant. "Chris Ant the Mum! Short for Christina. And this is Chris Ant the Son. Short for Christopher."

Mickey snorted, but a smile tugged at her pouty lips. "You forgot one," she said.

"Did I?" Dad handed the paper and pencil to her.

She bent over it and scribbled for a few minutes. When she straightened, she turned the paper around and pointed to her contribution, an even bigger ant with crossed eyes and a tongue hanging out, and a back end that was more butt than insect. She pointed to it with the pencil. "Chris Ant the Bum. Short for biggest di — jerk wad in school."

I burst out laughing, stood, and threw my arms out. "Chris Ant the Bum!"

Dad flashed a broad smile and started chanting, "Chris Ant the Bum! Chris Ant the Bum! Chris Ant the Bum!" pumping his fist in the air in time with the words. Soon, we were both chanting along with him, marching around the table like the world's weirdest parade.

I wrench myself away from the memory and wipe my face, but a smile lingers as I reply to Evie's post.

@Evelyn Wells yes, he loved them. Thank you, and really, don't worry about not being able to come. I completely understand.

I post the response and skim the rest of the page, this time paying a little more attention to the outpouring of love for Dad. It's still indescribably painful, but the good feelings are there, too. The beautiful memories.

I'm about to close the page when a notification pops up that Mickey has replied to my comment, and I can't help but take a peek.

@Kat Gray Chris Ant the Bum!!!

This time, my tears are more happy than miserable.

I click a heart onto her comment, then close the browser and glance over at Holly.

Except she's not beside me on the couch anymore.

My heart leaps into my throat, but the panic barely has a chance to take hold before I spot her wandering toward the glass-enclosed fireplace at the far end of the room. She stops, transfixed, as she stares up at the Hearth Wall and points.

My breath catches. "Do you know what that is? Do you want to be on the wall?"

She only looks at me, blinks, and points again.

God, I wish I could talk to her. I really need to work on that if she's going to be with me for a while.

There's no way I'm ever going to figure out what she wants, but I hope adding her to the ranks of kids will be fun for her, even if that's not what she's trying to say. I want to do it, even if Drew shows up tonight to announce he's taking her home. I want to uphold my parents' number-one rule.

Everyone who stays here is family.

"Let's put you on the wall," I say to Holly and hold out a hand. She frowns briefly, but she slips her hand in mine.

I lead her to the linen closet to the left of the fireplace and open the folding door. I'm relieved to find that everything is still where my parents kept it. One thing my father hasn't changed. The third shelf from the bottom holds all the Hearth Wall supplies. A small stack of profile forms, rows and rows of acrylic paint, a jar holding paintbrushes and markers, rubbing alcohol to clean up the paint. And of course, the Polaroid camera.

I pick it up and look in the bubble to make sure it has film. Four pictures left. "Okay, we're in business!" I announce and push aside the cringe this time. I decide that no matter how we end up communicating, I'll keep talking around her. She can't hear me, but maybe she can read lips. Or she'll learn to.

From the moment I start the process of adding Holly to the wall, things feel . . . right. Like she belongs here. She poses in front of the fireplace and watches in awe as her picture develops on the little plastic square. She picks a sunshiny yellow for her handprint. I write her name down as Holly Gray, then fill in the profile questions with my best guesses.

When I tack the paper onto the Hearth Wall with the others, Holly smiles and claps, and I swoop her into a hug.

It's the brightest moment I've had for a long, long time.

Afterward, I settle her on the couch so I can clean things up. I'm putting the Polaroid back in the linen closet when I notice something on the shelf above the supplies. An envelope propped against a small, dented, olive-drab metal tackle box that I recognize as belonging to my father.

He kept that box full of caramel creams, his favorite candy. Whenever any of us kids wanted one, he made a big production out of it, as if getting to have a five-cent piece of candy was like Willie Wonka finding the golden ticket. And of course, all the theatrics made them taste way better than they actually were.

The envelope has my name on the front of it.

Frowning, I reach up and take it down. It is greeting-card-sized, but it isn't thick or heavy enough to contain a card. The flap is tucked into the back of the envelope rather than sealed shut.

Inside, there's a single sheet of paper. A half-sheet, actually. And it's printed with a note.

Look inside the box, Kat. See what kind of man your father really was.

A strangled cry escapes me, and I throw both the envelope and the note. They don't go far, only flutter to the floor in front of me. Reflexively, I look toward Holly as if she's somehow in danger from this discovery, but she's fine. Still on the couch, engrossed in *Powerpuff Girls*.

I start shivering as I look from the note to the tackle box. Someone has been inside this house — and the cadence and contents of the note sound a lot like the Facebook message from "Daddy Dearest." There's no way for me to tell when whoever is doing this left the envelope, either. This is the first time I've opened the linen closet since I came home.

Maybe I should call the police. There could be fingerprints on the paper, and I could show them the screenshot of the message, even though I can't prove they're from the same person.

But first, I'm going to have to look in the box.

Something tells me I *really* don't want to do that.

My hands are shaking as I reach for it. I lift the box off the shelf, and it rattles on the way down. It feels empty, but I hear faint sounds from inside. Something sliding around and gently bonking against the edges. I pause and take a few deep breaths, then flip the latch and open the lid.

There's a single object inside. A Polaroid photograph.

And the subject of that photo is so horrific that I nearly vomit on the spot.

It's Naomi. Sixteen or seventeen years old, staring at the camera and striking a sultry pose. The picture was taken in her bedroom — she had the single-bed downstairs room, where the oldest foster kid always got to stay because they needed extra privacy.

And she is entirely naked.

She couldn't have taken the photo herself. Her entire body is in the frame, and the Polaroid doesn't have a timer function. Someone else snapped this picture.

Dad, what did you do?

I'm instantly appalled as the thought crosses my mind. There's no way in hell my dad had anything to do with this, even if some troll wants me to think that.

Still, it's damned hard to come up with another explanation for the existence of this picture. Which was in my father's box.

No. I refuse to even entertain the idea. Someone is screwing with me, trying to get into my head. The worst part is that I can't even begin to imagine *why* anyone would do that.

I'm also horrified that they've been in this house, and I'm definitely making sure every window and door is locked tight before we go to bed tonight.

Meanwhile, even if I know this wasn't my dad's doing, it looks bad. I need to hide it somewhere until I figure out what to do with it.

I set the box on a shelf, snag the note and stuff it back in the envelope, then throw it into the container, on top of that awful photo. Maybe I could stick the whole thing in the attic somewhere. Then again, I'll probably need to get more stuff for Holly from up there, and I don't want to keep being reminded of its existence.

Suddenly, I remember something that swims up from the depths of my mind. Alina and I used to play a game we called 'secret spies.' We'd write cryptic notes with clues on them pointing to the 'classified documents' and hide them in our spy drop in the basement.

Which was a loose stone in the retaining wall that looked flush with the surface but came out easy if you knew where to press. And there was a roomy hollow spot behind it.

That's where I'll put the box. No one will find it there, and I can decide how to handle it after I get through the next few days.

After I bury my father.

CHAPTER 9

The Journal

I hate it here more every day.

The mom is clueless and insipid. I learned that word in school here: *insipid*. She's always trying to compliment me about some stupid thing like my shoes or my hair when I know she doesn't mean a word of it. They have a bio kid, after all. She's keeping up the pretense like a champ, and nothing I do ever seems to break her.

But the dad? I can work with the dad. He's weak. I've seen him snap when the mom's not paying attention. He's got wandering eyes, too. The way he looks at me sometimes . . .

The dad is my ticket to surviving for as long as I have to stay here.

How long am I going to have to stay here?

If it's much longer, I might lose my mind.

CHAPTER 10

"It's just . . . bizarre. Like she came out of nowhere."

Drew's voice drifts from my phone. I have it on speaker, lying on the coffee table while I sit on the couch with Holly. She's freshly bathed and wearing blue Scooby Doo pajamas. I was trying to decide where we'd sleep when he called to tell me the news.

The police found absolutely nothing. No parent or guardian reporting a recently missing little girl. No one recognized the photo they took of her last night — not in the neighborhood, at any schools, daycares, or local business. Not on the Facebook page. No incapacitating accidents or deaths where a child should have been present but wasn't.

In this case, no news is weird news.

"They're going to keep looking, of course," Drew says. "Broaden the search, increase the media coverage. Even if she's local, she's not necessarily from the city. Her family could be in Granby, Hannibal, Volney . . . well, you know. 'Local' is kind of a sprawling term around here."

"Yeah, there's a lot of ground to cover." That's the rule more than the exception in Central New York. You have cities, then a bunch of towns clustered around it that may or may not link into the city's municipal systems depending on the individual town's wealth. Syracuse is the same way, with its 'surrounding communities.' There's North Syracuse and East Syracuse, Mattydale, Solvay, Dewitt, Nedrow, and a whole bunch more.

They're all sort of Syracuse, like Volney, West Volney, and the rest are sort of Fulton. And some areas are better than others.

"I can't believe no one's looking for her." Drew sounds upset, almost angry, and I can't blame him. With bruises that couldn't have come from a bush and a distinct lack of interest in finding her, it definitely feels like she's been abandoned. He sighs and clears his throat. "Are you doing okay with her? Again, I'm sorry I had to ask—"

"No, it's okay. *We're* okay," I interrupt him with a smile for Holly. The television is muted, playing a My Little Pony cartoon, but she glances at me whenever I start talking. I think she feels the vibrations of my voice through the couch. "It's a challenge not being able to talk to her, but she's an absolute sweetheart. So easygoing."

"Oh, that's great to hear," he says. "Speaking of communicating, I asked the department for someone who knows sign language so we can find out whether she's been taught it. If she has, it'll help a lot. We could ask her questions and check with schools and tutors to see if she's been in a program somewhere. But I told them to hold off sending them until . . . well, the day after tomorrow," he finishes awkwardly.

"I appreciate that," I tell him and mean it. Tomorrow is going to be hell, so the fewer things I have to try to accomplish, the better.

For a split second, I think about telling him what I found in the linen closet. I doubt he'll believe Dad had anything to do with it either, and I want to tell *somebody*. I'm so creeped out about whoever is screwing with me.

But I can't, because no matter what his opinion is, he's a social worker. And I think he'd be obligated to report it.

"I'll be there for all of it," Drew adds. "I took the day off."

The caring in his voice makes me tear up again. Why didn't I try harder to keep in touch with him? "Thank you. That really means a lot," I say. I glance at Holly, then past her to the wall above the fireplace. "I added her to the Hearth Wall today. Remember that?"

He gives a delighted laugh. "How could I forget? Except maybe I did, a little. What did I say I liked again . . . sunshine and rainbows or something lame like that?"

"Close enough." I snort laughter. "You like smiling and playing outside. And you dislike really big snakes."

"*Really* big snakes? I had to get that 'really' in there, like normal-big snakes are fine but not *really* big ones. Jeez, what was I thinking?" He chuckles again. "And you liked your camera, right? What did you put for Holly?"

I'm touched that he remembers my page, although the mention of 'camera' makes me shudder. "Let's see. She likes macaroni and cheese — she likes it a lot, actually — and dislikes being alone. Also true. And for her fun fact, I wrote '*I am brave, strong, and loved.*' Corny, right?"

"No," he says with a rasp in his voice. "Not corny at all."

So much for lightening the mood.

"Listen, I'd better try to get her to bed," I say. I'm still hoping to run her stuffed animal through the washer and dryer tonight after she's asleep. She's been clinging to the toy all day, and she got upset when I wouldn't let her take it in the bathtub. I had to set it on a chair so she could see it while she bathed. "I . . . well, I guess I'll see you tomorrow."

"Definitely. Goodnight, Kat."

"Goodnight."

He hangs up first, and I leave the phone where it is and grab the remote. Holly looks at me when I turn off the TV. "Well, kiddo, why don't we try to get some sleep?" I say, then stand and hold a hand out to her.

She clambers off the couch. After a pause, she grabs her dirt-smudged cat with one arm and reaches for me with the other.

"We really have to wash your friend." I smile and lead her toward the stairs. "For now, we'll both sleep in my room. See how that goes."

I don't want to leave her alone on her first night sleeping in a strange house. I have no idea if she'll sleep through the night, if she has any nocturnal issues like nightmares or sleepwalking. Until I figure out a way to communicate with her, we'll sleep in the same room. In the same bed, at least for tonight.

And with any luck, my own nocturnal issue won't visit me again.

CHAPTER 11

What is that?

I swear I heard a noise, but I can't move. It's so dark. Are my eyes open? Am I awake?

Something chimes in the darkness. Is that my phone? I don't think it's ever made a sound like that, and I can't see the screen lighting up. I try to grab for it, but my arm won't obey my brain's command.

Bang-bang-bang.

My heart kicks into high gear. I *did* hear something. It's coming from outside.

Marisol!

No, not Marisol. Holly.

Panic makes it worse. I can't let it take me. I have to calm down.

Breathe. Move. One step at a time.

I draw in a breath, then release. Feel my chest rise and fall.

These are my lungs, and they're under my command. My body is my own. I can move when I want to, like right now. I'm going to move my finger.

The instant I think it, my finger taps the sheet. Once, twice, three times. Like the sound I heard. I concentrate until I'm pointing at the ceiling.

I *can* breathe. I *can* move.

Okay. Five things I can see.

The bedroom door.

My robe hanging on the back of it.

The clock on the table—

Bang-bang-bang-bang.

This time, the strange chime follows the thumping sound, and my half-paralyzed brain finally recognizes it.

It's the doorbell.

My bleary gaze focuses on the clock to find it's almost three in the morning, and a sharpening swell of fear infuses me. Something is wrong. With an effort so great that I nearly scream, I force myself to move, to turn toward the other side of the bed.

Holly is still beside me. Sleeping, unbothered by the noise.

Some of the immediate panic eases, but I remain tense as I carefully peel the covers off, then sit up and swing my legs to the floor. There is never a good reason to ring a doorbell at three in the morning — and whatever it is, I don't want to face it. I've had my fill of bad news. What else could have possibly gone wrong?

Even as I try to find some excuse not to answer this middle-of-the-night summons, there's another round of knocking and doorbell-ringing.

You know it's the police. It has to be.

I'm on my feet before I can second-guess anything, grabbing my robe and easing the door open. It does pretty much have to be the police, unless it's someone who is somehow at the wrong house.

Or a crazy person.

Before my mind can fly off on a tangent and convince me there's an ax murderer at my door, I reach the stairs and catch faint red-and-blue flickers in the living room. So yes, it's the police. Why would they be here now? Did they find Holly's parents? Would they really drag me out of bed at this hour if they did?

Don't catastrophize, I admonish myself again as I pad down the stairs and head for the front entrance. I unlock the deadbolt, draw a deep breath, and pull the door open.

The tall, uniformed officer has sandy-brown, buzz-cut hair and apologetic brown eyes, and the silver nameplate on his uniform says WADE. It takes me a minute, but I recognize him as one of the officers who was at the hospital, taking my statement. There's another figure in the passenger seat of the squad car parked at the curb beyond him, probably his partner, whose name escapes me.

I don't remember them mentioning they were with the Fulton police. I assumed they were Oswego city cops, but I suppose it makes sense that they'd respond, since the girl was found in Fulton.

"Mrs. Martin?" the officer says.

My stomach gives a nasty twist. "It's Gray. Katrina Gray."

"Right. Sorry about that." He does actually look sorry. He hooks his thumbs in his belt loops and leans aside, trying to look past me into the house. "Ma'am, we had a report of a child in peril at this address. I'm sorry to wake you, but under the circumstances, we did have to respond. Is everything okay here?"

"What?" I stammer, too shocked to be angry at what he's insinuating. "*Peril?*"

"Yes, ma'am. Are you and the child okay?" he repeats. "Is there anyone else in the house?"

"I . . . no, there's no one else. Of course not." I shake my head and squeeze my eyes shut briefly. "What's going on? What report? She's in—"

A clotted cry from upstairs silences me. I barely register the look of alarm on the officer's face before I pivot and run across the living room, up the stairs, and into my bedroom. Holly is sitting bolt upright in bed, the lines of her body rigid and trembling. But she's not looking at the open door or the empty spot where I was when she fell asleep.

She's looking out the window, her eyes wide with terror.

Outside, I see only moonlight and shadows shifting in the breeze. Damn it, why didn't I fix the light? I got a new bulb along with the groceries earlier, but replacing it slipped my mind. I'll have to do it tomorrow.

No. Not tomorrow, either.

As I rush to the bed and touch her shoulder to get her attention, I hear footsteps coming up the stairs. The officer *came into the house.* I grit my teeth against an angry shout and sit on the edge of the bed, holding an arm out for Holly. She whimpers as she crawls up beside me, and I stroke her hair, my gaze on the doorway.

"She's fine," I say as calmly as I can when Officer Wade steps into the doorway. "She just had a really hard day, and she doesn't like to be alone. As you can probably imagine."

I hope the look I give him conveys that him and his 'report' are the reason she was alone.

"All right, ma'am. Sorry to bother you," he says.

"Wait." Since he's here anyway, maybe he can help put my mind at ease. "When I came up here, she was staring out the window. She might have seen something." *Like whoever shoved her toy into my hedge and made her get trapped.* "But the back yard light is blown. Can you please see if there's anything or anyone out there?"

It could be that she's traumatized by the sight of the mangled hedge, but I'd like to make sure that's all it is.

Officer Wade frowns. "Did she mention that she saw — oh, crap. I'm sorry." He has the grace to look sheepish as he apparently remembers that she can't 'mention' anything. "Of course. We'll check it out."

"Thank you."

He turns and walks away. I hear a crackling fuzz sound, then a murmured voice as he presumably talks to his partner outside. Part of me wants to go after him and demand to know about this clearly bullshit report they received, but I know he won't tell me anything.

Maybe I'll ask Drew if he can find out.

Holly's shaking has subsided, and now she's twisting beneath my arm, trying to look around the bed. It dawns on me that she's searching for her stuffed cat, which I managed to wash and throw in the dryer before I went to sleep.

I get her attention and try to mimic her holding the toy by grabbing a pillow. "I gave her a bath," I say. "Do you want to go get her?"

She looks at me for a minute, then reaches out and clutches the bottom of the pillow. When I let go, she slowly draws it to her chest and hugs it with a confused expression.

"Oh, no, sweetie. You can have your cat." I stand and extend a hand, then change my mind and pick her up. She's still sleepy and a little disoriented, and I don't want her stumbling down the stairs in the semi-dark. I also want to avoid turning on all the lights if I can, because that will wake both of us right up.

She leans into me, still hugging the pillow.

I carry her downstairs and through the house to the laundry room off the kitchen. Through the small window above the washer and dryer, I catch the unsteady flicker and sweep of light as the police search the back yard. Honestly, it was probably nothing. If there was someone out there, they'd have found them by now. But I'm still uneasy.

She looked so scared, staring into the darkness.

There's enough light from the under-counter illumination in the kitchen to wash the laundry room in pale visibility. I shift Holly onto one hip, then open the dryer and crouch to reach inside. The stuffed toy is the only thing in there. I grab it, pull it out, and hold it up in front of her.

She lights up like a beacon. When I tuck it in between us next to the pillow, she buries her face in the cat's velvety surface and releases a happy sigh.

My heart is melting.

I head back, but instead of going upstairs, I settle with Holly on the couch. Officer Wade will likely check back in after they find nothing outside, and I don't want him tromping through the house again. Holly places the pillow at one end of the couch, then smiles at me and throws her free arm around my neck before she lies down, cuddling the stuffed animal.

She falls asleep within minutes, before the police finish their search.

I cover her with the blanket from the back of the couch, then get up and head for the front door. I'll stand there and wait so the officers don't ring the doorbell again. When I open it to the balmy evening, I realize they'd turned the car's flashing lights off. I hadn't even noticed the lack of red-and-blue pulses when I came down the second time.

Before long, I hear footsteps approaching down the driveway from the back yard. Officer Wade is in the lead, but his partner is not the same one who was at the hospital with him. It was definitely two men there. This officer is a dark-haired woman with pale eyes and a watchful expression. She's still sweeping a flashlight across the property on both sides of the driveway, and I wonder if she's looking for evidence that someone was here. At least she seems thorough.

This time, they both come to the door. Officer Wade jogs up the wide cement steps to the stoop while his partner lags behind, passing the beam across the small front yard that is no longer bursting with well-tended flowers but features the same neat grass as the back.

"Ma'am." He gives me a nod. "It doesn't appear that anyone has been in your yard."

"Okay. Thank you for checking." My gaze drifts beyond him to the woman, who's approaching the steps slowly, her head down as if studying the ground for clues. "Can I ask, what was this report you received?"

I know they aren't going to tell me, but I have to pose the question anyway. Officer Wade opens his mouth, his expression suggesting he's about to give me the official no-comment line. But before he can say anything, the woman starts up the steps and says, "Clearly, it was a bunch of bullshit."

I know that voice.

I know that *face*.

"Oh my God. Alina?"

"Kit-Kat!" She bumps past Officer Wade, and before I can say another word, she throws her arms around me.

I can't help it. I hug her back fiercely, and I start sobbing.

"Oh, Kat. I know." Alina's voice is thick as she squeezes me tighter. The hug seems to last forever. When she starts easing back, I try to get myself under control, turning my face away to wipe the tears.

Alina sniffles and coughs. "Hey, Bennie. Do you mind waiting in the car for a few?" she asks the other officer.

Benjamin. That was his first name. I remember now.

He grunts. "Fine. You could've told me you knew the . . . person here, you know."

I don't like the pause he uses. Was he going to say 'suspect?'

"I didn't know she was staying here," Alina fires back. "You could've told me her name, since you already met her."

Officer Wade — Bennie — huffs. "Fine. I'll call it in." He pauses and offers me another nod. "Sorry again for the trouble, ma'am."

"It's fine," I say, even though it's not. "Thank you."

Alina and I watch him walk down the steps, across the front path to the sidewalk. He circles the front of the squad car and climbs in the driver's side.

"He's so damn serious all the time," Alina snorts, then turns to me with a smile. "I am *so* glad to see you, Kat. I'm sorry about Bennie. If I knew it was you here, I would've been at the door myself."

"It's great to see you, too," I reply out of hand, my mind on a hundred questions I want to ask her. But the first thing that pops out is, "Why didn't you say you were a cop?"

Alina was one of the first people I invited to the Facebook group. Though I haven't seen her, we've interacted and even message-chatted a bunch of times, but her profession never came up once.

She smirks. "It's not advisable to advertise on social media that you're a cop. Some people get testy," she says. "Besides, it's not who I am. It's only a job."

There's a hint of reproach in her words, but I'm not sure where it's coming from or what it's directed at. So I decide not to address it. Instead, I refer back to her comment about why she didn't come to the door with her partner. "So . . . who did you think would be here?"

Her brow wrinkles. "Clara. I was a little mad about that, honestly. That's why I didn't come to the door. Kinda glad I was wrong, though."

"Wait." I blink. "Was Clara living here with Dad?"

"No. She's got her own house somewhere on the other side of the river," she says. "I just thought . . . Okay, I don't know what I thought. Anyway. She's not here, and you are."

"Yep. Here I am." Despite being thrilled to see her, I need to know more about what happened. And maybe Alina will tell me without her partner here. "Do you know anything about why you guys had to come out here?" I ask.

Alina rolls her eyes. "It must've been a prank, and if I find out who did it, I'm gonna kick their ass," she says. "We got an 'anonymous tip,' somebody claiming they saw a woman at this address locking a child in a shed."

"Jesus," I whisper, definitely not seeing the lighter side here. "Who would do that?"

"Probably some bored kid. And the number was private, so we can't even look it up," Alina says. "I know cop shows say we can, but that's bullshit, too."

Cop shows. My lagging brain finally tries and fails to reconcile Alina Cruz with Armed Cop. "I can't believe you became a police officer."

"Right? Me, neither. It's kind of a long story, and I'll definitely tell it to you soon." Her smile flashes back. "Welcome home, Kit-Kat."

"Thank you." Coming from Alina, the sentiment actually feels good. I have to bite my tongue to stop myself from crying again. I want to haul her into the house, make us a pot of coffee, and talk for hours. I want to apologize for never checking up on her after she left Dad's — she was sixteen, and she would've been in the system for two more years.

But I can't do any of that. It's three in the morning, Alina is obviously working, and I have a child sleeping in the house who might wake up and panic any second.

"Well, I'd better get moving," Alina says, as if she's reading my mind. "Lots of crime to fight, you know." She smirks and makes a sweeping gesture around the quiet neighborhood. "Listen . . . I hope it doesn't sound too awful to say that I'll see you tomorrow."

My smile feels genuine. "Not at all."

This time, I'm the one to initiate a hug.

CHAPTER 12

Holly and I are having breakfast in the living room. Or at least Holly is. I don't have much of an appetite.

I'm surprised I didn't have another episode this morning. I haven't gotten a full night's sleep since I came home, and the day of my father's funeral seems like a prime candidate for paralyzing nightmares. Especially after the middle-of-the-night police visit over . . . what? A prank? Someone with a vendetta against me?

Or maybe it's not about me. Maybe it's about Holly.

Either way, I can't figure out why anyone would make up a story about me locking her in the shed. If it was her actual parents, they could have gone to the police and simply gotten her back. I couldn't have done anything about it.

And if it's about me, who would've done it? Naomi is my first thought. She must know I'm in town, since she clearly knows about Dad. I'm honestly not sure if she still lives in Fulton, but she certainly knows the house and the address. Would she know about Holly, though? And if she does, why do *this* specific thing?

Then again, Naomi never seemed to need a reason to lash out about anything.

The worst part about what happened with her was that she seemed to be getting better. She lived with us for three years and spent the first of those years hating everyone and everything. But then, slowly, she started to warm up. By her senior year of high school, she was tolerant and occasionally borderline friendly.

At least until just before spring break — which was when she snapped.

I still have no idea what happened. She never told anyone why. She came home after the last day of school before the break and just . . . went after me. Screaming, calling me the worst names I'd ever heard at that point in my life. Getting physical. Before I really understood what was happening, she'd pushed me down the stairs. Broke my arm.

That was when Dad tried to have DSS place her somewhere else. Which, my mind insists on pointing out, would make sense if he'd been taking nude photos of her.

No. No *way*. There has to be some other explanation for that picture.

Anyway, Mom talked him out of it. She explained to me, much later, that it would've been worse if we sent Naomi away for what she did. That you don't give up on people because they make mistakes. I didn't really understand at the time. I do now, but for a while back then, I was so mad at my mother.

Because Naomi never calmed down after that. She reverted to worse than she'd been when she first arrived, and after she graduated high school, she couldn't get away from us fast enough. It took a month after the school year ended for them to get her into assisted housing, and it felt like the longest month of my life.

So maybe Naomi did call the cops on me — once again, for no particular reason, like whatever set her off back then.

Or maybe it was Tyler.

Chills race through me, and I shudder and nearly spill the coffee I'm holding in both hands. He's not only out of prison. He's in the area, apparently flogging the book he wrote while he was incarcerated. And I know he blames me for putting him there in the first place.

Me . . . and Lynette. We both testified against him.

Because he did it, goddamn it.

There's no way it could have been anyone else. Tyler and Marisol were alone in the house. All the doors and windows were locked. Both of them were upstairs in their respective bedrooms. She had sleeping pills in her system, the kind Tyler occasionally used. He admitted giving them to her. And his fingerprints were all over the pillow he used to—

I close my eyes and take a few slow, deep breaths. Somehow, even if getting a lawyer didn't help, I won't let Tyler get away with what he's done. That includes making up a story about me to the police, if he's the one who called them.

But I can't focus on that now. I need to get through today.

I set my coffee down and watch Holly for a moment. She's finished her bowl of cereal and taken a few bites of toast, and her attention is wandering away from the laptop in front of her. I had the idea to find a child-friendly YouTube video for learning sign language to see if she recognized any of it, but she hasn't responded at all to the smiling woman on the screen.

"Okay. Let's turn this off," I say, reaching for the track pad to close the browser. "Are you all done eating?" I gesture to her bowl and the small plate with the half-eaten toast.

She studies my face, then slowly reaches for the toast. Her expression falls as she starts bringing it toward her mouth. Clearly, she doesn't want to eat any more.

Does she think I'm telling her that she has to?

"Oh, no. It's okay." I gently cover her hand and take the now-cold food, then set it on the plate. "You don't have to finish it. I was only asking if you're done."

Even as I speak, frustration fills me. I wish I could talk to her. I wish I knew *anything* about her. Her real name, what her life has been like, how she got here. But I know this isn't easy for her, either, and I'm determined to be patient.

She looks from the plate to me, uncertain. I smile and shake my head, trying to convey that she doesn't have to eat more and that it's okay.

Finally, she lifts a wavering smile.

"That's right," I say, hoping she does understand. "You're good. We're good."

Suddenly, she climbs down from the couch and stands, facing me. She holds her arms down and places one hand over the other in front of her legs. It seems like a deliberate gesture. Is she signing something? If it's ASL, wouldn't she have reacted to the video?

Then I realize she's squirming in place a little.

"Oh! You have to . . . go to the bathroom?" I get up and repeat the gesture.

She nods.

My heart flutters as I beam at her, take her hand, and lead her to the downstairs bathroom. She goes right in and shuts the door, and I want to shout and pump my fist in triumph. This is definitely what she meant to say.

Even this tiny communication between us feels like a huge step forward.

While I wait for her, I look up the ASL sign for bathroom on my phone — but it's not what she did. The bathroom sign is to form a letter T, with a thumb tucked between the first and second finger of a closed fist, and shake it back and forth.

Still, her gesture meant bathroom. Maybe she has ways to convey other things, too. We can definitely work on that. In the meantime, this is an encouraging development. I'll take all the positives I can get.

As I'm looking at my phone, it pings with a notification. A new Facebook message. My gut sours, and I don't breathe until I open it and see it's from Mickey.

Honey, I'm so sorry. I can't make it down there for the funeral. Lizbeth is running a fever, and her throat's really sore and bright red. Think she caught the strep that's going

around school, so I need to take her to the doctor's. But I
was going to ask, since you're back home, maybe we can get
together sometime next week? Would love to see you!

I can't help but smile. Of everyone in our Facebook group, I've gotten to know grownup Mickey the most. She has a longtime partner, Cedar, but they're not married because, in her words, 'he's just as Bohemian as me, darling.' They have two kids together. Lizbeth is currently nine, and her brother, Lennon, is eleven. They live in Mexico — the town thirty minutes north of Fulton, not the country.

Though I'm sad she can't make it, because I know she really wanted to, my smile lingers as I type.

No worries, I completely understand. Would love to see you
too! Message me after you get Lizbeth taken care of and let
me know a good day. I've got nothing planned.

As I send the response, I'm surprised to discover that I mean it. I actually want to hang out with a person in real life, not just online. Maybe my self-imposed isolation hasn't left me hopeless and alone forever.

Maybe I'm not an utterly ruined human being, after all.

CHAPTER 13

If one more person tells me that Dad is in a better place, I'm going to punch them.

At least right now, no one but the minister is talking. I'd thought the funeral would drag on forever in that stuffy church with hundreds of people crammed into it and more standing outside, listening to the services over a loudspeaker. Dad was famous, after all, even if it was only locally.

But that all passed in a blur of tears and aching misery and people talking at me, all saying basically the same thing.

It's the graveside service that feels like it's taking hours.

What is he even saying? I wonder as the minister drones on about having many rooms in his father's house. As far as I knew, my dad was not a religious man. But he'd apparently specified all these arrangements ahead of time, down to the church and the clergy he wanted to officiate. So maybe he'd started attending services.

Another thing I might have known if I hadn't been such a shitty daughter.

At least not everyone who attended the funeral came to the cemetery, though there are still over a hundred people here. They're gathered in clumps and knots on the grass, leaving respectable spaces around the nearby graves. Only the occasional sob or sniffle competes with the minister's intonations.

My attention wanders, and I start looking anywhere but at the gaping hole surrounded by violent green Astroturf and the gleaming oblong box suspended above it. I stare past the minister, across the rolling hills of Mt. Adnah Cemetery, where my father is being laid to rest beside my mother. And my daughter.

My body clenches like a fist with the thought, and I close my eyes and start breathing slowly, deliberately. In through my nose, out through my mouth. If I don't, I'm going to start wailing — and I'm afraid I won't be able to stop.

A hand gently grasps mine. I exhale shakily, open my eyes, and turn toward Drew, who searches my face with deep concern. I nod to tell him I'm okay, and he offers a tight smile and squeezes briefly before releasing my hand.

I'm not okay. But I have to be, for now.

A flicker of movement somewhere off in the near distance catches my attention. I look that way and spot a figure half-hidden behind a tree, several rows back, watching us. Watching *me*. My heart rate instantly ramps up, and I nearly gasp and grab for Drew before I recognize the person.

Lynette.

My heart breaks looking at her. Though we never got the chance to make it official, Dad was her grandfather, too. I hate the idea of her standing alone back there, thinking she doesn't belong or isn't welcome.

Then again, maybe that's not what she's thinking at all. Maybe she's thinking she doesn't want to be anywhere near me.

Part of me still wants to go to her and invite her to join us. But before I can decide whether I should, she notices me noticing her.

And she's gone.

My breath shudders out of me, and I force myself to return my attention to the service.

Finally, the minister wraps it up and tells us to go with God. I heave an inward sigh of relief as I slowly back away from the hole, not quite ready to face hearing even more condolences and he's-in-a-better-place crap while I work my way back through the crowd to the vehicles.

The first thing I check on is Holly. She's been a real trooper through all this, sticking close to me without once fidgeting or poking around. She's still toting the stuffed cat around like a talisman, clutched tightly under one arm while she holds my hand with the other.

She looks up at me and yawns so widely, I can see her back teeth.

"Getting sleepy, huh?" I mutter with a smile. "One more car ride, then we can get something to eat, and I'm sure you'll be able to take a nap."

Of course, she has no idea what I'm saying, but she seems satisfied.

Just then, Drew gently nudges me with an elbow. "Hey," he murmurs near my ear. "Isn't that Bryon Halloway?"

I turn, follow his gaze, and see DNC's morning anchor approaching with a woman I assume is his wife. I'd met Bryon a few times as a child. Occasionally, my dad would take me to work with him for a few hours, and I'd get to sit in the booth and watch the live broadcast. They're both fifty-something, him with dark, silver-streaked hair and her with platinum blonde that might be dyed. His wife is a few inches taller than him.

I wonder how he ended up having Naomi as a co-anchor and why Marcia Matthews is doing the weather instead of Leslie Brandt, the weekend forecaster. But I'm certainly not going to ask Bryon about that now.

They reach us and exchange a few words with Drew, then Bryon extends a hand to me. "Katrina," he says, his blue eyes wavering in the sunlight. "How are you holding up?"

He's the first person to ask me that instead of offering trite phrases, and I almost burst into tears on the spot. A few slip out anyway as I accept his warm, firm grip. "Well, you know," I manage in a trembling voice. "Not great."

"I know. Such a shock. Joe was the absolute picture of health." Bryon is using his smooth, deep news voice, but I don't think he intends to be patronizing. I don't think he even realizes he's doing it. He and my dad were good friends, and he looks almost as distraught as I feel. "This is my wife, Cody," he says, indicating the tall platinum blonde. "Cody, this is Katrina Gray."

Instead of holding out a hand, Cody comes in for a hug.

I'm startled, and I stiffen for half a second before I relax and let the hug happen. Cody Halloway looks angular, but she's firm and comforting, and she smells like a fresh spring rain. A sob escapes me despite my best efforts.

She rubs my back. "Oh, honey, I'm so sorry. It's never easy losing someone."

At least she sounds like she means it.

We separate, and I realize most of the graveside attendees are dispersing. Drew is thanking them for coming and gently directing them around me and the Halloways, saying we hope to see them at the reception. Again, I feel a swell of gratitude for him.

"And who's this young lady?" Bryon makes no sudden moves toward Holly. He merely smiles down at her. "What a pretty cat you have there," he says.

Holly lifts her head toward him and blinks.

"Her name is Holly. She's deaf," I explain so he knows she's not being rude. "She's staying with me for a while."

Thankfully, neither of them questions that any further. "God, I'm sorry, Katrina. I hardly know what to say." Bryon offers a sad smile and shakes his head. "It just happened so fast. I mean, he was upset that morning, but he didn't seem sick at all."

"Upset?" I echo.

"Yes, he was . . . distracted. Almost missed his cue for the nine o'clock segment." Bryon's lips press together as he stares off briefly. "Apparently, someone came to the studio to talk to him. Texted him or something. He said it was urgent."

My brow furrows. "Who was it?"

"No idea. He met them outside."

Icy fingers of disquiet squeeze my heart. What was so urgent that would make my father step out in the middle of work? He was the consummate professional, even during the hard months after my mother died.

"Well, we'd better get out of the way." Bryon shakes my hand again, and Cody does the same. "We'll meet you at the VFW."

I give an absent nod. "Yes, thank you. See you there."

They drift off, and I try to calm my whirling mind. Was something wrong when my father died? Should I be suspicious of this mystery visitor? He died of a stroke, but like I knew and Bryon confirmed, he shouldn't have. His health was excellent.

Was it triggered by stress? Or maybe something more ominous?

As I struggle to concentrate on getting out of here, knowing I have to at least say something to the minister before I can leave, there's a tug on my dress. I look down. Holly bites her lip and makes the same gesture she did earlier this morning, one hand over the other in front of her legs.

"Oh, okay, sweetie," I tell her, though of course she can't hear me. When Drew gives me a confused look, I nod at Holly. "That means she has to go to the bathroom. We figured it out this morning."

"You did? That's great news!" Drew smiles and looks from me to her. "I can take her, if you want. I know you still have a few things to wrap up." He pauses, and his brows furrow. "Wait, are there even bathrooms here?"

Nodding, I point to the white house at the edge of the cemetery that borders East Broadway. "Yes. In there. And that would be great, if she'll go with you." The sooner we can leave, the better.

I catch Holly's attention, then repeat her 'bathroom' gesture and point to Drew. "Hold your hand out," I tell him.

He does. After a glance at me, Holly gives the tiniest smile and slips her hand in his.

Drew looks like he might cry. He's clearly touched that she trusts him. "Come on, Holly, let's go potty," he says — then his eyes bulge, and he slaps his free hand over his mouth. A muted snort comes from beneath it.

Oh my God, is he *laughing*? It takes me a minute, but I finally realize why.

Come on, Barbie, let's go potty.

I can see him, an awkward, gangly thirteen-year-old with orange corkscrew curls, livid freckles, and a penchant for good-natured mischief. I was helping Alina with her math homework, and we were listening to music. Aqua's *Barbie Girl* came on, and at the exact right moment, my bedroom door flew open and Drew burst in, a naked Barbie in one hand and a little plastic toilet from the Barbie Dream House in the other. He'd shrieked that altered line along with the song at the top of his lungs, giggling like a maniac.

We squealed and threw pillows at him. After he ducked out of the room, Alina and I collapsed in laughter.

Now, I'm struggling to hold back a laugh, too.

With Drew and Holly gone, I start looking for the minister. But before I spot him, a familiar countenance swims into view. Her blonde hair is starting to gray, and her bloodshot blue eyes are leaking a stream of constant tears.

"Clara," I breathe. Still feeling guilty that I practically forgot her existence, I hold out my arms, and she falls into them. I didn't even realize she was here — and I definitely should have. She was probably the closest person to him, especially over the last five years. She should have been sitting with me at the funeral in the designated family section.

Yet I didn't even bother looking for her.

"Oh, Kat. It's so awful. I'm so, so sorry," she sobs, still hugging me. "Your father is such a dear man—" She breaks off and looks up at me, horrified. Probably at her use of the present tense. "Was, I mean," she corrects, sniffling noisily as she swipes at her face. "I'm such a mess. I'm sorry."

"No, please. I completely understand." I wish I'd gotten to know her better. Her grief is as real as mine, and grief is always a little easier when you can share it. "*I'm* sorry for *your* loss*,*" I tell her. "Even though I hate that stupid saying."

A startled, watery chuckle bursts from her. "Oh, me too, sweetie. It's the worst, isn't it? Right up there with 'he's in a better place.'"

I can't help a smile as she echoes my sentiments. "Exactly," I agree.

"And then there's all this . . . fuss." She waves a hand around at the crowd, then leans in and lowers her voice. "You know, most of these people just want to be seen coming here. They don't care about Joe at all."

Now, I'm remembering something else about Clara Crawford. She's refreshingly blunt.

I like her for that.

"Anyway. Oh, my." She's still sobbing faintly, hitching every few breaths. She digs around in an oversized purse hanging from her arm and comes out with an open travel pack of tissues. "Want one? I must've gone through a dozen of these in the past few days."

"Yes, please." She extends the plastic package, and I extract a tissue.

She takes one out and blows her nose with a resounding honk, then fishes an empty plastic sleeve from her purse and tucks the used tissue in. "I won't bother with my face. No tissue's going to fix this." She gestures at her running makeup with a rueful smirk. "Listen, sweetie, I just wanted to make sure it's okay with you if I come to the reception. I know it's limited attendance, but—"

"Of course you can," I interrupt before she can finish that sentence and break my heart further. "You're family, too."

Her smile is full of warmth. "Thank you so much, Kat. It means a lot to hear you say that."

Instead of responding, I pull her into another hug. "It's the truth," I tell her. "I'll see you there."

Clara excuses herself to 'freshen her face' before the reception. For a moment, I watch her make her way across the grass and down the nearest hill with a vague ache in my chest. Though I hadn't spent much time with her before my world fell apart, she still feels familiar. Like another piece of home.

I hope I can gather them all back to me. Because now more than ever, I need every scrap of home I can get.

CHAPTER 14

After the relative calm coolness of the cemetery, the reception feels even more crowded than the funeral.

We're holding it at the VFW in Hastings because the Fulton one isn't big enough. Even here, the private event room is full, every seat at every table taken and more guests standing, spilling out into the main area by the pool table, or mingling with the patrons at the bar. The two long tables against the back and side walls, filled with food at the beginning, have been decimated and picked over. And stragglers are still arriving.

I'm sitting at a back table with Alina and Drew. Holly is next to me, lost in a coloring book one of the auxiliary ladies found for her. Bryon and Cody Halloway are here somewhere, too. I haven't seen Clara yet, but after she practically broke down at the cemetery, I suspect she's taking her time, trying to pull herself together.

People keep coming up to me with greetings and more condolences, but I'm not paying as much attention as I should. I'm all peopled out. Thinking that phrase almost makes me smile. It was one of my dad's favorites, especially after he had to attend some busy function or event as 'that weather guy.'

So when yet another shadow darkens our table, I almost don't bother looking up. At least until Alina lets out a gasp — a happy one — and Drew rumbles, "Holy shit."

I raise my head, and the face smiling down at me is the best kind of shock to my system.

"Blake!" I'm on my feet, throwing my arms around him, then I have to move aside so Drew and Alina can make their way over for hugs. A lump catches in my throat as I watch them greet each other in the same long-lost-friends way I'd met them when I came back.

Blake was with us for a year. My junior year of high school, to be exact. Before he came to stay with us, Drew had the 'boys' bedroom' upstairs to himself, so he grumbled a little about having to share a room again. But Blake fit in with the three of us so quickly, me, Drew, and Alina, that it felt like we'd known him forever.

And eventually, Drew admitted that he loved having a 'real brother' to balance out his annoying sisters.

"Guys." Blake is grinning, though unshed tears gleam in his vivid green eyes. He grew up movie-star handsome, with artfully tousled blond hair, chiseled features, and a lean but solid figure. "I mean, wow. Look at us."

"Talk about wow!" Alina waggles her eyebrows. "You got pretty, Fox."

Another latent memory surfaces. Alina had a nickname for everybody. I was Kit-Kat, Blake was Fox after the X-Files character because his last name is Mulder. Drew was Sunshine because his hair looks like a sunset, and he was always smiling.

And when Mom and Dad were out of earshot, Naomi was Twatosaurus Rex.

Blake snorts and ducks his head. "Pretty?"

"Hey, at least you're not 'adorable.'" Drew makes air quotes and shoots a mock glare at Alina. From what I gathered at the start of the reception, the two of them saw each other most recently out of us, but that was still several years ago. And they both still live in Fulton.

The fact that they haven't stayed close either only makes me feel a little less bad.

Alina chuckles and plants a loud kiss on his cheek. "Aw, you know I love you, bro."

"Ew. Sister germs," Drew intones.

We all laugh at that. And for a moment, I feel better than I have in a very long time.

"So." Blake squeezes my hand, then looks past me at the table. "Who's this small, sleepy person back here?"

My brow furrows, and I glance over my shoulder. Holly's arms are folded on the coloring book with her head resting on them. Her eyes are fluttering closed.

I don't blame her. It's been an exhausting day already.

"Um. This is Holly. She's . . . a long story, but she's with me." I share a look with Drew, and he smiles encouragingly. "I'm fostering her for now."

"That's really great, Kat," he says. "He'd be proud of you. They both would."

I know he means Mom and Dad. And now the tears are threatening all over again.

Drew looks at the uncomfortable position Holly's in. "There's nobody in the back room by the kitchen right now," he tells me. "Those tables have benches. Maybe you could lay her down for a quick nap? I'll ask the staff if they have anything resembling pillows or blankets."

"Oh, that's a great idea. Thank you." I turn and touch Holly's shoulder to get her attention. When I start to pick her up, she reaches for me and wraps her arms around my neck.

For one selfish second, I wish they'd never find her parents. I wish I could keep her.

After she's settled in place, I look at Blake and Alina. Drew is already slipping through the crowd, looking for a staff member. "Will you guys be here for a while? I'd love to catch up with you as soon as I can."

"Definitely," Blake says.

Alina nods in agreement. "Not going anywhere, Kit-Kat."

"Thank you so much. I think she just needs a few minutes of peace and quiet." *Honestly, so do I*, I add silently.

I make my way along the back wall food table to the doorway from the event room to the back. It's a smaller space, one side dedicated to a diner-style kitchen and three fixed tables with plain wooden bench seats along the other. A door on the far side of the room leads outside.

There's a stack of coats on the farthest table, and mine is buried in there somewhere. I take a few steps toward it, thinking I'll extricate it and fold it up so she'll have at least a slight cushion for her head. But before I can figure out how to get to my coat without putting Holly down or shoving the whole pile on the floor, Drew comes in with a barstool cushion and a flat bedsheet.

"Best they can do, and it's better than nothing." He smiles, skirts around me, and puts the pillow down on the far end of the nearest bench.

"That'll work."

It takes me a few minutes, but I get Holly settled with her head on the pillow, then cover her with the sheet. She doesn't take up the whole bench, so I sit on the end beside her.

"Are you okay back here?" Drew asks. "Do you need anything?"

I wave him off. "I'm fine." It's likely he wants to go back out and talk to Blake, and I don't mind. He's been by my side all day. "I'm just going to let her rest for a bit, then we'll come back out."

"Okay. Text me if you need anything, though."

"I will. Thank you."

He returns to the busy room, and I lean my head back and close my eyes. Being here feels so surreal. My emotions keep flickering back and forth. One minute, I'm thrilled to be with my siblings after so long apart. The next, deep sorrow gut-punches me when I remember *why* I'm here with them.

It's the world's worst roller coaster, and I want to get off.

I'm not sure how long I've been sitting there, trying to shut out the world, when someone says, "Oh, Kat, there you are. You doing okay, sweetie?"

The foggy, raspy voice is Clara's. I think. I open my eyes to confirm it and find her standing a few feet away, wringing her hands. It looks like she gave up on trying to save her makeup, because it's all washed off now. Her eyes are red-rimmed and watery, and her nose is bright pink. Probably from blowing it so much. She looks like a stiff breeze would blow her over.

"What about you?" I slide from the booth, careful not to disturb Holly, and give her a hug. "Here, do you want to sit with me for a while?"

"Thank you." She flickers a smile and heads for the opposite side of the table as I resume my seat. "Well. Here we are," she says, looking around the small room. "I don't think I've ever been to this VFW before."

"It's a good place. Everyone here is so nice." While I was growing up, we had almost every bigger-than-average gathering here. Milestone birthdays and anniversaries, graduations, wedding receptions, and these 'celebrations of life.' My mother's was here, too. "So . . . did you get something to eat?"

I hold back a groan. Could I have said anything lamer? I want to talk to her like a normal person, but I don't know what to say. *I'm sorry I didn't try harder to make friends with you* sounds terrible. I also don't want to make small talk about her job, since I don't know anything beyond that she's a nurse.

"Oh, no. Not too hungry," she says, folding her hands on the table. She cranes her head slightly to peer at the sleeping figure on the bench, and a gentle smile lifts her lips. "She's beautiful. I forgot to tell you that at the service," she says. "She looks just like her mother."

An involuntary wince contorts my features. "She's . . . uh, not mine," I stammer. "I'm taking care of her. I . . ."

Clara's face falls. "Oh, I'm so sorry," she moans. "I shouldn't assume."

"No, it's fine. Really." I reach across the table and lay my hand on hers. "I think she looks like Marisol, too."

Speaking my daughter's name aloud is a nick to my soul, every time, but I can't keep hiding from what happened. I've done that for far too long.

"She really does, the angel." Clara's smile returns. "Kat, I hope you don't think . . . well, with your father gone, I wanted you to know. I don't expect or want anything of his. The house, the car, the money. Everything goes to you, like he wanted."

There's no bitterness in her tone, and I'm once again floored by her bluntness. As well as the fact that she expects nothing. "Oh, I didn't think . . . I mean, he has a will, I guess, but I haven't seen it yet."

"And you're his sole beneficiary, which is exactly the way it should be." It's Clara's turn to pat my hand. "I wasn't sure if you'd think . . . well, you know. Younger woman and all. As if I could be called young." She gives a rueful snort. "Anyway, Joe and I never wanted to combine things. I had my house, my job, my finances, and he had his. We were happier that way. We simply enjoyed each other's company." Her smile grows distant, and a tear slips down her cheek. "I loved your father very much, and I just hope you and I can be friends."

I'm on the verge of sobbing myself. "I'd be happy to do that."

Yet even as I try to open myself to the idea of having relationships again, I can't help remembering that I wouldn't be here if my father wasn't dead.

And that it shouldn't have taken losing him for me to come home.

CHAPTER 15

Almost everyone from our party is gone now. The main bar is busier than ever, but the reception guests have trickled away in singles and small groups until only Alina and I remain. Drew and Blake stayed to help clean up, but they left a few minutes ago to head their separate ways.

Blake promised to stay in touch, and I really hope he does.

I tie up the last trash bag, dust my hands off, and look around the room. "I think that's it," I announce, smiling at Alina. "Thanks for the help."

"No problem," she says. "You ready to get out of here?"

"Definitely. Oh, wait a second." I turn to Holly, who's been quite the little helper, and make her bathroom gesture. "Do you need to go, sweetheart?"

She smiles and shakes her head.

"No? Okay, let's go for a ride." I pantomime a steering wheel, like I did when we drove to Walmart.

Holly nods.

"Oh my God!" Alina squeals, clapping her hands. "You're talking to her, right? She understands you?"

"Well, sort of." My broad smile matches hers. "It doesn't seem like she knows sign language, but we figured out 'bathroom' this morning. That's the first time she reacted to 'driving,' though."

"That is *great*." Alina grins at her. "Well, I need to pee before we go. Meet you in the parking lot?"

"Sounds good."

Alina heads for the single bathroom in the private area, and I take Holly's hand and lead her out, past the pool table, and through the main exit. There are still plenty of cars in the lot. I'm parked in the back row, and I'm not sure where Alina parked or even what her car looks like. I'm assuming she didn't drive a squad car here.

I head for my Taurus and press the fob to unlock it. In the brief, chirping flash of light, I see two people getting out of a blue SUV several spaces down from my car. They don't head inside right away, but I don't think anything of it until I'm buckling Holly into her booster seat, and I hear footsteps crossing the asphalt toward me.

Did somebody forget something and come back? Or maybe they're late arrivals. It's a few minutes past seven, the stated time the reception ended, so they're a little *too* late if that's the case.

The footsteps stop. "That you, Kat?" a voice says.

My blood runs cold. That voice can't belong to who I think it does.

At least, it better not.

I hold up a finger to Holly, hoping she understands that I won't be long, then straighten slowly and turn. The cold in me flashes into hot, boiling fury.

Tyler fucking Martin is standing there like he didn't murder my daughter and get away with it.

For a long moment, I can't force any words out. He's lost weight since I last saw him — probably too much. His cheekbones are a touch too sharp, his joints too prominent, his waist too tapered. Like Guy Pearce in *Memento*. And he's not alone. The woman, the *girl* who stands just behind and to the side of him, can't be older than twenty. Blonde-haired and blue-eyed, like me. Like Marisol.

Before I can even think about what I'm doing, my arm comes up, and I smack the son of a bitch across his smug face. Hard.

"What the *hell* do you think you're doing, showing up here?" I nearly shout as he reels back, and his hand shoots up to cradle his face. My voice echoes across the parking lot, and a few heads of the people in the outdoor smoking area turn. "You need to get the fuck away from me, right now."

My fierce glower practically dares him to say something about me hitting him.

If he does, I think I might hit him again.

Instead, he rubs his cheek, then holds up both hands in a gesture of surrender and backs up a step, nearly bumping into the girl. I can't even begin to imagine what he's doing with her — and I thought I couldn't hate him any more. "Hey, whoa. I just wanted to talk to you for a minute," he says. "You've seen the news, haven't you? You know I'm innocent."

"Bullshit," I snarl through clenched teeth. "I don't give a damn what fancy lawyer tricks they pulled. You are unbelievable, showing up at my father's funeral, you sick, murdering asshole!"

The blonde girl gasps. "Oh, no, your father? I'm so—"

"Shut up," Tyler snaps at her. "I said I'd handle this."

"Oh, you son of a bitch." I'm aware that my volume is rising even louder, but I can't stop myself. "What, you think you're a badass now because you were in prison? *Where you still belong?*" I look at the girl. "I don't know you, but I'm happy to give you a ride somewhere away from him, if you want."

In my peripheral vision, I see someone running across the parking lot. I'm pretty sure it's Alina. Suddenly, I wish she'd brought her gun with her, because I'd shoot this bastard and call it self-defense.

"Don't be stupid, Kat." There's a warning glint in Tyler's eyes that I don't like at all. "It's your fault I got convicted. You and that lying little bitch Lynette. I spent five years in prison, and I *didn't do anything, goddamn it!*"

"Hey! Step back from her *right now*, sir."

Damn. I've never heard Alina sound anything like that. She's developed a cop voice, and it's intimidating as hell.

Tyler's face contorts, and he moves back again. This time, he bumps the blonde, who looks incredibly uncomfortable. "Who are you?" he grunts, his eyes narrowing.

"I'm a police officer, *sir.*" Alina reaches my side as she launches the last word in a mocking drawl. I know she's not armed, but she has a hand at her side beneath her jacket, as if there's a gun there. "I'm gonna need you to return to your vehicle and get in."

For an instant, I think he's not going to leave. But he finally pulls a face, grabs the blonde's hand, and stalks off without another word.

Alina and I stay where we are, watching until they climb into the SUV, then start the engine. I half expect Tyler to peel out and rush past us, veering too close in some ridiculous display of pettiness, but he backs out and eases away in the opposite direction at normal parking lot speed.

"What a prick." Alina whooshes out a breath, then turns to hug me. "You okay, hon?"

"I'm fine," I murmur, trying not to betray how shaken I am, how it feels like even my veins are vibrating. I remember wondering if Tyler was the one who made the false call to the police about me, and now I'm thinking it's possible. He obviously knew I was in town.

Alina pulls back with a frown. "You sure?"

"Yeah. Sorry." I let out a long exhale. "He was not the person I needed to see today."

"Speaking of people we don't need to see," she says, panning an exaggerated gaze across the parking lot. "Did you notice how she couldn't even be bothered to show up today?"

"She who?" I ask, remembering how offended Alina seemed when she thought Clara was staying at Dad's house. Maybe that's who she means. I hadn't seen the two of them interacting at any point today — and I'm still not sure what Alina has against Clara.

But she grins and waggles her eyebrows. "Twatosaurus Rex."

I nearly choke on my own spit. "Oh, God, stop right there. If you say that three times, she'll appear and bite our heads off."

Personally, I'd have been more surprised if Naomi *had* shown up.

Again, I find myself wanting to confess what I found in the linen closet at the house. But telling Alina could be even worse than telling Drew, because then I'd be reporting it directly to the cops. Or at least *a* cop. She wouldn't be able to ignore the implications, and there would be an investigation.

I can't handle that. At least, not yet. So instead, I say, "She was probably too busy being on TV."

Alina grunts. "Don't you think it's funny how Naomi is suddenly a morning news anchor on the same show, the day after Joe died?"

Her comment brings my unease surging back. Morning anchor is a prime spot, not typically given to people with zero experience in broadcasting. And — not that I've watched every news channel or podcast ever — but I don't think Naomi is a seasoned news veteran.

Dad was a meteorologist, and it's not like Naomi took over his slot. She wouldn't have even been hired as a direct result of him dying. There's no way the network would have plucked someone completely new from nowhere and shoved them into the morning co-anchor seat overnight, so she must've already been hired when it happened.

Still, the timing is suspicious. And there was what Bryon said about my father having a mysterious visitor at the studio the morning he died.

Was it Naomi?

"Yeah. It's funny," I finally say. "You don't happen to know how she landed that spot, do you?"

"Hell, no. I haven't spoken to her since the day she left the house, and good riddance."

A small pat on my legs has me glancing down. I look at Holly, and she stretches her arms toward me, trying to smother a yawn.

"Oh, sweetie." I scoop her up and shift her onto my side, then give Alina an apologetic smile. "I'd better get this one home before she ends up falling asleep on the parking lot."

"Right! Yeah, no problem." Alina gives me a one-armed hug, then waves at Holly. "Goodnight, honey. Kat, I'll message you tomorrow? Maybe we can plan to hang out and do something fun while you're in town. Take the kiddo to Thunder Island or something."

I'm touched that she wants to include Holly. "We'll definitely do something," I say. "Thank you for being here today."

"Of course."

Alina heads across the lot, presumably to her car, and I open my back door to buckle Holly into her seat. Part of me is relieved this day is over. The rest of me wishes it hadn't come for many, many years yet.

And now, I have to wonder if someone made sure my father wouldn't get all those years he should've had left.

CHAPTER 16

The whole world is trembling.

Are we having an earthquake?

I suck in a startled breath and open my eyes. At least I'm not paralyzed, but it still takes me a moment to figure out what's going on. It's the middle of the night. I'm in my room, and the bed is shaking.

No, *I'm* shaking. Holly is shaking me.

I turn toward her as fast as I can. She's on her knees beside me, her eyes wide with the same fear she showed last night. And she's pointing out the window.

My heart twists as I stare at the darkened rectangle. At least the light hasn't come on. I managed to replace the bulb this morning before the funeral, so hopefully the lack of light means we don't have an intruder.

Like whoever left that note in the closet for me.

"Okay, sweetheart." I sit up and urge Holly farther onto the bed, so she's behind me. "I'll see if anything is out there."

I already know I'm not going to find anything, but I get up and walk the short distance to the window. The back yard is full of wavering shadows, as always. I stare down at it for several minutes, trying to adjust my vision, looking for some hint of what scared Holly.

There's nothing. At least, not that I can see.

I head back to the bed, so exhausted that my bones hurt. This is the third middle-of-the-night scare in a row. And for some reason, it doesn't feel like an accident. But I can't stop it if I don't know what's happening.

Holly is pushed against the headboard, clutching her knees to her chest. I sit on the bed, scooch up next to her, and lay a hand on her arm.

She's vibrating like a live wire.

"Oh, honey." I drape an arm around her small form, and she leans into me, still trembling. Her gaze remains fixed on the window. Maybe she really is having some kind of PTSD reaction to what happened to her out there. If that's the case, she can't tell me. I can't even take her to a psychiatrist for help, because I doubt Fulton has any therapists who specialize in deaf children who have no way to communicate.

Clearly, neither of us is ready to relax. I'll take her downstairs for a snack and some warm milk, then maybe we can try going back to sleep. I give her a gentle squeeze, then slip out of bed and pad across the room to turn the light on.

That's when I notice something smudgy on the window.

"What the . . ." I blink a few times to adjust to the light as I head closer and peer at the spot. When I make out what it is, the bottom drops out of my stomach.

It's a handprint. An adult-sized handprint.

On the *outside* of my second-floor window.

"Oh my God!" I gasp, turning to snatch Holly off the bed. I grab my phone from the bedside table as I hustle from the room and downstairs. My heart is pounding in my ears, and I'm on the verge of bundling her in the car and heading straight to the police station.

Then I think, how hard are they going to laugh if I show up to report a handprint on my window?

Damn it, I need more than that.

At the bottom of the stairs, I stop and open the entryway closet. I'm relieved to find what I hoped would still be in there — a softball bat. It belonged to my dad, and he always stashed it there when not in use as a kind of kid-friendly home defense weapon.

I grab it with my free hand and continue with Holly to the kitchen, where I settle her at the table. "Can you stay here for me, just for a minute?" I ask her.

It's not a shock when she doesn't reply, but it kind of looks like she understands. I hope.

I make the 'one-minute' gesture to reinforce that I'll be right back, then head to the kitchen door. I unlock it and twist the knob, but it doesn't move. A frown creases my brow. I jiggle it a few times, then let go and look at it. The thumb turn is up and down, but I can never remember which way is locked and which is unlocked. Did I actually lock it just now? Did I leave it open *all day* during the funeral and the services?

I twist the thumb turn the other way, then try the knob. It turns easily.

"Shit," I mutter as I step aside and pull the door open. At first, I'm mentally reviewing this morning, trying to remember whether I locked the door after I installed the new bulb. Which is why I don't immediately notice the broken glass on the patio, glittering in the wedge of light thrown from the kitchen.

When I do, my initial flash of panic turns to anger.

The light bulb has been removed again. Shattered again. This wasn't an accident the first time, and it's not now.

Someone has been coming into the back yard at night.

And maybe they're still out there, right now.

"Hey!" I shout into the darkness. "Who's there?"

Unsurprisingly, no one replies to admit they're trespassing.

I rush back into the kitchen and get the flashlight from its outlet, then give Holly another one-minute sign as I head to the open doorway. Still gripping the softball bat, I thumb the flashlight on and pass the beam across the yard.

Almost immediately, I spot something on the ground to the right, where my bedroom window is. A break in the neat, uniform grass. I step outside and approach cautiously, still panning the flashlight around in case someone *is* back here. When I reach the spot, I find that it's actually two breaks. Small, flattened rectangle areas of torn ground with deep circular divots in the middle, about five feet out from the house and directly in line with my window.

My stomach rolls. I think I know what those marks are.

I whirl and point the beam toward the shed. The padlock is hanging open from the hasp, the metal bar flipped back.

And there's a piece of paper taped to the shed door.

Terror and fury roil through me as I hurry across the yard and stop at the shed. The note is a half-sheet, same as the one in the linen closet. And the message freezes my bones.

What do you think of Saint Joe Gray now, Kat? That wasn't his only nasty secret. Another one lies behind this door. This, and so much more.

I yank the note down and shove it in the pocket of my pajamas. Once again, I need to take several deep breaths before I summon the courage to look.

When I pull the door open, a shiver racks me from head to toe.

Dad's extendable ladder is lying in the middle of the shed floor, the bottom of its legs caked with dirt and grass.

"What the hell?" I shout at no one in particular. No wonder Holly was so terrified. She definitely saw something — or rather, some*one* — through the window. And there's no way she can tell me who it was.

But at least now, I've got plenty of reasons to call the police.

* * *

"Well, we can file a report, but I'll be honest with you," Officer Everett says. "Probably not gonna find who did it."

"If anyone did," Officer Spears adds.

I bristle. "What's that supposed to mean?"

I knew Alina had taken the night off so she wouldn't have to pull a long shift after spending most of the day at Dad's services, so I didn't expect her or Officer Wade to respond to my call. However, I also didn't expect them to send Tweedledum and Tweedledumber, otherwise known as Officers Everett and Spears.

I'd already shown them everything except the note, including yet another mark I'd noticed when I took them outside — a pair of greasy smudges on the siding beneath the window, spaced roughly the same as the divots in the ground.

It didn't take a genius to see someone had placed the ladder against the house, climbed it, and pressed a hand against the window.

Apparently, Officer Spears was not a genius.

"Miss Gray, you said this was your dad's place," Spears begins. He and Everett are standing by the back door while Holly and I are at the kitchen table. Holly is picking at a bowl of Goldfish crackers with her head resting on the table, her legs gently scissoring in an apparent bid to stay awake. "You've only been here a few days, right? So maybe he used the ladder before you got here."

"Do you really think I haven't been in the back yard the whole time I was here?" I fling back. "Yesterday, the shed was locked and the ladder was clean and hanging on the wall inside. Tonight, as you saw, the ladder was on the floor and dirty. It was clearly used—"

"How do we know you didn't use it?" Spears interrupts.

"Hold on, let's calm down." Everett holds up a hand and shoots his partner a look. "It does appear that someone opened the shed and used the ladder to climb up to the window," he says. "You said the back door was unlocked, and the padlock key was hanging next to it. Now, I'm not saying it's your fault that someone trespassed," he rushes to add when I open my mouth.

I exhale sharply. "Okay. What *are* you saying?"

"I'm saying, unless you've got security cameras out there I didn't see, there's probably no way to find out who did it. And at best, if you want to press charges, it'll be destruction of property and you might get twenty bucks for the light bulb. In about a month."

"This wouldn't be considered harassment?" I demand. "What about the neighbors? Maybe they saw something."

"We can ask the folks on either side, but it was the middle of the night. Even if they were awake, they're probably too far away to make out features in the dark. And the place behind you is vacant. Been up for sale for a year or so."

I grit my teeth. "Can't you take fingerprints from the window or something?"

Spears snorts, and a muscle jumps in Everett's jaw. "First, that handprint is smudged to hell," Everett says. "Second, even if we got a viable print, we'd only find a match if the person is in the system. Which is highly unlikely."

"So you're not going to do anything," I say.

Everett shrugs. "Like I said, we can file a report. That way, if you ever find out who it was, we'll have a record of the activity. Or if they do anything more serious than trespassing and destruction of property."

Fantastic. The idea of filing a report that'll sit around collecting virtual dust until whoever this is does something worse does not fill me with confidence.

I almost decide to tell them about the note, after all. But I can't, because then I'd have to tell them all of it.

"Fine," I say at last. "Please do file a report."

It looks like I'll have to figure this out myself.

The Tweedles ask a few more questions, take some half-hearted notes, and finally leave. After they're gone, I check and double-check both doors to make sure they're locked, my heart thrumming the whole time. I hate feeling so terrified within the walls that kept me safe and happy for so much of my life. I need to stop whoever is doing this. But the police aren't going to help, and much as I hate to admit it, I can't do it on my own.

Drew is coming over tomorrow. Not as my brother, but as Holly's social worker — though I'm hoping he'll be my brother, too.

It's time I confided in someone. And I definitely trust him.

Right now, though, Holly and I need sleep. I think she's more than ready, though I worry that if I bring her back to my bedroom, she'll only freak out all over again. Not that I blame her in the least. I know I can't stop her from being scared every time she looks out that particular window.

So I'll change the situation so she doesn't have to keep waking up to the source of her fear.

I smile and reach over to rub her arm. "How about we sleep in a different room? There's plenty to choose from."

Of course, she doesn't know what I'm saying. Still, she's willing enough to come with me when I stand from the table and extend a hand to her.

The house technically has four bedrooms, but my parents set it up with five. The master bedroom is next to mine and also has a window overlooking the back yard. Even if it didn't, I wouldn't have taken her in there. I haven't been able to bring myself to even open the door to that room since I came back.

The two bedrooms at the front of the house overlooking the street were the 'girls' room' and the 'boys' room.' Each has two sets of bunkbeds, a single and a double-single, though usually no more than two kids stayed in a room at a time. There's also the downstairs bedroom for the oldest, last inhabited by Naomi.

I consider the downstairs bedroom for the sake of convenience, but it really isn't very big. Instead, we head upstairs, and I bring Holly to the girls' room. I open the door, and as it swings inward, I'm struck with an almost painful wave of nostalgia.

The hallway night lights show enough of the space for my memory to fill in the rest of the blanks. The white painted bunkbeds with colorful bedding and chalkboards at the end of each bunk for the girls to write their names on and decorate. The desks with laptops on either side of the room. The big-screen TV, the filled bookshelf, the toy box, the Barbie Dream House.

So many girls came and went from this room. So many sisters.

I didn't know how amazing my childhood was until this moment.

While I'm processing all this, Holly rushes past me into the room. She flits from desk to toy box to Dream House to bunkbed, clearly delighted.

I probably should've brought her here in the first place. Most of the toys are technically for kids ten and up, but there are plenty she can play with. And I can go through and remove anything that might be dangerous.

"Okay, this is your room now," I say as I step inside. "We have to get back to bed, but you can definitely play in here tomorrow." I place my hands together, hold them up, and rest my head on them, then point to the double bed on the bottom of the right-hand bunk.

I won't leave her alone all night until we can communicate more — and I have an idea that I want to try tomorrow. For now, I'm fine with sleeping in here.

But Holly climbs onto the bottom single bunk on the left. She snuggles under the blanket, lies down, and points from me to the double bed.

"You want me to sleep there?" I smile and walk over to the bunk. "I get it. You're a big girl, and you can sleep in your own bed."

She doesn't respond, but she returns the smile as I crawl under the covers across from her. She gives a huge yawn, and her eyes start fluttering.

She's out, and I'm not far behind.

CHAPTER 17

Drew's visit for an initial home inspection is scheduled for 11 a.m., and he arrives on the dot to find Holly napping on the couch and me looking like I'm auditioning for *Night of the Living Dead*. I tell him we had a rough night and promise to elaborate after he does his thing.

It doesn't take long. He knows this house, and not much has changed since he was a foster here.

Afterward, the two of us sit with cups of coffee in the dining room, so I can see Holly if she wakes up, and I tell him everything that's been happening since I came back.

Well, almost everything. I leave out the picture of Naomi.

When I finish, he looks horrified. "So you told the police all this, and they're *still* not going to look into it?"

"Well, maybe not all of it," I admit. "They don't know about the note or the Facebook message."

"You need to tell them. Whoever this is, they're threatening you."

"That's the thing. Technically, they're not." It sure as hell *feels* threatening, and I'm convinced there's a real danger to me somewhere in this, but the only thing they've promised is that I'll know 'the truth' about my father.

Drew frowns. "I guess. You should still tell them, though. I mean, some guy was creeping in your second-floor bedroom window!"

I shudder at the memory of seeing that handprint, knowing someone had been staring at me and Holly through the window moments before I found it. "Or some girl," I say.

"Right. It could be anybody."

I heave a sigh. "Yeah. But if I had to guess, I'd say it's either Tyler or Naomi."

Drew looks at me quizzically. "Why Naomi?"

"Because she hates me?" I throw up my hands. "She was angry at everybody, all the time. I know she lives in the city somewhere, and I think something's up about how she started working at DNC right after Dad died. Plus . . . I don't know." I stretch my arms over the table and groan. "Do you have any idea why she got so pissed at me and tried to kill me the last few months she was here?"

"No. Whatever it was, she wouldn't talk about it." Drew's constant cheerful expression fades. "I know you guys didn't like her, and I don't blame you. She really was awful a lot of the time. But . . ."

I look at him. "Wait, 'you guys?' Are you saying you did like her?"

"I tried to, as much as she'd let me." He shrugs. "She talked to me sometimes. Do you know why she was in foster care?"

"No. You know Mom and Dad didn't tell us any of that stuff." My parents didn't want anyone to feel judged or labeled by their pasts. Everyone got a fresh start in this house. Of course, that didn't stop the kids from swapping stories, so we found out most of their reasons anyway. Not Naomi, though. She wouldn't talk to anyone.

Except Drew, apparently.

He hesitates like he's deciding whether or not he should tell me. Finally, he says, "Her mother forgot her."

"Like, she left her in a store or something?"

"No. Forgot she existed." Drew winces, and a visible shudder moves through him. "She took off with her boyfriend and left her daughter home alone. For ten days. Naomi was seven."

"Jesus," I whisper.

"Day six, she ran out of food and started eating dry dog food they had left over from a dog that died a year before." He keeps talking in a rush, like he's desperate to pour out the rest of the story before he loses his nerve. "Day nine, she was trying to climb a bookshelf because she thought her mother kept money in a jar on the highest shelf, but it fell over on top of her.

"It broke her leg and her collarbone. She couldn't get out from under it, so she laid there in agony for twenty-four hours. Finally, she started picking up whatever she could reach and chucking it at the nearest window. She managed to break it, then kept throwing stuff outside. Somebody finally called the cops." He stops and draws a shaky breath. "The ambulance was in the driveway when her mother finally came back. And she didn't even go to the hospital with her."

Much as I'm not a fan of Naomi, tears prick my eyes. "That's awful."

"Yeah. Then she went straight from there to Stereotypical Foster Land," Drew says. "The first family was a kids-for-paycheck type, and the second fostered because they couldn't get pregnant, then they did and stopped caring about the fosters in favor of the golden bio-child. The worst part is that after a bunch of bad fosters, her mom somehow cleaned up enough to get custody of her again."

"Jesus. How is that even possible?"

Drew shakes his head. "Broken system, foster care shortage, caseworker overload . . . take your pick. Anyway, she was with her mother for less than a year before she got forgotten again. She was older, so she survived for a month until the police showed up because her mother had been evicted for not paying rent, and they were vacating the premises. That was when they sent her here.

"Before she lived with us, she spent her whole life with no one looking out for her. She expected Mom and Dad to do the same . . . because of you."

I swallow and meet his gaze. "So that's why she hated me?"

"At first, yeah, but she was getting better. I don't know what happened that last time." He exhales, slow and forceful. "Anyway, that's the reason I went into social work. For kids like Naomi. And Holly." He smiles toward the living room.

I definitely feel bad for judging Naomi now. I can't rule out the idea that she's harassing me, because she pushed me down the stairs for reasons still unknown and might still be holding a grudge. But she's moved down a few pegs on my pointless little suspect list.

"Do you think it might be one of Holly's parents?" I ask Drew. "Whoever keeps screwing with me, I mean."

Drew frowns. "If it is, that means they definitely shouldn't have custody of her. No one's gone to the police looking for her, so if a parent is harassing you, it's probably because they'd get arrested if they went to the cops."

"And we still have no idea who those parents might be, right?"

"Right." Drew shakes his head and starts gathering the paperwork. "I called around to every deaf and deaf-friendly school in a hundred-mile radius and sent her photo out to them, just in case. No one recognizes her. It's like she fell from the sky into your hedge."

I glance in Holly's direction. "I still think someone put her there on purpose."

"I mean, maybe, but why?" he says. "That would mean either they picked a random house to leave her, or they were targeting you to . . . what, hope you'd take care of her? Frame you for harming a child? Who'd want to do that?"

The words make something click in my head, and I blurt out, "Tyler."

Drew gapes at me. "What?"

"Tyler," I repeat. "I told you guys he showed up at the VFW last night, the bastard, but I didn't tell you why. He claims he wants me to believe he's innocent, but he also threatened me and Lynette."

"Wait, he threatened you? And who's Lynette? Hold on. I think I saw that name in your foster record. Was she . . ."

I nod. "She was my foster daughter. And I guess he didn't threaten us, at least not directly. It was more the way he looked, the way he sounded." It's my turn to shudder. "He blames us for him going to prison. We both testified against him, and Lynette . . . she's the one who found Marisol's body."

It's hard for me to say and looks hard for Drew to hear, because his eyes well up. "I'm so sorry, Kat. About your daughter. I'm sorry I wasn't there for you then."

"No, don't apologize for that," I insist gently. "No one could've been there for me, because I wouldn't let them. I'm just glad you're here now."

He smiles. "Me, too."

Now that I've had the idea, I can't get it out of my head. It must be Tyler. He wants me to suffer the same way he did. Except he deserved it, and he still does.

I can't go to the police with ideas, though. So I'll have to do everything in my power to stop him myself, and that starts with warning Lynette.

CHAPTER 18

The Journal

If I have to participate in one more 'family activity,' I'm going to scream.

The mom is relentless. She keeps acting like we're all in this together, on equal footing, but there's a clear us-and-them thing going on. And she's definitely blind to it. There's a million little ways she favors the bio kid over anyone else — who, by the way, is an obnoxious twerp.

I was right about the dad, though. He's a closet creep. I've caught him trying to sneak a peek at me while I'm in the bathroom or changing in my room. A few times, I've given him an eyeful while pretending not to notice he's watching.

I know what I have to do. When the time comes, I'm not going to like it. He's so *old*. It's gross. But it's got to happen.

It's the only way to make *her* happy. The only way I can get out of here, away from these fake people. To make her take me back.

Even though I hate her almost as much as them.

CHAPTER 19

After Drew headed out, Holly was just waking up. This time, I had her help me with the Walmart order, which would hopefully accomplish several things. One was getting the tools for the idea I'd had to communicate with Holly. Another was showing her the food to see if she wanted to choose something to eat. She did — she pointed to rainbow Goldfish crackers, so I ordered two bags of them.

Finally, I want to try to catch Lynette and pray she'll at least not run off.

I requested the same pickup window as our first visit, hoping she'll be working at that time. If she isn't the one who brings the order out, I'm determined to ask whoever does if she's there, if she'll talk to me. She was at the cemetery yesterday. Maybe that means she's open to letting me explain and apologize.

If not, I want to at least warn her about Tyler.

I catch a lucky break when Holly and I pull around the back of the Walmart. Or at least I hope so. There's one other car parked in slot 5, and Lynette is loading groceries into the trunk.

I swing wide around her and park in the first slot by the door. I don't want this to feel like an ambush, but it's the only way I can make sure she sees me and has to walk by. I'll try not to make a scene. But even if she refuses to talk to me, there's at least one thing I have to let her know. I fully intend to convey it by any means necessary.

Holly is in her passenger seat, engrossed in a game. Before we left the house, I dug out an old Android tablet, charged it up, and loaded it with a few age-appropriate apps. She's playing one called Kitty Town that lets her find hidden cats and move them around a virtual town. And of course, her non-virtual stuffed cat is tucked in beside her.

I hate to feel like I'm abandoning her to a screen, but I also don't want her to sit quietly and do nothing, like a broken doll, until our communication improves.

I'm glad to see her having fun.

After I park and turn off the engine, I get Holly's attention and give her the holding-up-a-finger sign that I hope she reads as 'I won't be long.' She gives me a bare nod, then returns to hunting kitties. I can't help smiling. She may be deaf, but she's like any other kid when it comes to electronics.

It's a warm day, so I leave the AC running and crack both front windows before I get out of the car. I walk around the trunk and up the passenger side, then lean against the door where Holly can see me and get my attention if she needs it. And I wait.

The wait isn't long. Less than a minute after I'm in position, Lynette slams the trunk of the car she's working at shut, then walks halfway to the open driver's side window, dragging the cart behind her. "You're all set," she tells the driver, her voice thin with distance.

Whoever's in the car waves and mutters something I can't make out. Lynette nods, turns away, and heads back toward the store.

She doesn't see me until she's covered half the distance. Then, she slows and looks up, and a fleeting expression crosses her face.

It almost looks like fear.

Whatever it was, it's swallowed by a scowl. She's a beautiful young woman, even wearing that sour expression, with her blonde hair in an upswept braid and her amber eyes narrowed and sparking. High spots of color form on her cheeks, and her full lips twitch.

"Lynette." The word rasps from my throat, and I'm not sure I can say anything more. I can see in her eyes how badly I've hurt her. It wasn't intentional, but that's no real excuse.

And I have to keep going, or she may get hurt a lot worse than with what I did.

"Can we talk for a minute?" I finally say. "Please?"

Her mouth curls into a sneer. "Why?"

"Because I want to apologize."

She huffs. "Oh, it's *way* too late for that."

"I know, but I'd like to anyway. If you'll let me."

We stare at each other for what feels like forever. At last, the rigid lines of her body soften a touch, and she props an arm on the empty cart handle and sighs. "Fine. Go for it."

The relief that fills me is tempered by the knowledge that even though I have the chance to apologize, she probably won't accept it. Still, I press on. "I . . ." Whatever I'd planned to say dies in my throat, so I clear it and try again. "Sorry is nowhere close to good enough," I tell her. "I was going to list all my excuses for doing what I did, but it was inexcusable. You absolutely should hold it against me. But for whatever it's worth . . . I am so, so sorry."

I make myself stop talking before I can shove my foot further into my mouth and hold my breath, waiting.

Lynette studies me with an expression I can't interpret. Then, she gives me the tiniest smile. "You're pretty good at apologies."

"Thank you." My own smile is much bigger. I don't expect this to usher in a new era where Lynette isn't angry with me, but it's a start. One small step toward reconciliation, if that's at all possible.

"Mm." She straightens and grabs the cart handle with both hands. "I gotta get back to work. Thanks for the apology."

"Oh . . . wait. There's something I need to tell you." I glance into the car, as if Holly might somehow overhear. She's still absorbed in the tablet. "Do you know that Tyler is in town somewhere?"

Lynette rolls her eyes. "Unfortunately."

My heart jackknifes into my throat. "Has he talked to you?"

"Nah, I've just seen him around," she says. "Why? Does *he* want to apologize?"

"No. I'm worried he's going to come after you. Maybe hurt you." I fold my arms around my waist. "He's pissed. Blaming the two of us for putting him in jail for no reason, so he claims." I won't tell her what he called her. She doesn't need to hear that.

Anger floods her face. "No reason? He *murdered* Marisol!"

Hearing her say that is like a warm blanket of vindication. I have to be careful, though, because he's now innocent in the eyes of the law. Though I'm glad Lynette thinks it's bullshit, too. "He's been exonerated, and it seems like he convinced himself he's innocent," I state, trying to hedge my bets. "The important thing is that he's furious. If he approaches you, I want—"

I cut myself off before I start telling her what to do. Instead, I make it a question. "Will you try not to engage with him? Call the police instead? I . . . just don't want anything to happen to you because of him."

She seems surprised, and I hope it's not because she didn't think I cared about her. "Yeah, okay," she says. "Appreciate the heads-up."

"No problem."

Lynette starts to walk away, then stops behind my trunk. "Are you staying at Grandpa Joe's place?" she asks.

The bittersweet pang of her calling him *Grandpa* almost undoes me. "Yes," I reply. "For the foreseeable future, anyway."

"I could stop by for a visit." Her voice is almost a whisper, and she looks away as she says it. "Maybe tomorrow night? I work two jobs, so it'd be pretty late. Around eleven?"

I have to fight the urge to scream my affirmative and jump up and down with joy. "That sounds fantastic," I manage in a somewhat normal voice. "Do you still like cookie brownies with cream cheese frosting?"

"I love them," she says after a heavy pause, still not looking at me.

"I'll have some waiting for us, then."

She half-turns, like she's going to say something else, then changes her mind. "See ya," she says, hustling toward the employee door with her cart.

After it closes behind her, I stay outside the car until my breath stops hitching, my shoulders stop heaving, and the tears stop flowing. Then I wipe my face with a sleeve as I walk back to the driver's side. I climb in and flash Holly a smile. "Maybe today is turning into a good day, after all," I announce.

She doesn't hear me, but I choose to believe she shares the sentiment.

CHAPTER 20

When we got home and brought our Walmart haul inside, I decided to take advantage of the warm spring day. So, Holly and I packed up and headed to the playground. It's only four blocks away from my parents' house, so we walked.

She loves the swings and the slide, as far as I can tell. The monkey bars, not so much. I think the next time we come, we'll wear bathing suits and hit the mini water park.

I'm already envisioning a future where Holly stays with me. Where I work outside in the summer while she plays. Find a tutor to teach both her and me sign language. Enroll her in school. Teach her to drive. See her off to her prom. Everything I never got to do with my own daughter.

But I can't think like that. Nothing is certain, especially in foster care.

As we walk back, I'm thinking about the best way to execute my communication idea. I have the tools now, but they need a little modification. There's a stack of old magazines somewhere in the house. Barring that, I can probably print some pictures.

Lost in thought, I don't notice the car that's slowing down as it approaches us from the opposite side of the street, coming from the direction of the house, until it stops in the middle of the road. I look up, startled, and involuntarily clutch Holly's hand.

It's a blue SUV.

But it's not the one Tyler had at the VFW. This one is smaller, a lighter blue, and there's a woman driving. A familiar woman. The new co-anchor of the morning news show on DNC.

Naomi stares at me through the windshield. She doesn't look angry. She looks . . . blank.

I'm not sure what to do. She's just sitting there idling in the street. Hands on the wheel, eyes on me. If she notices Holly, she makes no indication that she knows or cares about the girl.

Part of me wants to rush into the road, screaming and pounding on her window. But I don't do it — because of Holly, and because of the story Drew told me. Because the other part of me wants to give her the benefit of the doubt.

I don't know what she wants, though. She's still staring. Motionless. No expression.

Just as I decide to approach her car to see if she reacts, she starts driving again. Slowly, picking up speed after she passes us. I pivot to watch, wondering if she's going to turn around and come back. Stop on this side of the street to say whatever she wants to say.

She gets about four blocks down, then slows and makes a right turn.

Into a driveway.

Oh, my God. Does she *live* on this street?

Heart pounding, I turn back toward the house and start walking with Holly. I don't even want to think about this right now. It's possible that she's visiting someone, but if she does live there, any of the things that happened over the past few days could've easily been her.

Maybe I need to consider security cameras, after all.

* * *

After dinner, Holly and I sit in the living room. She's been watching cartoons while I finish my little project, and I think it's ready now.

I turn off the TV, and Holly immediately looks at me with curiosity.

"Okay. We're going to try something here." I gesture at the coffee table, where I've laid everything out. "Hopefully, this is going to help you and me talk to each other a little more."

I have a bowl of Goldfish crackers, a cup of juice, the tablet, the coloring book, and a Barbie doll on the table. There's also a new purchase I made today. It's a toddler toy with nine oversized, squishy colored buttons that light up when you press them. I've glued a picture to each button. The device has a carrying handle, and I've attached a keychain sound button to it. The button lets you record a sound that it plays back when pressed.

"Are you ready to try?" I place the button toy on the couch between us. "Watch this."

Making sure she's paying attention, I reach out and press the top left button with a picture of food on it. Then, I pick up the bowl of crackers and eat a few. I put the bowl down, press the top middle button that displays a glass with a straw. And I pick up the juice and have a sip.

Holly watches me, though she doesn't have much of a reaction.

"Do you want to try?" I turn the toy toward her and point to the top left button.

She stares at it for a minute. Her gaze flicks to me, then back to the button. She presses it.

I grab the Goldfish bowl and hold it out to her.

After a brief hesitation, she takes a small handful of crackers. She pops one in her mouth and watches me while she chews, almost like she's wondering if I'm going to stop her.

I give her a thumbs-up.

She smiles and continues until she's eaten them all. When she finishes, I point to the second button. "Are you thirsty now?" I ask. "Try the button."

Again, she stares at it, but she presses it a bit faster than the first time.

I hand her the juice glass. She takes it, and I give her a thumbs-up. So she drinks a few swallows and puts it back on the coffee table, close to her.

"That's right. These buttons are so you can have a snack when you're hungry and a drink when you're thirsty." That's too complicated to convey in a simple picture, but I'm hopeful that she'll grasp the concept after we've used the device for a while.

Encouraged, I walk her through the next few. Coloring book, tablet, toy. With each button, I pick up the corresponding object, briefly play with it, and put it down. Then, I have her press the buttons and hand her the objects.

For some of these, I'll have to eventually expand the demonstration. I want to show her that food, drink, and toy don't just mean Goldfish crackers, juice, and Barbie dolls. I can tackle those one at a time over the next few days, though. For now, I only want to show her that when she pushes a button, I'll know she wants something and will get it for her.

The next button is a toilet. She already has a way to communicate that, but I included it to reinforce the idea that pushing buttons means telling me what she wants or needs.

For this one, I stand, make the gesture she uses, and press the button. Then, I walk around the couch and toward the downstairs bathroom, looking at her while I do. The door is visible over the back of the couch. I step into the bathroom, close the door for a few seconds, and come out. After she presses the button, I hold a hand out for her and lead her to the bathroom, then back to the couch.

I have a button for 'outside' that's a picture of a sun for her to use if she wants to play in the back yard. Some of the new purchases are for that. Sidewalk chalk, bubbles, a bouncy ball. She can also hopefully use it if she wants to go to the playground. But I don't have the outdoor toys set up yet, and 'play outside' is a nebulous concept, so I don't introduce it yet.

The next button is also not easy to convey. It's a picture of a little girl sleeping, so she can tell me if she's tired and wants to take a nap or go to bed. I have a pillow on the couch, and I press the button, then lie down on the pillow to show her. I turn the device toward her and point to the sleep button. When she presses it, I hand her the pillow.

She takes it, frowns, and hands it back.

We'll have to work on that one later.

The last of the nine buttons on the device is a picture of a mother and child hugging. I stand with the device, smile and press the button, then crouch to hug her where she's sitting. Still at her level, I put the toy on the couch.

Before I can point to the hug button, she presses it, then launches off the couch, into my arms.

I don't bother choking back the sob that rises in my throat.

After a good, long hug, she sits down and looks at the light-up toy for a moment. She points to the sunshine button and looks at me questioningly.

"That's for playing outside," I tell her. "We can't do that yet." As I speak, I shake my head. At least I've cleaned up the broken glass, but it's getting dark, and I need to replace the light bulb yet again.

Holly pauses, looks back at the device, and picks up the keychain attached to the handle. I glued a picture of me to the button and recorded a sound on it. This one is going to be hard to explain, too, but it's the most important one.

The device came with a remote fob to activate the light and sound, so it can be used to find lost keys, but it does the same thing when the physical button is pressed. I take the fob from my pocket and hold up a finger, then walk away and duck behind the couch, out of sight.

I press the fob, and the button flashes and calls out, "Help!" in an automated female voice. At the sound, I pop up from behind the couch.

Holly giggles.

It's the sweetest sound I ever heard, and it's so unex-pected that happy tears spring to my eyes. I could listen to her laugh all day.

I duck back down and press the fob again.

"Help!"

When I spring up, she laughs even harder. The next time I duck, she presses the button first and giggle-snorts at my jack-in-the-box routine.

If this works the way I want it to, she can use the sound button to get my attention when I'm not looking, if she's in another room, or if we get separated. After the initial giggle fit dies down, we work with the button for a while. I alternate between the 'wait' gesture and moving farther away to hide.

Eventually, I reach the dining room and stand behind the wall next to the entrance. When I hear "Help!" from the living room, I rush in and stop in front of her, flashing a thumbs-up. "Great job!" I enthuse, then reach down to press the hug but-ton and follow through with a squeeze.

I sit back on the couch beside her. So far, this is encour-aging progress. I know she should really learn actual sign lan-guage and get more thorough testing to see if hearing aids or even cochlear implants will help her, but for now, the ability to communicate more than 'bathroom' or 'drive' is huge.

"So, is there anything you'd like right now?" I gesture to the light-up toy.

Holly studies the buttons as if seriously considering the question, then presses the one for the tablet.

I laugh. "Of course you want that." I turn the tablet on, load the Kitty Town app, and hand it to her. Within seconds, she's absorbed in the colorful game.

I start clearing the coffee table, intending to set up my laptop and check my work emails while she's playing. As I'm stashing the Barbie doll and coloring book on an end table shelf, the doorbell rings.

The sound sends a jolt through me. I'm not expecting anyone, and awful scenarios start flashing across my mind.

It's the police responding to another false report. It's Drew with news about Holly's parents, coming to take her away. It's Naomi, ready to say or do whatever she couldn't earlier in the street.

I almost decide not to answer it, but my car is in the driveway and the lights are on. Whoever it is must know I'm here.

Reluctantly, I shuffle toward the front door. The heavy curtains across the glass panes on the inside prevent me from seeing out, though they're mostly to keep people from looking in. As I reach for the door handle, I try to peep through the side and catch a glimpse of whoever's out there, but I don't see anything.

I frown and pull the door open.

There's no one here. No person standing at the door, no vehicle at the curb.

Instead, there's a large, thick manila envelope in the middle of the stoop. *Katrina* is written across a folded piece of paper taped to the outside.

I'm not getting a good vibe from this package.

Part of me wants to leave it there and pretend I never saw it, but I can't. I have to know what's in it.

Curiosity killed the Kat.

The phrase pings through me like an arrow to the heart. I was a nosy child — my mother called me 'enthusiastically inquisitive' — and Dad used to say that whenever I poked too far and risked hurting myself.

Whatever this package is feels like a risk. But it's one I'm going to take.

I pick up the envelope, which is heavier than it looks, then close and lock the door and carry it inside to the couch. Holly briefly looks up from her game and smiles. I return the expression, and she goes back to her kitties.

Slowly, I peel the taped paper from the outside of the envelope and unfold the note. It's handwritten in black ink, and the more I read, the harder my stomach lurches.

Kat,

I'm sorry about last night. I was out of line, and I shouldn't have yelled at you. You have to understand my frustration. Five years is a long time to spend in prison when you didn't do anything.

And I didn't do anything, Kat. I swear it. Whatever else you may think of me, I loved Marisol and I would never hurt her.

Here are copies of the evidence that exonerated me. Some of it is technical. I included my lawyer's notes that explain it all, and also a copy of my book. Please, please look at the evidence. I need you to know that I'm innocent.

Sincerely,
Tyler Martin

When I reach the end of the note, I'm close to crumpling it up and screaming in rage. He gave me a copy of his goddamned book, the one he's using to profit from my daughter's death? I can't believe I ever loved this man, who writes empty, florid notes with such a pompous undertone. And that signature. *Sincerely, Tyler Martin.* He's even scribbled his phone number after the name. As if I'm some business executive he's pitching for a movie deal.

Not his ex-wife, whose child he murdered.

Instinctively, I carry the whole thing to the kitchen, intending to throw it away. But I pause halfway to the trash can.

What if it's true? What if, somehow, Tyler is innocent? Whatever is in this envelope, it must be pretty damned convincing, or they wouldn't have let him go.

If he really didn't do it, I have to know. Not for Tyler's sake. Innocent or not, I want nothing to do with him ever again after the way he treated that girl last night.

I have to know because if Tyler didn't kill my daughter, whoever did is still out there.

And they need to pay.

I can't bring myself to open the envelope yet, though. Instead, I stow it in a kitchen drawer with a stack of appliance warranties and instruction manuals, then return to the living room. Tonight is not the night to tear down my worldview and replace it with horrified uncertainty.

It's a night to celebrate successes. And one of them is sitting on my couch, waiting for me.

CHAPTER 21

I hear something. At least, I think I do.

My eyes are open before I realize I was asleep. It's not dark, but it's not light, either. Everything is a gray, crisscrossed haze.

And I can't move.

Come on, wake up! I'm not as muddled as I usually am during an episode, and my inability to get up is more frustrating than terrifying. I heard something . . . or did I? The noise wasn't right, but it feels more like the memory of a sound. Something that infiltrated a dream I can't quite remember.

I strain to move an arm or a leg, even though I know that never works. The effort makes my heart pound in my ears, and panic creeps in.

This is the worst part. The paralysis. Your brain believes you're moving, but your body won't respond — and it feels like dying.

I have to calm myself. Go through the countdown.

Five things I can see.

The crisscross pattern above me is the straps for the upper bunk. The gray haze is the mattress. I see the pale peach edges of the fitted sheet. The wall to my right. The single bunkbed with Holly sleeping in the bottom to my left.

My heart begins to slow.

Four things I can feel.

A pillow beneath my head. A blanket on top of me. My heart slamming in my chest.

My foot flicking impatiently, trying to reach the floor and get me up.

I can move my foot.

Ignoring the rest of the countdown, I swing my leg to the floor, then the other, and sit up. Pain flares through my overtaxed body, but it doesn't last long. I glance over Holly first. She's sleeping soundly, her calico cat tucked under one arm while the fingers of her other hand curl loosely around the light board. The noise didn't come from her.

In fact, there's hardly any sound at all. Only Holly's slow, even breathing and a whisper of wind from outside.

It's barely light out, the edge of dawn. I pick up my phone from the small stand beside the bed to check the time. Not quite 5:30 in the morning. I haven't gotten a single full night's sleep in this house since I came back.

I want to curl up and grab a few more hours while I can, but something feels off. I don't think the noise I heard is what woke me. That still seems distant, like part of a dream. Yet an uneasy feeling lingers, and I know I'm not going to get back to sleep.

I sigh and push to my feet, stretching my arms over my head. Maybe a hot shower will relax me. As I ease from the stretch and pivot to snag my phone, I glance through the sheer curtains and out the window overlooking the road.

There's a blue SUV parked across the street. Naomi is leaning against it with her arms crossed, staring at the house.

Instantly enraged, I grab my bathrobe and race from the room, putting it on as I sprint down the stairs. I dash to the front door, yank it open, and lunge out onto the stoop. "What the hell do you want?" I shout.

Naomi's eyes pop wide, and her mouth forms an *O* of surprise. She jerks upright and scrambles to grab the driver's side door handle.

"Naomi! What are you doing here?" I move across the stoop and down the first step. The concrete is cold against my bare feet, and the bandaged one starts throbbing. I still haven't fully healed from stepping on that broken light bulb.

She doesn't even look at me when I speak. She wrenches the door open and practically throws herself into the driver's seat. The door slams shut, and she starts the engine and peels away without fastening her seat belt.

Damn it, what was that about? Between yesterday's stare-off in the street and this crazy stalker behavior, I'm just about convinced she's the one behind everything. The only thing that doesn't fit is Holly, but maybe she has nothing to do with it. Maybe whoever abandoned her is truly gone, and all the other stuff is Naomi doing inexplicable Naomi things.

I can't go after her now. I have Holly, and Naomi was dressed in professional clothing, so she's likely heading to work. Somehow, I have to confront her, but it won't be right this minute. Which is probably for the best. Naomi's anger has never felt rational, so I need to be the calm one if I'm going to make sense of what she's doing.

As I turn to go back inside, something catches my eye. A flash of color where none belongs. I look toward the driveway and spot it right away. Behind my parked car, spatters of arterial red stand out on the ground, vivid against the gray asphalt surface.

Is that . . . blood?

I'm shivering and dizzy as I make my way across the front lawn, stepping carefully with my bare feet. As I get closer, it looks less like blood and more like paint. Still, that doesn't completely relieve me. Whatever it is, it shouldn't be there.

I reach the car and stare at the splashes. Definitely paint. I look down the driveway toward the road, then up it toward the back yard. I can see the shed from here.

The shed that's liberally splashed with the same stuff trailing down the rest of the driveway. And the paint isn't all that's wrong back there.

Rather than run down the driveway barefoot, I go back into the house. I shove my feet into my sneakers by the front door, not bothering to hunt down a pair of socks. On my way to the back door, I focus on my breathing. In through the nose, out through the mouth. Slow and steady. I'm so shaken that if I don't get enough oxygen to my brain, I'll hyperventilate and pass out.

And the sight that greets me when I open the door to the back yard does nothing to calm me down.

The shed is ruined.

It's not only the red paint, which is bad enough, because somehow the color looks exactly like fresh blood. The structure itself is decimated. Shingles torn from the roof. Boards pried from the walls. The door taken off its hinges and propped drunkenly aside, still attached with the padlock. All the shelving has been removed.

Tools, shelving, boards, and shingles are scattered across the yard, some of the detritus also splashed with red. And inside what remains of the small building, several floorboards were pried up and tossed out. There's a crumbling hole dug into the ground beneath and a dirty shovel lying on the remnants of the floorboards beside it.

The dirt from the hole is flung all over the inside, clumping on the walls and smearing through gloops of paint.

Those sounds I heard in my sleep. It must've been this.

Half-dazed, I make my way across the yard toward the destruction, careful not to step on tools or boards. I'm starting to get a better picture of what happened, and it worries me more with every revelation. What appears random is careful, almost methodical. The roof shingles were cut with a knife. The nails were pried from the boards to remove them. The door hinges and shelf brackets were unscrewed and disassembled.

None of this was done in a destructive rage, except maybe the digging.

This took hours of work, done as quietly as possible.

Naomi is insane.

I don't want to look any closer, but I have to. I remember the note on the shed, the one that claimed my father had a secret behind the door. And I can't help but feel this was done to show me the alleged secret.

Whatever it is, I need to know.

I reach the entrance and stare inside at the missing floorboards and the hole in the ground. There's something there in the dirt at the bottom, protruding like an exposed tree root. It's wrinkled and leathery, almost spider-like, though it's much larger than a spider.

Is that . . .

Before my brain completes the thought, a piercing noise fills my head. I fall to my knees, barely noticing when one of them lands on a busted board and drives splinters into my skin. Because the noise is my own scream as I recognize the object jutting from the disturbed earth.

It's a human hand.

CHAPTER 22

I feel like I'm going to end up meeting the entire Fulton police department before this unfolding nightmare ends.

Two officers arrived almost immediately after I called 911 and managed to explain that there was a body buried under my shed. Their nametags said WALTERS and RUBIO. Officer Walters is a tall, stern, solid woman shaped like a rectangle. Her partner, Rubio, has far more curves, and he looks half-asleep.

They told me to wait inside while they started 'processing the scene' and that more officers were en route. Over the next fifteen minutes or so, what seemed like a dozen squad cars and at least one ambulance choked my street and drew the neighbors out in droves to stare.

I didn't catch all their names. I know there's a detective out there somewhere with the uniforms, and he's going to come inside and question me soon. At least all the commotion hasn't woken Holly yet, and I'm grateful for that.

The last vehicle to arrive was a red Jetta. And I could have cried with relief when Alina climbed out, wearing a sweat suit and carrying coffee and donuts from Dunkin. She'd just gotten off shift when my call came in, and she didn't hesitate to come over for moral support.

I'm still shaking when Alina and I sit down at the kitchen table, and it takes several minutes before my body finally stills. After I explain everything to her, she looks as washed-out and shocked as I feel. "I can't believe it," she murmurs. "And you think *Naomi* dug up this . . . body?"

"Definitely. I mean, she was right in front of the house, just standing there. And yesterday, she stopped driving in the middle of the road and sat there staring at me for, like, five minutes."

Okay, so it probably wasn't five minutes, though it felt like forever. And if I really think about it, it's possible Naomi didn't do it. She was in a jacket and blouse over a pencil skirt with high heels, impeccably groomed, flawless makeup. She didn't look like someone who'd spent hours un-building a shed and digging a hole.

But she could've done it, then gone home and got cleaned up and dressed before she came back to gloat.

It's not like she lives very far.

Alina shakes her head, then takes a sip of her coffee. "I don't know. This is crazy," she says. "How is there somebody buried under the shed? And whoever did this, they knew the body was there. Like, do you think Naomi murdered someone and, what, tried to frame you for it?"

No. She tried to frame Dad.

I haven't told Alina or the police about the note I found on the shed door. Which, I know, is a massive mistake. I should've officially reported it when Drew suggested it. Now, the longer I wait, the worse it's going to look. They're definitely going to think my father is a murderer.

"Maybe?" I finally say.

Alina frowns. "That's really flimsy. What do you think she wants?"

"No idea. She hates me, and that's always been enough."

"Maybe she was jealous. You know, bio daughter, parents love you best, and now that Daddy Joe's gone, you get everything."

137

The bitter note in her tone takes my breath away. I've never heard her mention anything like this. Alina always seems genuinely happy for everyone when good things happen and sympathetic over the bad things, even if her own situation is worse.

Has she really felt this way, all these years?

"Alina," I say carefully. "Are *you* jealous of me?"

Her expression flashes into something unreadable. For a second, she looks distant — and almost angry. Then she blinks and offers a weak chuckle. "No, of course not," she says. "I was trying to channel my inner twat, you know? I'm just tired. It's been a long shift, and then I find out there's a dead person buried in the yard of the house I grew up in. Sorry about that."

I'm not sure I fully believe her, but I'm willing to let it go.

I want to change the subject and not think about the awful discovery, but I'm not sure what to talk about. Which actually makes me a little sad. I haven't talked to her in so long that I have no idea who she is now. My sister is practically a stranger to me.

Then, I remember what she said the first night I saw her in town, when she answered the false report with Officer Wade. After I said I couldn't believe she became a police officer.

It's kind of a long story, and I'll definitely tell it to you soon.

"So." I drink some of my coffee and pluck a frosted donut from the open box beside us, though I'm not sure I'll be able to eat it. My guts are churning like a storm drain. "You promised me a long story about how you became a cop."

Alina perks up slightly. "You're right! I did say that." She's already started eating a white-frosted taillight, and she takes another bite and chews thoughtfully. "Well. I have to warn you, it's not entirely a happy story. There's a good ending, though."

The idea that something bad happened to her almost makes me change my mind about hearing it. Because maybe it's something I could have stopped if I'd stayed in contact, and maybe I'm about to feel worse than I already do.

No. Refusing to hear other people's sorrows in order to preserve your own happiness is the coward's way out, especially with people you care about. I won't do that to her.

"I'd still love to hear it, if you want to tell me," I say.

"Okay. Here goes." She drags in a long breath through her nose, purses her lips, and blows it out. "After DSS decided we couldn't stay here, you know, I was sixteen. If I wasn't here, I wanted to be on my own. They wouldn't let me, of course. And they were right that I still needed care . . . just not the care they gave me." She rolled her eyes.

I want to ask if they put her in a state home, but I have a feeling it was worse than that. I stay quiet and let her keep talking.

"They placed me with a family in Granby Center. Out in the boonies," she says. "I use 'family' loosely here. The parents had two kids in middle school, a girl and a boy, and an adult son who lived there with his girlfriend and her two kids, a baby and a toddler. House wasn't nearly big enough. I have no idea how they managed to keep their foster status. Likely they didn't tell DSS the son and family lived there."

I picture the cramped quarters, see Alina probably sleeping in the closet or the basement or something, and shudder. "That's awful. I hate fosters like that."

"Trust me, that is not the awful part. It sucked, but . . ." She releases a shuddering breath. "The father didn't want another daughter. He was looking for more of a side piece."

"Oh, God," I rasp. "Did he . . ."

She's already shaking her head. "He didn't rape me, though it wasn't for lack of trying. Either he'd get interrupted with so many people in the house, or I'd manage to fend him off. He also threatened me. Said if I told my social worker about him, he'd kill me. And I believed him."

I think I'm going to be sick. "How is there a happy ending here?"

"Believe me, it's *very* happy." She offers a slanted smile. "I wanted out of there the second I turned eighteen, so I did my homework. Figured out how much money I'd need to get my own place faster than waiting for social services to put me on section eight. I got a job at a nearby gas station, saved every penny for a security deposit, and kept an eye out for anywhere I could work full-time straight out of high school that would support me. The police were hiring. They paid enough, and I qualified."

I can't help frowning. "That doesn't sound very happy."

"It gets better." She pauses for another slug of coffee. "The reason I believed he'd kill me was that he was a meth cooker, with a network of violent assholes dealing for him."

"Holy shit," I blurt, briefly wondering if the guy who screwed up Evie was part of this man's violent network. "That's not better!"

"No, the better part is that a few years after I became a cop, I busted the son of a bitch." Alina grins broadly. "He got thirty years for drug distribution, then killed a guy in prison for 'disrespecting' him. So now he's serving a life sentence. Best of all, that bastard will never lay a hand on his daughter."

"Oh my God, Alina." I'm out of my chair, circling the table to hug her. "I'm so sorry that happened to you. But also, you're amazing."

She's smiling when I pull back. "I know, right?"

At that moment, a figure darkens the open back door. "Ms. Gray," a male voice calls. "May I have a word?"

I exchange a look with Alina. She gets up and follows me to the back door.

The man standing there is tall and thin with dark hair and a pencil mustache. He's not wearing a uniform, but there's a badge and a gun clipped to his belt.

"Detective Dereck Wyetta," he introduces himself, then nods at Alina. "Morning, Officer Cruz."

"Wyetta." She returns the nod. "Any idea what's going on here?"

"Well, that's what I'm hoping to find out, with Ms. Gray's help."

At least he hasn't called me *Mrs. Martin.* "I already told the first officers everything I know," I say to the detective. "When I saw what happened out here, I didn't touch anything. You should be arresting Naomi Young."

"Kit-Kat, don't," Alina warns under her breath.

Wyetta's features remain impassive. "We'll be interviewing the person you saw outside this morning and canvassing the area to see if there are any witnesses," he says. "Meanwhile, I need to ask you a few questions. Can I come inside?"

It's on the tip of my tongue to fire back something like *do I have a choice?* when I hear the front door opening. It slams shut, and a familiar voice shouts, "Kat! Oh my God, are you okay? Where are you?"

Drew. He must've heard about units dispatched to an address where one of his charges resides. Alina and I exchange a glance, and I call out, "In the kitchen."

He rushes through, comes straight to me, and gives me a hug. I'm close to tears when he pulls back and does the same to Alina. Something about Drew always feels safe, like an older-brother vibe, even though he's a few years younger than me and a year younger than Alina.

"What's happening?" he demands, looking at the detective now.

Wyetta arches an eyebrow. "That's what we're all trying to figure out here, Mr . . . ?"

"Seaborn. Drew Seaborn." He points to his laminated DSS badge. "I'm the caseworker for Kat's foster daughter. And Kat and Alina's brother."

The detective looks slowly between us. "Interesting," he says. "Maybe we could all sit down and have a little chat."

I don't see how that can be avoided now, so I invite Wyetta inside.

This is going to be a very long morning.

CHAPTER 23

The house doesn't clear out until almost noon, though Detective Wyetta informed me that he'd probably be back tomorrow for more questions.

Drew told him about the note I found on the shed. Not that I blamed him for it. I'm actually grateful it came from Drew instead of me. The detective thundered at me a little for 'withholding evidence,' but a few well-placed glares from Alina calmed him down. The police took the note with them.

I can tell they already think my dad is responsible for this, even though there isn't a chance he could be. He never would've murdered someone, and he sure as hell wouldn't have buried a body beneath his own shed.

But until we know more about *whose* body it is and what happened to them, there's not much I can do. I mean, maybe it's not even a murder case. The body had obviously been in the ground for a long time. Possibly even before my parents bought this house.

I shove the thoughts from my mind. If I keep trying to 'solve' this with almost no information, I'll drive myself insane. I need to focus on trying to salvage what I can of this day.

By now, Holly is up and dressed, and we've had a late breakfast. I've decided that we're going to spend today trying to relax, so we're going to the playground again. This time, we'll attempt playing in the water park.

I couldn't find a bathing suit that would fit Holly, so we're both dressed in shorts and T-shirts. Holly is playing on the tablet while I pack a bag with towels, dry clothes, snacks, drinks, and sunscreen. I'm not sure if the changing rooms at the playground are open for the season yet, so I'm planning to drive over in case we have to go home wet.

As I'm in the kitchen, keeping an eye on Holly at the table while I fill a few Ziploc bags with rainbow Goldfish, my phone rings. The screen says Clara C.

I almost forgot that I programmed her number in when we talked at Dad's reception.

"Hello?" I answer, trying to sound cheerful.

"Oh, Kat, hello," Clara says. "I hope I'm not bothering you. Do you have a few minutes?"

I shift the phone to pin it against my shoulder while I pack up food. "Of course. Is everything okay?"

"Well, as good as it can be," she replies on a heavy sigh. "I really just wanted to see how you were holding up. Are you still in town?"

I should probably tell her that I'm not holding up at all, that I found a dead body in my back yard this morning. She'll hear about it sooner or later, anyway. But for now, I don't want to pile any more grief on her.

"Yes, I'm still around. I'm staying at Dad's place for . . . a while." For the first time, I think about the fact that staying here permanently is an option. The house is mine and paid off, and I can do my job from anywhere. It's not like I had some exciting life in Syracuse to get back to, either. I barely know enough people there to call anyone by name.

Plus, if I get to keep Holly, DSS won't like me moving to a different county.

The thought is so huge that it threatens to overwhelm me. I push it aside for the moment so I can talk to Clara. "Anyway, I'm doing okay," I lie. "Hanging in there. How about you?"

"Oh, I'm still here," she says. "They've got your father's permanent stone in at the cemetery, right next to dear Audrey. It looks beautiful. Have you seen it?"

"Not yet, but I will soon." For some reason, I'm surprised to hear her say my mother's name. "Did you know Mom?"

"I never had the pleasure of meeting her. Your father talked about her all the time, though. Sometimes, I feel like I know her." I can hear the smile in her voice. "I'd tell him about my Lionel, too. He was a good man." After a long pause, she muses, "I think that's why Joe and I weren't in a rush to blend our lives. We'd both lost our soulmates."

My eyes start watering, and once more, I feel awful for staying away so long. For not spending enough time with Dad to know that he still talked about how much he loved Mom, even to his girlfriend. For not getting to know this woman who was probably my father's best friend.

"I'm so sorry about your husband," I say. "Ugh. Sorry about saying sorry. You'd think I wouldn't forget how lame that sounds after hearing it a thousand times the other day."

Clara laughs, and I chuckle with her. "Oh, honey, it's fine," she says. "Listen, do you need anything, for yourself or the little girl who's staying with you? I bake a mean tuna noodle casserole."

I can't help smiling. Casseroles . . . yet another overblown funeral tradition. "We're fine right now, but thank you so much for the offer."

"Any time. You just let me know if there's anything I can do, even if it's listening to you talk. We should get together for that coffee soon."

"Yes," I tell her. "I've got a busy day tomorrow, but can I give you a call on Sunday?"

"Of course, sweetie. Call me anytime."

We end the call, and I start to put the phone down when I notice a handful of unread notifications. They must've come in while the detective was 'interviewing' us.

I pull the top menu down to look at the details. There are a few new posts on the Fulton Grays page, and I have messages from Mickey and Evie. The one from Evie is asking about the funeral, how it went, whether her flowers arrived. God, the funeral seems so long ago already, though it's been less than two days.

I reply to Evie, thanking her again for the arrangement, then read Mickey's message.

> *Hey! So I can arrange to come down there either Thursday or Friday next week, whichever day works for you. I'm thinking late lunch, maybe a drink or two, and we can walk around being all nostalgic and shit. Hit up Scoops or The Big Dipper for ice cream. Hell, we could go bowling! What say you?*

My heart sinks further with every word I read. I'd completely forgotten about making tentative plans to see Mickey. I don't even remember if I told her about Holly staying with me, and with everything that's happening, I'm not sure I'll be able to hang out.

It takes me a few minutes to compose a reply as I tap out and delete a bunch of different explanations, trying to cram all the huge things she doesn't know about into as few words as possible. Finally, I settle on a message and send it.

> *So here's the thing. I might have to postpone. I'm dealing with a police thing, and did I mention that I'm sort of a temporary mother at the moment? I'm taking care of a little girl, fostering her until they figure things out with her parents. How's the week after next looking for you?*

I feel bad that I'm underplaying so much, but I don't want to drop a bunch of huge bombs all at once. She'll want more of an explanation than I'm able to give. Hopefully, she'll understand, and we can dish on everything when things calm down and we can finally get together.

It's not long before a reply comes in.

Oh my God, girl! You have a POLICE THING? I'm officially dying of curiosity. You're not under arrest, are you? Okay, what about this, we have a video chat this weekend? You can tell me all about your foster girl and your police thing, and I can tell you about The Great Strep Throat Incident.

I snort a laugh in spite of myself and text back.

No, not under arrest. Sounds good! Drop me a message when you're free.

She replies with a thumbs-up.

I smile faintly as I close the app and look over my preparations for the playground. After tucking the last few snacks into the outside pockets of the duffle bag, I turn to Holly. She's still playing on the tablet, but she looks up when I wave. "How about we go have some fun together?" I say and make the 'driving' gesture.

She beams and gives me a thumbs-up.

"Yes! It's time to practice the last piece of the puzzle." I reach for her light toy on the table beside her and press the 'sunshine' button. "Let's go play outside."

I try to ignore the sinking feeling that the sunshine button won't get as much use as I'd hoped for a while, since the back yard is a crime scene. Every time I stop distracting myself, I start seeing that hand jutting out from the ground, a frozen claw reaching for a rescue that will never come. I don't even want to speculate about the identity of the body or the possibility that my father had anything to do with it.

I'll have to face it soon enough. For now, we've got sprinklers to run through and swings to ride.

CHAPTER 24

I pace my living room, alternately staring at the front door, then the stairs as I walk back and forth. The urge to check my phone is ever-present, but pointless, since I know she doesn't have my number.

It's almost 11:30, and Lynette isn't here yet.

I should've tried to get some way to contact her. I've been thinking that maybe I can find her on Facebook, but I don't want her to feel like I'm pushing her. It's a miracle that she's willing to talk to me at all.

That is, if she is actually willing. Maybe she stood me up.

It feels surreal, getting so worked up about this when just this morning, I found a body buried in the back yard. But I still don't have any details on that, and I was hoping Lynette's visit would be, if not a pleasant distraction, at least a productive one.

I won't tell her what happened. Not yet. I don't want her to freak out before I get the chance to explain myself and beg her forgiveness.

Still, I'm not sure how long I should wait for her, especially since I'm worried about Holly, who's asleep upstairs. She has her light box, and I used the remote fob to make sure I could hear the sound button from down here. But we haven't practiced much with me being in another room, let alone another floor.

I'm so nervous that when the doorbell finally rings, at first I think it's my phone. I wonder who's calling, even though it sounds nothing like my ringtone. I pull myself together, then wipe my damp palms on my jeans and open the door.

"Lynette, hi." I realize I'm too brightly enthusiastic, smiling too hard, but I can't seem to help myself. "Please come in."

Ugh. I sound like a game-show hostess.

I move away from the door, and Lynette steps inside slowly. She's wearing a plain black T-shirt under a nylon jacket and some kind of dark uniform pants, and her hair is pulled back in a simple ponytail. "Hi," she says, her gaze skating around the living room as if she's expecting a trap. "Sorry I'm late. We got busy right before I was supposed to clock out."

"It's no problem. I'm glad you made it."

I close the door behind her and lead her to the couch. I've made the promised brownies, arranged them on a big plate with a few smaller plates and napkins laid out on the coffee table. "Cookie brownies," I announce in my stupid game-show-hostess voice. "Would you like a glass of milk? I mean, well . . . something to drink?" I fumble. She's an adult now, and she might not appreciate her terrible foster mother sucking up with the equivalent of cookies and milk.

But she smiles as she sits down. "Sure. Thank you."

"Great! I'll be right back."

After these messages! I think insanely.

I've *got* to stop using that voice.

I hustle out to the kitchen and grab two glasses from the cabinet. I've got whole milk for Holly and one percent for me, but I don't want to go back out there and ask Lynette which kind she wants. I'm afraid I'll start babbling something like *let's see what's behind door number one!* Instead, I grab the whole milk, figuring it'll go better with brownies, and pour both cups.

When I return to the living room, Lynette is standing at the far end, reading the Hearth Wall.

A hot flush of mortification fills me. She should be on that wall, part of the family, but I can't ask her to do it now. That would be adding insult to injury.

I clear my throat and force myself to stop sounding like I'm about to announce the grand prize. "Here you go," I say, setting the glasses on the coffee table. I take a seat and watch as Lynette scans the wall one last time, then turns and ambles back to the couch.

She sits, takes a brownie, and puts it on a small plate. "Where's the kid?"

"Huh?" I blurt, blinking a few times.

"You had a kid in the car, didn't you?"

"Oh. Yes." Could this be any more of a disaster? The foster child I inadvertently gave up on asking about the foster child I currently have. "She's sleeping," I say. "I, uh . . . I'm just watching her for a while."

I try to brace myself for more questions, but she doesn't ask any. Instead, she takes a bite of the frosted cookie brownie and closes her eyes as she chews. "This is good," she says after she swallows. "Thank you."

"I'm glad you like it."

The stilted conversation and long, awkward pauses might be worse than the game-show-hostess voice.

I fold my hands in my lap and pivot slightly toward her. "Lynette, there's something I want to tell you," I say. "If you're willing to listen."

She stares at me, then says, "Okay."

"Right." I draw a bracing breath. "Like I said earlier, this is not an excuse. I just want you to know . . ." I trail off and close my eyes, trying to organize everything I want to say into something coherent. "That weekend. The weekend after . . . after Marisol died." It's still so hard to say out loud that my daughter is dead. "I'd booked a little vacation for us. For the whole family. A cabin on Lake Ontario, at that campground you liked so much when we went before."

I pause, not sure if I should keep going. Will she feel better or worse, knowing what I intended to do but never actually did?

I've already started this, though. I need to get to the end.

It's hard to keep meeting her gaze, but I do it. "I had the adoption papers filled out and ready for you to sign," I tell her. "In fact, I still have them. They're expired, but I couldn't get rid of them. I . . . I was in such a dark place after Marisol." Despite my best intentions, I have to look away. "I've been there for years, if I'm being honest. And I'm just now coming out of it."

I make myself look back at her. Is that anger in her eyes? Sadness? I can't tell.

"I wanted you to know that I love you," I say, even though it sounds corny and trite. "Even though I acted like an idiot back then, and it's my fault that I lost you. I loved you then, and I love you now. I always will."

Lynette swallows hard and stands like a shot. "Can I use your bathroom?" she blurts.

"Um. Of course. It's—"

"I remember where it is."

She practically runs for it, and the door slams shut behind her.

I remain in place, stunned and confused. Was that a good sign or a bad one? Is she so mad that she can't stand to look at me? Is she crying and doesn't want me to see? Even as my mind spins through speculation, part of me is listening for Holly. Reacting in a general 'sleeping child plus loud noise is bad' way, though she certainly didn't hear the slam.

The wall clock marks five long minutes before Lynette emerges and shuffles back to the couch. She sinks onto the cushions, then slowly raises her gaze to mine.

Her eyes are red. So she was almost definitely crying.

I still don't know if that's good or bad.

"Thank you for that," she breathes. "I . . . I never knew you had the papers."

My heart practically soars.

I want to hug her, but that seems forward. Rushed. I'll let her make that move, if she wants to. For now, I'll silently rejoice that the adoption-that-wasn't does not seem to be a deal-breaker.

There's something else we should talk about, too. At least I've already broached this subject, so it won't come out of the blue. "Has Tyler tried to approach you?"

She shakes her head, her mouth full of brownie. She finishes the bite and swallows some milk. "Haven't seen him, and he doesn't know where I live."

"That's good." A slight frown furrows my brow as I recall my earlier thoughts when he left that envelope at my door. "Lynette, do you think there's a chance he really didn't do it?"

"Definitely not. I mean, he must have, right?" I can see the uncertainty in her eyes while she must be thinking the same thing I was. "But the court said he didn't. They let him go, I guess. So maybe . . . I don't know." Her shoulders slump. "He was the only one there," she mutters.

"Listen, even if it turns out he's innocent, you can't blame yourself," I tell her. "All you did was tell the truth. Nothing that happened was your fault."

Her breath shudders from her. "Do you think he's innocent?"

"I guess I don't know, either."

She frowns. "If it wasn't Tyler, do they know who did do it?"

"I don't think so." An idea occurs to me. Maybe I can end this uncertainty for both of us. "He left me copies of the evidence, because he wants me to believe him," I say. "I haven't looked at it yet. Do you want to look at it with me?"

Lynette considers it. Finally, she says, "Okay. Sure."

I head back to the kitchen and retrieve the thickly stuffed envelope from the drawer. It's a relief not to have to look at its contents alone, but I wonder if it's going to be too much for Lynette. The immediate, visceral effect of Marisol's death was far worse on her.

She's the one who found Marisol's body.

Lynette was out with friends from school. They saw a movie, then went to a late dinner. When she came home just before one in the morning, both Tyler and Marisol were in bed. Except when Lynette went into Marisol's room to sneak

151

the box of Reese's Pieces she'd bought her at the theater under her pillow for a morning surprise, she realized Marisol wasn't sleeping. She was stiff and contorted, her eyes bulging, her skin blue.

She'd been smothered to death.

Now, as I carry Tyler's 'proof' like the envelope is full of excrement, I realize something I'd never put together before. I know why I became a recluse after it happened.

I left the house, and Marisol died.

Therefore, if I didn't leave the house, nothing bad would happen. No one else would die.

Except someone did.

So, I left the house.

Lynette is watching me. Her gaze flicks to the manila envelope as I sit beside her. "Is that it? His proof?" There's unmistakable sarcasm in her tone.

"So he claims." I'm glad that we seem to be united on the subject of Tyler, but it's going to be hard to reconcile if this proof is definitive. And it has to be, doesn't it? The time for reasonable doubt is the trial, not the appeal. "I guess we'll find out."

My fingers want to shake as I unfold the clasp and lift the seal. I can feel the shape of a hardcover book on the bottom, but I don't want to see that at all. Instead, I grasp the sheaf of papers and pull them free, then drop the envelope with the book on the table.

"What's that?" Lynette reaches in and pulls the book out, holding it up in front of her to read the cover. "Ew. He wrote a book?"

"Apparently." I catch a glimpse of his 'author photo' on the back. He's wearing all black, trying to strike a serious pose that doesn't suit him. A kind of elbow-propped, almost resting his chin on his hand but not quite touching position, unsmiling. It's as pretentious as his note.

He was never that person.

Lynette wrinkles her nose and tosses the thing face-down on the empty envelope. "Gross," she pronounces.

I couldn't agree more.

The papers from the envelope consist of several stapled packets. DNA results, toxicology reports, and what looks like scientific articles that are labeled 'expert testimony.' I can barely make any sense out of it. As I flip through them, Lynette looks on, her expression stating she doesn't understand, either.

Finally, I find the lawyer's notes Tyler mentioned. The language is still stiff, peppered with jargon and legalese, but I get the gist of what they're saying.

It feels like a chasm has opened in my core, and everything inside me is sliding into the abyss.

"What . . . what does that say?" Lynette whispers.

"It says he didn't do it." My voice is raspy, and I try to force a swallow past the sudden dryness in my throat. I point to the section of the lawyer's notes that discuss the toxicology report, which I thought they'd run on Marisol, but it's not about her.

"This says there was opium in Tyler's system," I explain. "It's what they use to make heroin. The report basically proves that at the . . . the victim's time of death, Tyler was physically incapable of doing . . . what was done to her."

I'm stammering the words, choking on them. The notes go into further detail, though they use sterile terms to describe smothering a five-year-old child to death with a pillow.

Lynette's brow furrows. "Tyler was on drugs?" she says. "But that doesn't mean he didn't do it. People kill people when they're on drugs all the time."

"Not with opium." I hate having to explain why Tyler is actually innocent. I don't want to reinforce it in my own mind, let alone Lynette's, but I need to know the truth. "It causes severe disorientation and muscle weakness. He would've barely been able to move."

I have no idea about the effects of opium, or any illegal drug, but the lawyer's statement makes it very clear. There's also an expert testimony to back it up.

And though I hate to admit it, Tyler was unusually groggy and out of it when I got to the hospital. In those precious few seconds when I first saw him and didn't think my husband had killed our daughter, I'd chalked it up to extreme grief. Then, I thought he'd been drinking.

It seems it wasn't *only* grief and alcohol, though.

Lynette's frown deepens. "Wait, how long was he doing drugs?"

"He wasn't, according to this," I tell her. "Something about levels consistent with a first-time user. They think he was dosed, somehow."

"But that doesn't make any sense!" Lynette exclaims, flinging her hands in the air.

She's right. It really doesn't. Unless someone came into the house, drugged Tyler, then killed Marisol. Which seems to be where this evidence is pointing.

I can't even imagine why anyone would do that, let alone who might be responsible. Especially considering the other major piece of evidence in these reports.

"That's not all they have, either." I indicate another section of the lawyer's notes. "Marisol had trace DNA under her fingernails. They didn't test it at first because Tyler was so apparently guilty. Locked house, two people, one dead. By the time he found a lawyer willing to dig deeper for an appeal, it was too degraded to identify, even if the person was in the system." I pause to heave a breath. "But they did determine it was a woman's DNA."

Lynette stills, and her face blanches. "A woman?" she croaks.

I can only nod.

She stares at me for a long time, uncomfortably blank. Then, her expression crumples. "Oh, God," she wails. "I put him in jail for nothing!"

She bursts into tears.

Immediately, I close the gap between us and put my arms around her, the idea of letting her initiate tossed by the wayside. She's still my daughter, at least in my heart, and I won't let her cry alone.

She leans into me. She's sobbing so hard that every heave shakes the couch. I rub her back, murmuring whatever words of comfort I can summon as her storm slowly subsides until she goes limp, occasionally jerking with a watery, hitching breath.

When she's quiet, I shift slightly so one arm is around her as she rests her head on my shoulder. "It's absolutely not your fault," I tell her, kindly but firmly. "Like I said, all you did was tell the truth. You couldn't have done anything more."

"I know, but . . ." She drags in a long, stuttering inhale. "I hated him," she whispers. "For no reason at all."

I can think of a few reasons to hate him, but I won't share them right now. "You can only work with what you know, honey."

I wince inwardly as the endearment leaves my lips. That's probably taking it too far. She may not have any more reasons to hate Tyler, but she has plenty to hate me. But either she doesn't mind, or she doesn't notice. I suspect it's the latter.

Lynette sniffles and swipes at her nose. "Eurgh. Sorry," she says. "Do you have any tissues?"

"Of course. I think they're in the bathroom. I'll grab them."

After a quick side hug, I extricate myself from the couch and head there. I'm not entirely sure that's where I saw the tissues, but when I flip on the bathroom light, I spot the box on the back of the toilet and bring it to Lynette.

She cleans her face off, and miraculously, we start chatting like normal people over brownies and milk. She tells me a little about her jobs — she works at Walmart and McDonald's — and I touch on my video-editing work. Neither of us mentions Tyler or Marisol again. Half an hour passes in a blink.

Eventually, she looks at her phone and sighs. "I'd better get home," she says. "I have a shift in the morning."

"Oh, I'm so sorry to keep you awake! Do you have to be up early?"

"Well, not *early*." She smirks. "I'm in at eleven, but that's basically morning for me. I'm usually up pretty late."

As I prepare to walk her out, I'm trying to figure out the best way to ask if I can see her again. I feel awful that she has to work two jobs to survive, and I wonder if she has anyone in the area she can rely on for help.

Lynette came to us from a truly broken home. Her father was physically abusive and kept both her and her mother on a tight leash, using the threat of further violence to keep their mouths shut. When Lynette ended up in the hospital at the age of thirteen, with four broken bones and bruising over more than fifty percent of her body, Myron Drummond tried to claim Lynette's mother had done it, and that she'd run off afterward.

However, in a moment of courage, Lynette confessed to the hospital staff that her father had beaten them both that night, and she thought he'd killed her mother.

Whether she was murdered and her body hidden, or she escaped and managed to disappear, Lynette's mother was never found. Her father was sentenced to life in prison. She had no siblings, and if any aunts or uncles existed, she didn't know about them.

Which made me abandoning her even worse.

We're almost at the door when I finally manage to blurt out, "Hey, do you want to hang out again sometime? When you're not working, I mean."

Wow, that sounds a lot dumber out loud than it did in my head.

Lynette looks at me, then flashes a hesitant smile. "Sure," she says. "Do you want my number? I can let you know when I have free time."

I try not to squeal like a teenager as we exchange numbers, and then she hugs me.

I hold the door open as she walks outside. She stops on the stoop and turns. "Grandpa Joe helped me out, you know," she says. "When I moved to Fulton. He helped me find an apartment, a car, a job. Gave me money sometimes."

My heart liquefies. I'm so glad that at least someone was there for her, and I hate that it wasn't me. It *should* have been me. "He was a good man."

"He was." She smiles. "See you later, Mama Kat."

Somehow, I manage to hold back the tears until she's in her car and driving away.

As I head back inside, I'm determined to pick up where Dad left off and help Lynette. That starts with keeping her safe, which means I have to do one more thing before I head up to bed.

I find Tyler's number on the note he wrote me and send off a text, not caring that it's the middle of the night.

Lynette and I know you're innocent, okay? Now leave us alone.

That's the only admission he'll ever get from me.

Part of me wants to explore this new information about my ex-husband and what it means. Not for him, but for me. Because despite the spectacular collapse of us, it wasn't always that way. Otherwise, I never would have married him in the first place.

Once upon a time, he'd been charming, considerate, funny, devoted . . . all those things that make a person good. He'd been one of those men who wouldn't hurt a fly, even though he could if he wanted to. Or so I thought.

After Marisol's death, a big part of the reason I withdrew from the world was because I didn't trust myself to interact with people. If I'd been so wrong about the man I married — a man who turned out capable of murdering a five-year-old — how could I ever know who was good and who wasn't?

The proof that he did not in fact commit such a monstrous act allows me to go a little easier on myself. Still, I can't forget, *won't* forget, that Tyler Martin is far from an angel. The way he was treating his 'date' is more than enough to demonstrate that.

Whether he's guilty of murder or not, I don't want him anywhere near me, or Lynette.

And this time, I *will* protect her.

CHAPTER 25

So many things are crashing through my mind right now that I can't focus. I can barely see the face in front of me, the moving lips. I can't feel my extremities. I am all stomach, swooping and see-sawing, buzzing with a constant, droning, high-pitched whine that has me on the verge of passing out.

The doorbell rang at a little after 10:30 this morning. It was Detective Wyetta — and friends. Alina was with them, and Drew arrived shortly after.

They know who the body is.

But it *can't* be.

I feel like I'm having an episode of sleep paralysis while I'm wide awake. Like I can't control any part of me. Somehow, I'm participating in an interview with Detective Wyetta, but it's like watching myself talk and nod and shake my head. I'm on autopilot.

I need to break out of this.

Come on. Five things you can see.

The detective's mouth moving, his thin lips twisting, exposing insanely white teeth. Holly sitting on my lap, confused and hiding from all the people in the house. A small dent in the vinyl toward the middle of the kitchen table. Drew in the dining room, giving a statement to a uniformed cop in a shaky voice. The sun burning a slanted line across the tiled floor through the open back door.

Four things you can feel.

Holly's slight, warm weight. The chair pressing against the backs of my thighs. Blood whooshing through my veins.

Sick. I feel sick.

Three things you can hear.

Bursts of chatter from cop CBs. Alina sobbing in the living room. Detective Wyetta's nasal breathing.

Two things you can smell.

Sweat. Fear.

One thing you can taste.

Dirt from Evie's grave.

". . . time you saw Evelyn Wells?"

The world rushes back into focus so swiftly that its vivid presence almost overwhelms me. I'm not sure I heard even the tail end of the question correctly. "Sorry, Detective Wyland—"

"Wyetta," he corrects me.

"Detective Wyetta. Can you repeat that?"

He looks at me like he's concerned for my sanity, and he probably should be. "I said, when was the last time you saw Evelyn Wells?"

That is definitely not something I know off the top of my head. I search the dusty halls of my memories for a moment I didn't know I should cherish. When I find it, I realize it's doubly precious — because it's also the last time I saw my mom.

"Christmas vacation, twelve years ago," I tell him. "I was home from college."

He nods and makes a note. "The start of the year she went missing, is that correct?"

"Yes."

"And who lived in your home at that time?"

"Mom and Dad." I pause and look at him. "Do I need to state their names?"

For a moment, the detective looks sad. "No. I actually knew your parents."

"You did?"

"Yes, but let's get through these questions first, please," he says. "We had Mr. and Mrs. Gray. Who else?"

"Everyone who's here, actually," I reply. "Drew Seaborn. Alina Cruz."

Detective Wyetta scribbles this down. "Not Naomi Young?"

"No. She left the summer before." I cock my head at him. "Why would you ask about her?"

"I heard you lodged a strenuous complaint against her," he says. "I am with the police, you know."

Was that a joke? I can't really tell with his dry tone. Not that I'm going to complain if it was. He's been far nicer than the other cops. Except Alina, of course.

"Anyway," the detective says. "Did anyone living at home at the time seem to have a problem with Evelyn? Any fighting or tension that you noticed?"

"Absolutely not." I want to shake my head and repeat myself for evidence, but I have enough presence of mind to know that vehement denial looks suspicious. Besides, Holly is starting to grow heavier on my lap. I think she's falling asleep, and I don't want to jar her with sudden movements. "Everybody loved Evie."

Everyone but Naomi. Who wasn't there at the time.

Though she *was* in Fulton.

Apparently, she's never left.

Now I'm thinking about Naomi again. And about the box in the basement. Could she have killed Evie? It's a massive stretch, but it's not impossible. Someone apparently made a fake Facebook account, pretended to be Evie, and spent years convincing me it was her. *Years.* That's how long I've been talking to 'Evie' online.

Someone knew she was buried beneath it. Wanted her found. Otherwise, no one would have ever thought to look there. When I didn't take the bait with the note, they decided to make sure I wouldn't miss her.

Maybe those someones — the fake Evie and the corpse digger — are both Naomi.

I've tuned out the detective again, but he's only watching me. Waiting for me to say something. I'm not sure what I'm supposed to tell him, though. Despite the horrific discovery in my parents' back yard, I'm determined not to mention the photograph. The one that can't be what it looks like.

"Are you *sure* it's Evie?" I say when Detective Wyetta doesn't comment further.

"Well, the DNA test says it is. So does the backpack full of Evelyn Wells' possessions that the body was wearing, which includes a journal and a few books with her name written in them all," he drawls. "I suppose, short of confirming with a Ouija board, we're as sure as we can be."

I want to snap at him, tell him that the sarcasm really isn't necessary, but I don't have the strength.

Evie is not in Florida, working in a retirement home full of lovely clients and living near a gorgeous white sand beach. Evie didn't make it through years of homelessness and drug abuse, only to turn her life around.

Evie never left Fulton. She never left this *house*.

Evie is dead.

And they think my father did it. All of them. The police, my siblings. They think he's a murderer.

I don't know what to think anymore.

"Okay, well, I told you about the fake Evie on Facebook," I say. "Is there any way you can . . . I don't know, trace who made the account? Whoever it is, they might be involved. Right?" *Naomi. I'm sure it's Naomi.*

The detective looks at me. "It doesn't actually work like that. We'd only be able to get that information directly from Facebook. Well, Meta, I suppose. Unless there's a murder confession somewhere in your message history, they probably won't give it to us." He frowns. "Wait, is there a murder confession?"

I shake my head. "She was pretending to be Evie. Not Evie's killer."

"How do you know it's a she?"

I almost say there's a picture of her, but of course, that must be fake, too. And he's right. Whoever's behind this profile could be literally anybody.

And if it's not Naomi, there's every chance I'll never know who it is until and unless they choose to reveal themselves.

"I'll tell you what, though." Detective Wyetta produces a phone from his pocket. "I'll give you my number, and you text me the profile link. I'll see if I can find out anything about it. Who knows? It might help."

"So you're not going to take my phone and process it for evidence?"

He smirks. It's the closest he's come to smiling since he arrived at my door. "Honestly, we try not to do that. People need their phones these days."

He reads out his number, and I open the conversation with 'Evie' to access the profile. My stomach burns at the sight of all those messages we exchanged, years of sharing our lives . . . all of it made up. Completely fictional.

Except that's not true. Only half of it was fictional. My half of the conversation was real.

Oh, my God. How much have I told this person? They know so much about me, and I know nothing about them.

My blood runs cold, and my hands shake as I send the message to the detective.

I could be in serious trouble here.

CHAPTER 26

Alina lives across the river from me on the same side of Broadway, the main road that cuts through Fulton from east to west. Her place is a cute two-bedroom Cape Cod on a quiet street named after a tree, like all the roads off West 1st Street South in this section. You can see the lake from her back yard.

Holly and I are here because my father's house is officially a crime scene, and the police are searching it from top to bottom.

If they find that box in the basement, I'm screwed. It's evidence, my fingerprints are all over it, and there's a note addressed to me inside it.

But there's nothing I can do about that now.

We're in the second bedroom, which contains a queen-sized bed, two end tables with lamps, a dresser, and a flat-screen TV with a Fire stick. Alina pointed out her active, signed-in apps before she left for her shift. She has Netflix, Hulu, Paramount Plus, Disney Plus, the Discovery Channel, and Shudder, which she said is a horror movie channel.

I have no interest in horror movies tonight, because I feel like I'm living one.

Holly is zonked out on the bed, exhausted after a long day, but I can't sleep. I've got a million things on my mind. For one, I feel terrible that Alina went to work after she couldn't have gotten more than four hours of sleep this morning, then spent most of her day being interrogated by her co-workers. Finding out the body was Evie clearly hit her hard. The way it hit all of us. But she insisted she was fine.

I suspect she wants to listen in on some station gossip and try to find out more about Evie's case.

I'm also absurdly touched that Alina not only invited me to stay the night, but trusts me in her home while she's not here. It's such a sisterly thing. Despite our years of no contact, she didn't hesitate to help me when I needed it.

It's the same with the others. Drew has gone above and beyond ever since I came home, and Lynette is talking to me again.

I hope I don't manage to screw everything up this time.

Besides that, I'm worried about the basement. That photo and what it means. If it's what it seems like at face value — and I still can't believe it is — who knows what else they might find? I've barely looked at anything in that house since I came back. Entire rooms left untouched. There's three thousand square feet of space, not counting the basement.

What if there are more horrific surprises waiting for me, like the note-writer suggested?

And of course, there's Naomi.

I grab my phone from the bedside table, flip it over. It's almost two in the morning now. I've been sitting here for over three hours, stewing and churning, unable to settle.

I'd thought of going onto the group, kicking 'Evie' off, then posting a warning to everyone that she was an impostor and not to engage with her. But I decided against it, at least until word gets out that the body's been identified. Instead, I've been messaging her profile.

I unlock the screen and open the app, despite the lack of notifications telling me she hasn't replied. I stare at the last several messages I sent after getting Holly to sleep. All of them are still unread.

Naomi, I know this is really you.
Why are you doing this?
Answer me.
Hello???
Naomi! What did you do?

It's pointless. I know it is, but I compose yet another message to the person behind the screen, the person who's not Evie and is probably Naomi.

Did you kill her? Just tell me that. It's not like I can prove it if you did.

As I send it, my mind drifts back over everything that's happened. Everything I can't help thinking points back to Naomi. Evie's body, the suggestive destruction of the shed, climbing the ladder to look in my bedroom window, calling the police on me. Holly abandoned in my back yard . . . which still doesn't make sense.

Even before that. The visitor who went to see my dad at work the day he died. At that point, Naomi had definitely been hired at the studio. They wouldn't hire her and start her on-air the same day.

My head throbs with frustration, and I stab out one last message.

Did you kill my dad?

I tap send and toss the phone back on the nightstand, then massage my temples. All this wheel-spinning is getting me nowhere. The problem is, I don't know where to direct my energies. Where to even begin untangling this series of disastrous dominoes.

My phone dings.

I snatch for it, my heart in my throat.

Joe Gray got what he deserved.

I stop breathing. Even while part of me screams in outrage and aching sorrow at the possibility that my father's death wasn't natural, I'm screenshotting the conversation in case she — or whoever — decides to delete the thread. Does this count as a confession?

Maybe I can get one.

Did you kill him? Tell me. How did you do it?

I spend the next ten minutes staring at the phone. No response arrives. My message remains unread.

A guttural cry escapes my throat, and I toss the device aside. Of course whoever this is won't confess to murder. They've been cultivating this charade for years. They are patient, and cunning, and evil.

And I can't sit around waiting for the police to find them.

Finally, I come to a decision. I'm going to do something about this. Tomorrow.

My mind made up, I lie back and slide under the blanket.

I fall asleep within minutes.

CHAPTER 27

If the police found the box in the basement, they didn't inform me about it.

We're allowed to return to the house in the morning. I tried to avert my gaze from the now-gaping hole in the back yard surrounded by crime scene tape when I pulled into the driveway, though I still took in far too much. I hustled Holly inside, and after a leisurely breakfast, we went on a tour of the house.

It looks like, for the most part, they put things back in place after they searched. All except for the master bedroom. I didn't spend much time in there, just long enough to note the mess. I'm not ready to face that yet.

And the box is right where I left it, the photo still inside.

Now, Holly and I are at the kitchen table having a snack. I'm working on a second cup of coffee, and Holly is occasionally eating a Goldfish while she chases virtual kitties. I may not be doing a great job at limiting her screen time, but so far, she's never complained when I indicate that it's time to stop playing with the tablet and do something else.

I've texted Drew to tell him about my plans for today and ask for his help. He's the only other person Holly seems comfortable with, and I don't want to bring her along. He agreed, but he expressed a few reservations about the soundness of the idea.

I told him I have to know. Have to *see* how she reacts.

He seemed to accept that.

As I finish the last of my coffee and debate whether I want a third, the doorbell rings. I'm beginning to hate that sound. Most likely, it's the police with more questions or demands to search something. I want them to find out who did this, but I seriously doubt they'll find answers to a twelve-year-old murder here.

I realize murder is an assumption, but it's a logical one. Why else would someone bury Evie's body, if not because they killed her?

The doorbell chimes again, and I sigh and push my chair back. "I'll be right back, sweetheart," I say to Holly, holding up a finger until she acknowledges with a nod and a thumbs-up. She's definitely come to understand the gesture.

I grumble my way through the dining room, then the living room, and open the door. The half-scowl forming on my face gives way to surprise. "Clara?"

She's standing on the stoop with a sturdy-looking cardboard box at her feet. Concern is etched into her features. "Hello, dear. I'm so sorry I didn't call first, but . . . my God, are you all right? What happened here?"

She must have seen the back yard. The mounds of dirt, the crime scene tape. I consider not telling her, so she won't worry, but she's bound to hear it on the news along with everyone else. Better for me to tell her first if she doesn't already know.

I glance over my shoulder. Holly's back is to the door, head down, lost in the world of Kitty Town. I step out onto the stoop and close the door most of the way, so I can still hear her if she presses the help button.

With no idea where to start, I dive right in.

"There was a body buried under the shed," I tell her. "The police dug it up."

"A body?" Clara repeats, dumbfounded. Then her face turns the color of cottage cheese, and her chin quivers. "You don't mean a *human* body . . . ?" she whispers.

I swallow and nod.

"Dear Lord, no. Oh, honey. I'm so sorry." She nudges the box aside, almost tripping over it, and hugs me.

She's trembling almost as hard as me.

"How *awful*," she rasps, slowly releasing me. "Are you all right? How did they find a buried body? Do they know who it is?" Tears pour down her cheeks as she fires questions, more horrified babbling than expecting any answers. Suddenly, she jerks into a rigid stance, and it looks like she's about to faint. "Oh, God. They don't think your father . . ."

"No. I'm sure he had nothing to do with it," I reassure her, even if the police think differently. "The body was buried there years ago. They haven't made a formal identification yet, but it's Evelyn Wells. My parents fostered her, and everyone thought she ran away."

"No. Little Evie?" Clara covers her mouth with a hand, and a few rapid sobs escape her. "That poor child," she whispers. "She was only fourteen, wasn't she? Your father talked about her, too. He felt so terrible that he wasn't able to find her."

I don't want to consider how unimaginably worse he'd have felt if he was still here, and he found out after all this time that Evie hadn't gone far at all.

Clara is openly weeping now. She fumbles in her purse and pulls out a half-empty tissue packet, then wipes her face and blows her nose. "Oh, what a terrible week," she says in a trembling voice. "At least there's one bright spot. I'm glad I've gotten to see you."

"Same here." I smile and go in for another hug.

We stay that way for a moment, then Clara pulls back with a startled, "Oh! I completely forgot the reason I came here in the first place." She gestures at the cardboard box. "These are your father's things," she says. "Everything he left

169

at my house over the years. Just trinkets, really, and a few photos, but I thought you might like to have them."

Her thoughtful earnestness brings tears to my eyes. "Clara, thank you so much," I say. "But you know, I think you should keep it."

"Really?" She blinks rapidly. "You wouldn't mind?"

"Definitely not. I have this whole house full of things to remember Dad by," I tell her. "If he left those at your house, I'm sure he would've wanted you to have them."

She beams at me. "Oh, honey, thank you," she says. "Like I said, they're just trinkets, but a few of them are dear to me. Especially the photographs."

"It's no problem. You're family." I glance back at the house again. "Listen, do you want to come in? Have that coffee we keep talking about?"

Her face falls. "I'm actually on my way to work," she says. "One of the girls called in sick. Oh, how about Tuesday afternoon?" she suggests. "I've got the day off. We could go to Backstreet Books, or maybe that new place, the 114 Reserve. Have you been there yet? It's a lovely atmosphere, and the owners are so nice."

I can't help smiling. Fulton may be a city, but sometimes it feels like a small town where everyone knows everyone.

Which is why it's so strange that absolutely no one recognizes Holly's picture.

I push the thought away. "That sounds great. I'd love to check out the new place."

"Wonderful! I'll text you, and we can figure out a time." Clara bends to pick up the box. "Thank you again for this. I really appreciate it. We'll talk soon, okay?"

"You got it."

I push the door open and step back inside, watching Clara head to her car at the curb. She didn't look too good a minute ago, when I thought she might faint, so I want to make sure she gets there without collapsing. She makes it, stows the box in the back seat, then waves to me across the roof before clambering into the driver's seat.

I wave back and head into the house, already turning my mind back to what I intend to do later today.

One way or another, I will get answers.

* * *

"Are you sure this is a good idea?" Drew asks for the dozenth time.

I huff at him. "No, but I'm doing it anyway."

Drew and Holly are sitting on the couch. She's got her stuffed cat, her light toy, and the tablet. There are snacks and drinks on the coffee table, and there's more food available in the kitchen. I've also brought the toy box from the boys' bedroom downstairs and placed some of the toys Holly likes in it. It's probably overkill, but this is the first time I've left her since the day she came into my life, and I'm as nervous as a mother leaving her infant with a new sitter.

Still, I'm by the door, resolutely putting my shoes on.

"Just promise that if anything goes wrong, you'll call me. Or 9-1-1," he says.

I stick out my tongue. "Yes, Mother."

"Ha-ha. That's *my* line, you know."

"We can share it." I cross the room to crouch in front of Holly. "I won't be gone long," I tell her, and hold up a finger. "Okay?"

She nods with a thumbs-up.

I give her a quick hug and straighten to address Drew. "You'll be okay, right? Thank you so much for doing this. Really."

"Yeah. I still don't think you should, but I get why you are." He smirks. "Do I need to press the hug button, or what?"

I laugh and hug him. "Thank you. I'll be back soon."

"You'd better."

Before my nerves can fail me, I hurry back across the room and out the door.

It's better, being outside. I feel like I've taken the first step already, and everything else is downhill. I'm not going to drive because I want the time to think, to harden my resolve. And if I'm driving, I might miss it.

I walk down the steps, reach the sidewalk, and turn left. It's a sunny afternoon, not as brutally hot as yesterday felt, but still warm. Pleasant, with a light breeze. For the first time since I've been back, I take the opportunity to look around.

It really is a lovely neighborhood. Not picture-perfect like those upscale New England towns with cookie-cutter pastel homes and perfectly manicured lawns, not rustic like a country setting. But it's charming. It has character. Some of these homes, like my parents', are more than a hundred years old. Others are newer. Some lots have huge, old towering trees reaching for the sky like stalwart sentries. Not all are the same type of tree, either. Others have short, wide trees, slender saplings, or no trees at all.

There are houses with and without front porches. Single stories, split levels, two stories, a few three-levels where they have full attics. Most are single-family homes, with the occasional larger, three- to four-apartment unit sprinkled in.

The sidewalks aren't perfect, but they're generally straight and even. The roads aren't perfectly smooth, but — well, the roads aren't great. Especially the side streets. However, they're passable, and the city keeps them up in the winter.

It's really a good place to live. To raise a family.

Why did it take me so long to realize that?

I've walked four blocks, and I see what I'm looking for ahead on the right. A little blue SUV in the driveway of a white two-story house that's as pin-neat as Naomi looks on television. It's a newer place, vinyl siding instead of wood. Gently sloping front lawn. Blue trim that practically matches the vehicle. Screened front porch surrounded by colorful, beautifully arranged bursts of flowers.

A girly-girl house.

I pause on the sidewalk and take a deep, settling breath before marching up the front walk. Up three steps, through the outer screen door, across the porch. I press the lighted doorbell and hear the muffled, cheerful chime from the other side.

It's not long before footsteps approach from inside. There's a click as a bolt is opened, then the knob turns and the door swings inward.

Naomi looks shockingly young. Her face is makeup-free, or at least it appears that way. Her hair is pulled into a high ponytail. She's wearing a spaghetti-strap top and leggings, and the toenails on her bare feet are painted with hot-pink polish.

Her mouth parts in surprise, and her eyebrows raise almost to her hairline. She looks like she's about to say something.

Then her expression drags down sharply. "No." She backs away and starts to close the door.

"Naomi, wait!" On impulse, I shove my foot in the gap. The door slams into my sneaker and bounces off. "Please," I say. "I just want to talk for a minute."

A somewhat misleading statement, but I need her not to run off. Not until I say what I have to say.

For a long moment, she doesn't move, until I'm convinced she's going to start bashing the door into my foot until I take it out of the way. Finally, she huffs a breath worthy of an exasperated teenager and pulls the door open, eyeing me warily. "Step back, and I'll think about it," she says.

I do so slowly, expecting her to slam the door in my face any second. Instead, she leans against the door frame, crosses her arms, and folds one ankle over the other. "Talk, then."

As I stare at her, my prepared rant falls away from my tongue. I remember the story Drew told me about Naomi's birth mother, about the foster families who came after that. How she spent so long being abandoned and neglected. Why she learned not to trust anyone.

And I can't do it. I can't come at her with a pile of accusations.

Even if they're true, she'll never admit to anything like that.

Instead, I say, "Did you hear about Evie?"

I watch her carefully. Her expression slackens, and the lines of her body droop slightly. "I did," she replies in a flat tone. "It's awful."

I can't tell if she's trying to hold back her emotions or if she doesn't care.

"Yes. It really is." I give it a minute to see if she adds anything else. "The police think Dad did it, you know? Killed her and buried her in the yard."

"He didn't," Naomi snaps immediately.

Is she saying that because she believes in Dad, or does she know he's innocent because she did it?

"I know that. But the police don't."

"Well, they'll probably figure it out."

What a scintillating conversation we're having.

Maybe I should try approaching this from another angle. "So, the other day," I say. "Why'd you stop in the middle of the road and stare at me?"

That gets a stronger reaction. She straightens, and her arms fall to her sides, hands clenching into fists. "You know what? Forget this. Just leave, Kat."

"What? Why are you so pissed off?" I feel my control slipping, and I'm losing the struggle to get it back. "Why do you hate me *so* much, Naomi? Everyone who tries to be nice to you, you bite their heads off for it. You killed Evie, didn't you? And you killed Dad!"

A red flush blossoms on her face. She takes a sharp breath and bares her teeth. "Get the hell off my porch, you crazy bitch!"

The door slams so hard that her front windows rattle.

I purse my lips and exhale. "That went well," I mutter.

CHAPTER 28

The Journal

Seriously, I'm going to kill the bio kid.

The dad is showing some resistance. I almost had him the other day, but then the bio kid had some sort of *malfunction* and we were interrupted. After that, he started acting like we'd never made progress toward the goal.

Not that he knows what the goal is, of course. In some ways, he's just as clueless as the mom.

This is taking so much longer than I thought. Every time there's a setback, I have to start being nicer to everyone and going along with the rah-rah-family stuff like I actually believe they've accepted me. And that's when I have to be careful.

Sometimes, I find myself thinking maybe they're not fake. Maybe they mean it.

Maybe I can stay for real.

I can't fall for that line, though. I have to get the dad back on track. She's counting on me — and there will be hell to pay if I don't.

Luckily, I have an advantage that no one knows about.

I know *all* his secrets.

CHAPTER 29

I haven't been to Tavern on the Lock since I was fifteen, but the place is exactly as I remember it. And it's bustling.

After the last few days we've had, I decided to take Holly out to dinner. We're sitting on the patio with a great view as the sun sets over the Oswego River. Water pouring over the nearby lock kicks up a billowing, misty spray that catches the golden pinks and reds of the dying light. The air smells fantastic, a heady mix of water, grass, and cooking food.

I'm enjoying a Barnacle Burger, a massive crab cake over greens, with a side of homemade breadsticks, and Holly chose a quesadilla and fries from the kids' menu. I was a little worried she liked the picture but wouldn't eat the food, but she dug right in. She's working on the last wedge now.

"This is good stuff, right?" I give Holly a thumbs-up, and she returns the gesture. "I think we need to get dessert, too. What do you say?"

"Did I hear someone say dessert?" Our waitress materializes beside the table. She's an upbeat young woman, auburn-haired and hazel-eyed, probably in her early twenties. She was immediately welcoming to both of us when we arrived, and when I told her Holly was deaf, she used as many hand gestures as possible while talking.

I smile up at her. "I think we're going for it, but we need a while to finish up here."

"Not a problem," she says with a smile. "Can I get you any refills on your drinks?"

Holly's chocolate milk is still halfway full, and I've barely touched my first refill of iced tea. "We're good for now. Thanks so much."

"Okay! Just wave if you need something."

The waitress zips off to another table, and I dip another bite of my crab cake into the remoulade sauce. "Good stuff," I repeat before popping it in my mouth.

As I'm reaching for my tea, a voice calls out, "Kat?"

The sound of it makes my spine crawl.

I give Holly the 'wait' gesture and turn toward the voice, already gritting my teeth. "Did I not make myself clear?" I say coldly to the approaching figure and his date — a far-too-young blonde woman, but not the same one he brought to the VFW. This one is a shorter, curvier model with heavier makeup. "Which word did you fail to understand, Tyler? Leave, us, or alone?"

He comes right up to the table with the blonde girl in tow. "So, you looked at the stuff," he says. "That's great. Did you read the book?"

"Get away from us."

"What the hell, Kat? I thought you said—" He cuts himself off with effort and calms down. "You know I didn't do it."

"I saw the evidence." I won't give him the satisfaction of agreeing. I told him once, in a text. That's all he gets.

He folds his arms. "Well?"

"Well, what?"

"Are you going to apologize?"

I'm so stunned that at first, I can't speak. The look I spear him with is pure ice. "Apologize?" I repeat. "Are you out of your goddamned mind?"

Heads are turning in our direction. I'm about to make a scene here, but I don't care.

Tyler's jaw sets. "I think you owe me that much."

"I don't owe you *anything*." I shoot to my feet so fast that he stumbles back a step. "I'm only going to say this one more time. Stay. Away. From me. And if you go near Lynette, I will call the police." I lean closer to him. "Maybe you didn't kill my daughter, but you're trying to *profit* from her *murder*, you absolute scumbag."

I'm keeping my voice low because this is no one else's business, but the girl with him seems to hear. Her eyes widen in shock.

Maybe I can save her from him. I face her fully, and tell her, "By the way, if you've been with him for longer than three days? He's cheating on you."

"Shut the hell up!" Tyler sputters.

"Excuse me," a loud female voice calls. It's our waitress, and she's glaring daggers at Tyler. "Is there a problem here, sir?"

Tyler sighs and holds his hands up. "No. No problem," he says, backing away.

"Help!"

Holly's sound button startles me. I turn toward her, but not before I catch Tyler glaring in her direction.

If he so much as tries to speak to her, I'll kill him.

"What do you need, sweetheart?" I ask, ignoring everyone else.

She pushes the toilet button.

"You got it." I hold a hand out, and she hops from the chair and takes it, half-hiding behind my legs. She's holding her light toy and her stuffed cat together in her free hand.

Without another word to Tyler, I brush past him and lead her inside.

The restroom is bright and quiet, soothing after the chaotic confrontation. Holly goes into a stall by herself. I have a feeling she doesn't really need to go that badly and just wanted to get away from the angry man — and honestly, I'm all for that. She can take all the time she wants.

Maybe he'll be gone by the time we come out.

I don't need the bathroom, though. I stand at the sink and wash my hands, splash some water on my face. As I'm pumping paper towels to dry off, the restroom door squeaks open and a short blonde woman breezes in.

It's Tyler's date.

"Hey." She gives me a nod and goes straight to the sink. But instead of washing her hands, she reaches up and pulls a few bobby pins from her hair.

Then, she removes it.

It's a blonde wig. The black hair beneath it is slicked tight to her skull, twisted into a flat bun on the back of her head. She watches me in the mirror the whole time.

"I told him to forget it and gave him a refund," she says as she stuffs the wig in the satchel purse slung across her shoulder. "I wanted you to know that."

A refund?

She must read the question in my eyes, because she laughs. "Yeah, you can't cheat on a girlfriend if you're paying for her," she says. "That one three days ago was a friend of mine. This creep goes for young and blonde, but after what you were saying back there, I think he's going to find his pickings slim around here."

I blink. "So, you're a . . ."

"Lady of the night?" She winks at me in the mirror. "The PC term these days is 'sex worker,' but yeah. That I am." She shakes her head and starts unwinding her bun. "I've got standards, though. And that guy doesn't meet 'em."

I'm horrified all over again. She's basically telling me that Tyler's been using his blood money to buy sex.

"Sorry to be the bearer of more bad news," the girl says. "It seems like you've had a lot of that. Anyway, thanks for the heads-up about him."

"No problem," I manage.

She shakes her hair out, then produces a brush from her purse and runs it through a few times. "Take care, hon. Your little girl is gorgeous, by the way. Looks just like you."

Before I can summon any kind of response, she's out the door.

I think Holly and I will have dessert at home tonight.

After she's done in the stall, I help her wash her hands, and we go straight to the cashier. I feel bad about not leaving the waitress's tip on the table, but the man at the register assures me she'll get the whole thing if I leave it with him. I pay the check with a debit card, hand over a twenty for the tip, and start walking Holly outside.

That's when I discover that Tyler did leave, but he hasn't gone far. He's in the parking lot, standing by his SUV and shouting into a phone.

And I'll have to walk past him to get to my car.

Cursing under my breath, I scoop Holly up and switch her to my hip, so she'll be on the side that's away from Tyler when we pass him.

As I start down the row, a memory surfaces from the depths of my past. A Saturday like today. Marisol was three, Lynette was fifteen. I'd taken Lynette to the mall for the afternoon, part of my promise to spend quality time with her without a toddler in tow — a girls' day out. When we got home, Tyler was standing in the open doorway, talking to a blonde girl on our porch. The girl rushed off as soon as I pulled the car into the driveway.

I asked Tyler who she was. He said she was a high school student doing a fundraiser, one of those c things with over-priced cookies, popcorn tins, and wrapping paper. Except she definitely wasn't carrying a catalog, and Christmas was a long way off from June.

And when we went inside, Marisol was asleep. An hour past her usual nap time.

A terrible suspicion washes over me, and fury descends like a curtain. I stalk the rest of the way to Tyler and smack the phone from his hands.

"Jesus Christ!" he shouts, jerking toward me. But I'm already backed away, out of his reach and protecting Holly. "You know, you're being an unbelievable bitch."

"Did you have a *sex worker* in our house the night our *daughter died*?" I hiss at him.

His stunned, sick expression and the way the color drains from him tells me everything.

"You deserve a lot worse than prison, Tyler."

I can't stand the sight of him for one second longer. I practically race the rest of the way to my car without looking back.

CHAPTER 30

Sleep isn't going to grace me with its presence anytime soon.

It's 11:30. I gave up trying to sleep an hour ago. Holly is slumbering away, and I'm glad she was able to settle after the encounter with Tyler. Unfortunately, that's not going to happen for me.

Every time I try to figure something out, things just get more tangled.

I'm sitting cross-legged on the couch, flipping through cable channels without seeing anything. I thought I knew who killed my daughter, but I don't. I thought my dad died of a stroke, but he didn't. Maybe. I thought Evie was alive and well in Florida, but she isn't.

I thought none of these things were connected. But maybe they are.

My slow television roulette lands on a sitcom. When a doorbell chimes, at first I think it's part of the show. It takes a minute for my brain to recognize the sound was louder than the television.

I'm on my feet and moving toward the door when I consider that it might be Tyler.

I decide to look. If it is him, I'll double back for the fireplace poker and come out swinging.

At the door, I pull the taut curtain back enough to peer outside.

It's Lynette.

Worry spikes, and I rush to open the door. "Are you okay?" I say by way of greeting. "Did Tyler try anything stupid?"

She blinks at me. "Uh, no. Haven't seen him. I just got off work."

"Good. Great." I step back and pull the door open the rest of the way. "Come on in. I mean, if you want to."

"Sorry I didn't text or anything." She looks even more tired than the last night she was here. After an uncertain pause, she walks inside and waits for me to close the door. "Did I wake you up?"

"Not at all."

She trails me toward the couch. I ask her if she wants something to drink, and she says anything cold would be great. While she sits, I find two cans of Sprite in the fridge and bring them out for us.

Before I can ask how she's doing or if she needs anything, she says, "Why are you so worried about Tyler? I thought he didn't do it."

"He didn't. But . . ." I bite my lip, wondering how much I should tell her about what I've learned tonight. I'm not even sure what to do with the information myself. Finally, I decide to answer her question with another question. "Lynette, did you ever see Tyler with another woman? Like he was cheating on me?"

She immediately drops her gaze and starts playing with the ring tab on her soda can.

"It's okay," I urge her. "You can tell me if you did."

She takes a deep breath and sighs it out. "Yeah. I mean, one time," she says. "It was after school. You know that restaurant at the bottom of the hill? They came out and got in his car." Her eyes cloud, and she frowns at the memory. "She was blonde like you, so I thought it *was* you at first. But she was way younger. Like she could've been in high school with me." Lynette looks disgusted.

I don't ask why she didn't tell me. No one wants to break that kind of news to their mother . . . or their maternal figure. And it certainly wasn't her responsibility to inform me of my husband's sick indiscretions.

At least my confrontation with Tyler may have served a useful purpose. He's so furious with me now that he may not bother harassing Lynette. Still, I want her to be careful and avoid engaging with him.

"Tyler isn't the man either of us thought he was," I say. "He didn't kill Marisol, but I still think he was indirectly responsible for her death. He was . . . not being a good parent." Fresh rage toward him sparks in me, but I tamp it down. "He's not worth feeling bad over."

Lynette shakes her head. "You know, I kind of don't anymore. I almost forgot about that girl until now. It was nasty." She shudders, then looks at me. "I'm sorry he did that to you."

"Thank you, but I'm fine." I smile and straighten my spine, as if I need to prove how fine I am that my ex-husband has been sleeping with barely legal sex workers at least since when we were married, maybe even before. "How are *you* doing?"

"Fine," she says, then blinks and seems to refocus. "Oh, crap. I came to see how you were doing, actually. I heard about that . . . um, the back yard? They said there was a body. Are you the one who found it?"

The idea that she stopped by because she was worried about me warms me to my core. "Yes, unfortunately." I won't go into detail about the vandalism that led to the discovery. "It was pretty bad, I'll admit. I knew her — she was my foster sister. We all thought she'd run away from home."

"Oh, man. That's so sad." Lynette looks toward the kitchen and grimaces, as if she can see through the exterior wall and picture me out there, discovering my dead sister. "Did the kid see it?" she asks.

The question throws me until I realize she means Holly. "I don't think she did," I tell her, running back through the day in question. I'm pretty sure she was by my side the whole time and nowhere near the back yard.

Lynette's eyes narrow so briefly that I'm not sure I didn't imagine it, but she nods. "That's good. It'd be pretty awful for a little kid," she says. "How do they think she got there?"

Again, I don't want to tell her the police think her Grandpa Joe is a murderer. So I say, "They're not sure. The police are looking into it."

She seems to accept the response.

We don't spend as much time talking as we did on her last visit. Lynette is yawning, droopy, and I worry about her driving when she's so tired. When she says she needs to go a few minutes later, I ask her if she wants to crash here.

She declines, says she sleeps better in her own bed. But she thanks me for the offer.

I walk her out and wave when she gets into her car. She looks so small and tired. And I can't help a lingering worry that there's something more happening with her than working two jobs. She seems . . . lost.

I wonder how much time she spent with Dad and realize that could easily be it. Maybe she visited him frequently. Of course, she's grieving him like I am, too — and if there's one thing grief is not, it's invigorating.

She may have lost a closer friend than I thought, and I need to step up.

This time, I want to be there for her the way she deserves.

CHAPTER 31

I just got off the phone with Detective Wyetta. He basically called to tell me no news is good news. They haven't determined anything conclusive. They have no cause of death and no evidence pointing to anyone responsible.

I suppose I'm glad he's keeping in touch, but I'm not sure how I feel about 'hey, just wanted to tell you that we know nothing.'

So I'm not in the best mood when the doorbell rings.

It's around noon, and Holly is napping on the couch after an early morning wakeup. I'd been thinking about joining her when the detective called. Yet another unexpected visitor is not going to help me catch up on all the sleep I keep missing.

Still, I grit my teeth and march to the door, half-hoping it's someone I can unleash my shortened temper on. Like a political canvasser. Or Tyler.

If I had a hundred guesses, I never would've come up with who it actually is.

"Naomi." I spin through all the ways I could respond and land on sarcasm. "Shouldn't you be preening for the cameras right now?"

She flinches like I'd screamed at her. "It's Memorial Day."

Right, the holiday thing. They'd have the weekend newscaster in today.

I'll never guess why she's here, so I don't try. I wait for her to say something — even though it seems like she's never going to. She's staring at me with that same blank, slack-jawed expression she wore during our middle-of-the-road silent showdown the other day.

At last, she shakes herself, and her shoulders square up. "May I come in, Kat?"

Naomi Young is full of surprises today.

My knee-jerk instinct is to slam the door in her face like she did to me, but that's not going to get me anywhere. I still want to know what she has to do with all this. I'm sure she's involved somehow. So, if she has something to say, I'll let her.

I step back from the entrance, wordlessly agreeing to her request.

She wanders past me, her movements uncertain. When she reaches the point where she can see the little girl sleeping on the couch, she freezes in place. "My God," she murmurs. "It's like seeing a ghost."

The ghost of who? I frown and close the door, and she jumps a little at the sound.

"Do you want some coffee?" I ask begrudgingly. If I can't sleep, I may as well caffeinate.

"Yes, please."

"Come on. Let's sit in the kitchen."

She follows me through, pointedly not looking at the couch as we pass it. I've already got a pot of coffee brewed from earlier. It's not going to be the best-tasting coffee in the world, but it should be drinkable. I pour two mugs, then put them on the table with cream and sugar.

Naomi is already sitting down, her back to the living room. I sit across from her and fix my coffee, and she does the same. She takes the first sip and struggles to hide a grimace, but she powers a polite expression through. "This is nice. Thank you."

She's probably a coffee snob who'd drink Starbucks if Fulton had one. I stir my mug, set the spoon aside, and gulp down a swallow.

And I almost gag on the stuff. It's bitter, oily, and lukewarm.

"Gah! It's *not* nice." I was so tired this morning, I didn't really check the time when Holly woke up and I made the pot. How long has it been sitting on the burner? Long enough for the four-hour auto timer to shut off, at least. "Sorry. This is awful. I can't even let *you* drink it."

I grab both mugs and dump them down the sink. Dad didn't like the taste of Keurig coffee, so he only had the standard drip brewer. I'll have to start a fresh pot and wait for it. I load ground coffee into the basket, pour in the water, and hit the power button.

When I return to the table, Naomi is almost smiling. "You're right. It was awful."

It really was. I want to grab a toothbrush and scrub the taste off my tongue.

There are all sorts of things I'd like to say right now, but I don't want a repeat of the incident at Naomi's front door. So, awkward as it is, I wait for her to start the conversation.

It takes her so long that by the time she starts talking, I've almost forgotten she was there.

"About the staring thing," she says, flicking a glance over her shoulder that doesn't quite make it. "I thought I was going crazy. I mean, what I saw was you walking down the street with Marisol, and . . ." She trails off with a shiver. "It took me a minute to figure out it wasn't her."

I start to relax, understanding, until a glaring issue jumps out at me. She's had nothing to do with my life since she turned eighteen.

"How do you know *anything* about Marisol?" I challenge her, failing to keep the heat in check.

She blinks. "Joe told me about her."

"He what?"

I don't mean to roar the words, but they still come out that way. Again, Naomi looks over her shoulder. As if she's worried I might wake Holly. She doesn't know Holly is deaf.

Her gaze meets mine, and she bites her lip. "He showed me pictures of her," she says. "He was so proud. He also told me what happened when . . . she died. I'm so sorry, Kat."

A childish part of me wants to tell her I don't need her sympathy, but I refrain. "Thank you," I say, because it's really the only possible response. "I didn't know you still talked to Dad."

"Yes, well. He was very kind to me, even after I was such a . . . what was it Alina used to call me when she thought I couldn't hear? Bitchzilla?"

I snort. "Actually, it was Twatosaurus Rex."

Naomi makes a choking sound, then starts cackling. "Oh my God, yes! That's it. So much better than Bitchzilla."

Her reaction startles a laugh from me. I'm dangerously close to warming to her.

"You know what's funny, though? I never would've admitted it, but . . . it actually made me happy. I had an Alina nickname like everybody else, even if it was a mean one." She smirks. "Pathetic, right?"

Damn it. I've passed dangerously close and gone straight to almost liking her.

But she still pushed me down the stairs and broke my arm. And possibly murdered two people.

"No. It's not pathetic." I give her a smile. There's no way I'm going to tell her about Drew sharing her life story with me, but I'm glad he did, so I can at least try to understand her.

The coffee machine wheezes and gurgles behind me. I'm thankful for the interruption, because as hard as I'm trying to remember why I suspect her of awful things, she's making it difficult not to tear up. "Let's try this coffee thing again," I say as I push up from the table and turn my back to her.

By the time I pour two fresh cups, I've regained my composure.

"Thank you. Again." Naomi nods as she fixes her coffee, then lifts the mug and sips. "Much better."

Another awkward silence settles over us. Naomi toys with the slim cross-body purse she's wearing, then looks at me over her cup. "So, when you came to my house . . ."

"I'm sorry about that. Really." I shouldn't have yelled at her.

She shakes her head. "I guess I almost get why you think that," she says with a sigh. "Thing is, when you told me about Evie, I didn't know it was her."

"Huh?" I think back to the conversation.

Did you hear about Evie?

I did.

"I figured it out. Right that minute, when you asked if I heard," she explains. "I knew about the body, but the police hadn't released an identification. They still haven't. When you said it was Evie, I freaked out." She gives me a strange look. "Are you *sure* it's Evie?"

Something in the way she says it gives me pause. "Why do you think it's not?"

"Because . . ." She chews the inside of her cheek. "I'm friends with her on Facebook. At least, I thought I was. She said she lives in Florida and—"

"Works in a retirement home," I interrupt. "Near the beach."

Her eyes stretch wide. "Exactly. You, too?"

"Yeah. I don't think it's her, though." *Joe Gray got what he deserved.*

Evie loved Dad. She loved everybody.

"Oh, my God. What is going on?" Naomi mutters, massaging a temple. She heaves a breath and fiddles with her purse again, then unzips it. "There's something I want to show you."

She pulls out a small envelope with her name printed on the front and nothing else. "This was in my mailbox the day before Joe's funeral." She slides it across the table. "My first day at DNC."

I pick it up and extract a folded piece of cream-colored paper. It's a half-sheet bearing a computer-printed note, just like the ones I've been finding.

Katrina didn't pass that photo around school.
It was Joe.

My stomach lurches, and my mind flashes to the box in the basement.

"That's why I was so mad at you," Naomi blurts before I can react. "Back when I broke your arm. I had a n — uh, an explicit picture I was going to give my boyfriend. I don't even remember who it was at the time. It was in my backpack, but when I got to school, I couldn't find it. And you were in my room that morning."

"I was?" It was so long ago, and most of my memories of that day involve Naomi attacking me. But then I remember how I was grumpy all day at school, and why. "That's right. I thought you took my heeled boots," I murmur.

"Well, I didn't. For the record." She smirks, but the expression fades fast. "Anyway, by lunch period that day, it seemed like every senior and half the juniors had that photo on their phones. Somebody took a picture of it and started texting it around. It spread fast." She raises an eyebrow. "It wasn't you, right?"

"No. No way." Even as much as I hate Naomi, I never would've done that to any girl. Or boy, for that matter.

"Yeah, I believed that part of the note. But . . . Joe?" She frowns and pokes the envelope. "How would he even get a bunch of high schoolers' numbers? And I wouldn't believe it, even if he did have the numbers," she rushes to add. "He was good to me. Helped me apply for college and financial aid. He got me the DNC job, too. I was really excited to work with him . . ."

She breaks off with a sob, and tears streak down her face.

"Sorry." She swipes them away with the back of her hand, then gestures at the note. "I just don't know what to make of . . . that."

Suddenly, I know I have to tell her.

"Naomi." A rush of guilt threatens to swallow me. "I think I've seen the photo you're talking about. Not back in high school, though. Is it a Polaroid?"

Her cheeks flush red, and she nods. "I kind of borrowed the Hearth Wall camera. I didn't want it on my phone," she says, then gasps. "Wait. How do you know it's a Polaroid? You couldn't tell from the picture that got passed around. You— I mean, whoever did it snapped a photo with their phone and put the Polaroid back in my bag. I guess so I wouldn't find out until it was too late." She frowns at me. "So how . . ."

"Because I found the actual photo." Shivers race through me. "It was in the linen closet, in Dad's box. The one he used to keep full of caramel creams."

She blanches. "No. I don't believe it," she says. "Joe didn't do it."

I agree, but I still bristle at the unspoken assertion. "But you think he killed Evie?"

"*No.*" She sounds shocked that I'd even suggest that. She raises her head and sighs at the ceiling, tapping her chin with a finger. "Maybe someone's trying to frame him? Like, ruin his reputation, his legacy. Who would do that, though?"

If it's not Naomi, I have no clue who it could be. But there's something else that needs addressing. The reason I was terrified Dad had done something horrific when I first saw the Polaroid. "Naomi, you didn't take that picture. You couldn't have. Your whole body and both arms are in the frame, and the camera doesn't have a timer," I say. "So who did?"

Her flush returns, a darker red than before. "Actually, it was Alina."

"What?"

"I literally had no one else to ask," she replies defensively. "You hated me, Evie was a child, and I sure as hell wasn't going to ask the boys."

I want to point out that she was a child, too. We all were, even Alina. But that's not important right now.

192

"So you never thought Alina, the one who knew the photograph existed, was the one who spread it around school?"

Naomi looks like she's just gotten an electric shock. "Oh, God."

I hate to even think it, but Alina makes sense for so much of this.

Just the other day, she'd more or less admitted she was jealous of me. Thought my parents loved me the most, and I got everything while the fosters got nothing. She'd tried to walk it back and claim she was talking about Naomi, but she sure as hell looked like she meant it.

She would've been jealous of Evie, too, even if she didn't show it. Evie was the special case, the one who got the rules bent for her. The one who had all the attention, even from Mom and Dad. She was sixteen when Evie 'ran away,' but it wasn't like teenagers couldn't be murderers.

And after my father failed to qualify for keeping his foster status, she was sent to live with a meth dealer who constantly tried to rape her for two years.

Plus, she's a police officer. If evidence of anything did end up filtering its way to the cops, she could probably do something about it. Alter it, or make it disappear.

Again, the only thing that doesn't fit is Holly.

I'm more convinced than ever that Holly was a coincidence, whether she ended up here deliberately or accidentally. The rest is all one person.

And that person might be Alina Cruz.

CHAPTER 32

The Journal

The dad thinks he's going to give me away. I know it.

Nobody sees the real him. You'd think he was a saint, the way they act. Such a great father. So caring.

Way more caring than they think.

I've been around men like him before, who think they're so slick, but I have to admit, he's better than most. It feels like he has the whole world fooled. Even the bio kid thinks he walks on water. And the mom really thinks he's invested in the whole foster-kids-are-real-kids-too scam.

Now, I can see it in his eyes. The calculations. The scheming. He knows that I know too much, and I can bring him down any time I want to.

But I've got people fooled, too. Including him.

He'll never see it coming.

CHAPTER 33

Naomi doesn't stay much longer. When she leaves, it's with the box containing her photograph. She deserves to do whatever she wants with it.

She mentioned something about setting it on fire.

As for me, I've come to a decision. I won't wait around for the police to decide that my dad was a murderer, because it's easy to convict someone who can't defend themselves. I'm going to figure out who's behind the fake Evie profile, who's been stalking and harassing me. Who really killed Evie and hated my dad enough to frame him for it.

I need help to do it, though. I'm not a cop, and they won't help me anyway, but I do know someone who can access records I can't.

Drew wasn't too thrilled about the idea, but he agreed to do what he can.

After Holly wakes from her nap, we have a quick lunch, and I tell her we're going for a drive. She's happy to go along. I pack a bag and load us into the car, heading for Mexico. That's where the Oswego County DSS is located. I thought about messaging Mickey to see if she wanted to grab lunch or coffee after my unofficial appointment with Drew, but it's a school day. I don't want to spring anything on her and make her feel bad for having to turn me down.

Besides, we're video chatting this Sunday evening. I'm hoping by then, I'll have a better idea of when we can get together for some quality time, without rushing our little reunion.

The drive is pleasant enough. There's little traffic on the back roads in late morning, and Holly alternates between playing on her tablet and looking out the window. It takes around half an hour to get there. When the building comes into sight, I'm dismayed but not surprised to find the big parking lot absolutely packed with vehicles.

Not surprised, because the office serves the whole county, which is one of the poorest in the state. They're perpetually overworked, understaffed, and confined by the boundaries of the slow-moving steamroller that is New York State bureaucracy. Social work is not for the faint of heart.

At least Drew knows we're coming. I prowl the parking lot rows until I find a space to squeeze into, then connect my phone to the Bluetooth and dial Drew's cell.

He answers on the second ring. "I take it you're here?"

"Yep," I tell him.

"Okay. I'm going to come down and get you," he says. "Meet me at the front entrance."

"Will do." He sounds flustered, and I feel bad because I've probably screwed up his day. "Drew . . . thank you for helping me with this," I say. "You have no idea how much I appreciate it."

He snorts. "Don't thank me yet. I'm not sure how much help I'm going to be," he tells me. "See you in a minute."

Frankly, anything he can find out will be more than the jack squat I have now.

* * *

Drew's office is way more fun than any social worker's quarters I've ever seen. He's clearly arranged things with the kids he works for in mind, and he's managed to do a lot in a small space. There's a kid-sized table and chairs stocked with coloring books and drawing supplies, a small bookshelf with selections ranging from picture books to young adult novels, a toy chest, a laptop, and even a Velcro ball dartboard.

Considering the minuscule budget DSS works with, I'm guessing he bought all this out of his own pocket, too.

I hadn't told him exactly what I wanted him to look into, so when I said I needed everything he could find on Alina, he balked pretty hard. Then, after I explained why, he came around to it. More or less.

Holly and I are sitting at the kids' table, me perched precariously on a chunky little plastic chair while we color a picture together, when Drew says, "Hmm. This is interesting."

I immediately look up. "How interesting?"

"Not sure yet," he murmurs, clicking a few more things on his desktop computer. He's been perusing documents and databases for more than half an hour at this point. "About three years after she became a cop, Alina was suspended for two weeks while they investigated her for planting evidence."

"Really?"

"Looks that way. Hang on, I'm going to see if I can find any more about it."

I'm relieved he took me seriously when I asked him to look into her. Especially since I couldn't explain or support every reason I had to suspect her. I definitely wasn't going to tell him she'd taken a nude photo of Naomi and spread it around to the kids at school. He was upset, too, but less at me and more at the possibility that Alina wasn't the ball of sunshine we all thought.

That part upsets me, too.

If Drew is starting to find things up, I need to pay attention. I signal to Holly that I'll be a minute and stand, stretching the kinks from my legs and back.

"Oh, here we go," Drew says, staring at the monitor.

I cross the small space between the table and his desk to stand in front of him. "Did you find something?"

"Yep. A useless factoid." He flashes a crooked smile. "She was cleared and reinstated. I mean, that should've been obvious, right? Since she's still a cop and all. I guess if you wanted to be negative, you could think she did plant the evidence and got away with it."

I'm not sure what to think. I don't *want* to think any of this about Alina.

"There's something else here." Drew clicks on the screen and hits a few keys. "She was arrested and sent to jail. Well . . . juvenile detention." He leans closer, his eyes narrowing. "For attempted murder, which was dropped down to assault and battery. Served six months."

My core ripples with unease. Alina didn't mention that little detail when she told me what happened after she left Dad's. Juvenile detention means she wouldn't have been eighteen yet. So, she'd tried to kill someone when she was still a teenager.

And possibly succeeded with a previous attempt.

Drew's eyes are glued to his monitor, unsmiling. "There's a gap in her records, at least as far as I can dig at the moment," he says. "I didn't bother doing the math before, but she didn't start with the police department until she was twenty-two. From when she left juvie until then, I can't find anything about her."

The ripples grow stronger. "That's not normal, right?"

"No. Usually, it's pretty easy to pull together a rough timeline of a person's life online with the tools I have. "I could probably do this with Naomi, too." He glances at me. "Are we still suspicious of her?"

"I don't know," I mutter. It feels like I don't know anything anymore.

I turn for a quick check on Holly and find her coloring away, her tongue poking from the corner of her mouth in concentration. Then I move to the side of Drew's desk, trying to get a look at the screen. Not that anything he's looking at makes sense to me. "So there's, what, four years unaccounted for?" I ask.

"Almost five, actually. I'm trying a different kind of search, to see if she was . . . oh."

The last word is a whisper as his computer chimes, and a window pops up with a list of what looks like references with hyperlinks. I don't know what it means, but from the look on Drew's face, it's nothing good.

"She was, um. Soliciting services. Advertising online." He guides the mouse until it hovers over one of the links. "Not sure I want to see this," he murmurs. "I mean, she's my *sister*."

Still, after a brief hesitation, he clicks on it.

Another window opens with a profile that lists what appears to be normal bio bullet points at first glance, but it's easy to see the euphemisms if you're looking for them. However, it's the photo that catches my attention. Definitely Alina. She looks so young, even with the heavy makeup she's wearing.

And whether it's dyed or a wig, her hair is blonde.

Drew points to a link beneath the picture that says *See more here*. "Listen, whatever we do, I am *not* clicking that," he croaks. "This is a work computer, and . . . like I said. Sister."

He doesn't have to. I don't need to see more. In fact, I wish I'd seen a lot less.

Why, Alina? I search the frozen face from my past, looking for some hint of the jealousy and rage that must have driven her. I'd never seen a single sign of it. How could I have missed something so huge?

Whatever the reason for my ignorance, that's not my most pressing concern at the moment.

I have to figure out how to stop her. Before she does something worse.

CHAPTER 34

Alina is at the house when Holly and I get back.

In fact, I can't pull into the driveway because she's walking down it from the back yard.

Oh, no. What was she doing back there?

. . . they investigated her for planting evidence.

I can't believe this. I'm so shaken that my vision blurs, and I slam on the brakes hard enough to jerk us forward and make Holly gasp. "Sorry, sweetheart," I murmur, not remembering for a moment that she can't hear me. I'm staring at Alina as she strolls toward the car, grinning and waving as if she hasn't been making sure everyone believes my father killed Evie.

Even with everything Drew found about her, I wanted to think there was some other explanation. He's promised to keep digging — whether he ends up finding reasons for her history that have nothing to do with Dad and Evie, or discovering proof that she was involved.

Until then, anything I say will be her word against mine, and her word will be taken, because she's a cop. I'd intended to act as if I didn't suspect her. Like nothing had happened to shatter the bonds of sisterhood we'd started rebuilding.

How can I do that now? Why was she in the back yard?

She hurries down the rest of the driveway and off to the side, near the stoop, so I can finish pulling in. My mind races as I ease the car into place and park. I hope the smile on my face doesn't look as outrageously fake as it feels.

What am I going to do? I can't confront her now. Not without any sort of proof, and definitely not if she planted something that will implicate Dad. I don't think I can act natural, either. This feels so much worse than the idea that it was Naomi.

This is a much deeper betrayal.

I can't handle it. But I have no choice.

I turn off the engine and slowly exhale the breath I'd been holding. Holly looks at me with uneasy inquisitiveness, as if she senses the shift in my mood. I can smile for her, a real smile, and I hold that expression as I give her the signal that I'll only be a minute, then open my door.

"Hey, girl!" Alina greets me cheerfully as I'm climbing out. "I wanted to see how you're doing, and . . ." She trails off and slides into concern as she takes me in, and I realize I'm not hiding my emotions as well as I'd hoped. "Oh my God, did something else happen? Is Holly okay?" She leans aside to peer past me into the car.

"She's fine." I wince inwardly at the snappy tone that emerges and scramble to backpedal. "I'm sorry. I haven't been sleeping well."

Concern floods her features, and she tilts her head. "I mean, it's not surprising, considering the circumstances," she says. "You've been through so much."

Is her sympathy genuine? How can I believe anything she says?

"Yeah, it's been crazy," I manage in what sounds like a normal tone to me. This time, my smile doesn't feel so forced. "Let me just get Holly out of the car."

"Of course. Do you need help with anything?" Her gaze scans the car, and it takes me a minute to realize what she's looking for. Shopping bags. She must've assumed that's why I wasn't home.

"Oh, no. We were just at the playground." The lie slips out easily, and my heart starts to settle into a more normal rhythm. "Thank you, though."

"No problem."

I circle the car and open Holly's door. Her cheeks are flushed, and her eyelids droop slightly. She'd nodded off a few times on the way back from Oswego but didn't settle into a deep sleep. It's probably better that she doesn't take a nap right now, since she already had one today.

After I unbuckle her, help her to the ground, and make sure she has a good grip on her stuffed animal and her light toy, I grab the bag and wait for Holly to step back before I close the door. She slides her hand into mine without prompting, and we walk around to join Alina.

"Hi, honey." Alina smiles at her and gives an exaggerated wave. "She is just the most adorable thing. Did Drew find out anything more about her?"

"Not yet. It's so strange that no one's ever seen her before." It feels surreal, chit-chatting about normal subjects while my chest roils with upset and uncertainty.

Holly's mouth stretches open in a huge yawn, and as awful as it is, I'm grateful for the excuse. "Well, I'd better get her inside," I say.

Alina blinks, then steps aside. "Oh, of course!"

I walk past her toward the stoop and climb the steps with Holly. It's on the tip of my tongue to say something along the lines of *thanks for checking up on me, see you later,* when I hear footsteps behind me.

She's following me into the house.

My body flashes cold, then hot. I can't help picturing Alina closing and locking the door behind us, then casually producing her gun and shooting me. Or grabbing the fireplace poker and bashing my brains out.

Come on. You're being ridiculous, Kat.

Alina would never do something like that.

She'll be subtler when she kills me. Like how she let everyone think Evie ran away.

I *have* to stop thinking like this.

When we get inside, Holly heads straight for the couch. She climbs up and makes herself comfortable, placing her calico cat beside her and the light toy in her lap. After a glance at me to see if I'm watching, she pushes the tablet button.

"Okay," I relent with a laugh and pull it out from the bag. "Not too long, though. It's almost bath and pajamas time." I mostly say that for Alina's benefit, to dissuade her from staying too long. I'm handling myself for now, but I won't be able to keep it up all night.

"Wow. You're really doing great with her," Alina says from behind me. "Do you think she'll end up staying with you?"

"I hope so," I murmur without turning as I hand Holly the tablet. Finally, I pull the smile back on and face my sister. "Sorry I wasn't home when you got here," I tell her, battling to keep the accusation from my tone. "So, what's up?"

"Oh! Geez, I'm an idiot." Alina smirks and mock-slaps herself in the forehead. "I should've texted first. I left my jacket here when . . ." The corners of her lips quirk down briefly. "I was looking to see if it was in the back yard. That's where I took it off, the morning with the . . . shed stuff. Then everything happened and I forgot. Have you seen it? It's black denim, cropped, with a built-in belt and a Betty Boop patch on the back."

Of course she has an excuse for being back there. I do remember her wearing that jacket when she got here, though. "No, I haven't seen it," I tell her, which is the truth. "Maybe your friends on the force took it with them."

Damn it. That definitely came out with a tone.

Alina cocks an eyebrow, then folds her arms and meets my gaze. "Okay, spill it," she says. "Something is wrong. What is it?"

At last, I realize how I can pass this off and hopefully keep her from finding out what I know about her.

"*Everything* is wrong." It's not hard to put a tremble in my voice. I shuffle toward the couch and plop down next to Holly, who flashes me a smile before going back to her game. "Losing Dad was enough, you know? Then there's the stalking, the vandalism, Evie . . ." I trail off with a sob. It's pure stress rather than sorrow, but it doesn't sound any different.

"Oh, Kat." Before I can think of a way to protest, Alina is crossing the space. She leans down and hugs me, and I barely prevent myself from stiffening and flinching away. Instead, I lean into her.

Thankfully, she backs off after a minute. "Listen, is there anything I can do for you?" she asks. "My next day off isn't until Wednesday night, but I'm flexible during the day. I can sleep when I get off or wait until before I go in."

Why does she have to act so nice? It only makes everything worse.

"You've done so much already," I say. "I appreciate it, but I'm . . ."

A sudden idea occurs to me. A way to see how she reacts without accusing her of anything outright.

"Actually, there might be something you can help me with."

She levels an earnest nod. "Name it."

I inhale through my nose. "The thing is, I don't think Dad had a stroke," I tell her. "I think someone killed him."

As I study her face, her eyes tighten and flash. Like she's angry.

"Kat, that's . . ." She shakes her head, her lips pressed into a firm line. "I mean, that's crazy."

"Is it?" There's no harm in telling her this, because I'm not going to add *and I think that someone was you.* "At the funeral, Bryon Halloway told me Dad had a visitor at the studio between segments, and he came back really upset. Bryon's trying to find out who it was."

That last part is a lie, but I want to push her. To see guilt or fear on her face.

204

Maybe even get a confession.

"No," she whispers, and shakes her head harder.

"I really think it's possible," I insist. "Are you able to access his files at work? Maybe if you can get your hands on autopsy results or a coroner's report—"

"Come on!" she rasps out. Tears slide down her face, fast and thick, and she starts trembling. "It was a stroke, Kat. It happened on *live television*. Do you know how many people watched him . . ." She trails into a shuddering sob. "Losing him was awful, but you can't seriously think it was murder."

My heart plummets into my gut.

She's denying it way too hard.

"You said you wanted to help," I toss back. "*I'm* the one who lost him, you know."

Alina reels back like I punched her. Every bit of color drains from her face, and her lips part, trembling and twitching.

The devastation etched on her face nearly kills me.

All at once, I'm desperate to take it back. To give her the benefit of the doubt, despite the mounting pile of signs that point to her guilt. To erase the incredible, callous pain I've inflicted on her.

But it's too late.

Without another word, Alina whirls and rushes across the room. She fumbles the door open and bolts outside. It slams behind her with relationship-killing finality.

What have I done?

CHAPTER 35

My phone rings on the kitchen counter while I'm cleaning up from our bedtime snack. I almost drop the glass I'm carrying in my haste to snatch it, praying that it's Alina.

Clara's name is flashing across the screen.

My lungs deflate, and I almost let it go to voicemail. Then I remember that we're supposed to meet for coffee tomorrow at 'the new place.' Maybe going out with a friend is exactly what I need. A break from the disaster my life has suddenly become in less than a week, a way to clear my head.

I answer with a smile in my voice, even if my face doesn't match. "Hi, Clara."

"Hello, Kat, dear." Her warm greeting penetrates me through the phone, and I manage to relax a few degrees. "How are you doing?"

"Oh, I'm . . ." I almost say *fine* before I remember that Clara shares my disdain for empty platitudes. "Taking it day by day," I finish. "And yourself?"

"Exactly the same," she says. "I hope I'm not calling too late?"

"Not at all." It's only eight o'clock. Normally, I'd be up for at least a few more hours, but tonight I'm going to try going to bed when Holly does. Which will be very soon, judging by the whole-body yawn she's engaged in at the kitchen table right now. "What's up?"

"I just wanted to make sure we were still on for tomorrow. Are you able to meet me there at one o'clock?"

"That sounds perfect." Suddenly, I realize that we never discussed Holly in terms of our coffee date. In fact, I haven't even gotten to explain how I ended up with her. I'd told Clara at the VFW that I was taking care of her, but that was it. "Hey, Clara," I say. "Do you mind if I bring someone along with me?"

She chuckles. "Of course not. I didn't know there was a man in your life, but I'd love to meet him. Or, wait . . . it could be a woman, couldn't it? Either way."

I smile. "Actually, it's a little girl."

"Oh! Do you mean that sweet child you had at the reception? That would be a delight," she says. "What's her name?"

"Holly." I'll have to explain more tomorrow. For now, the little girl in question is fading fast. "And speaking of her, someone needs to be tucked into bed," I tell Clara. "So, we'll see you tomorrow at one o'clock."

"Wonderful. Looking forward to it, dear!"

"Me, too."

I end the call, slide the phone in my pocket, and check the back door lock again before I walk to the kitchen table. Holly is rubbing her eyes and fighting another yawn. She blinks at me sleepily.

"Looks like it's about that time, huh?" I smile and push the bed button on her light toy. "Shall we head upstairs?"

Holly looks from the button to me, then shakes her head.

"Sweetie, it's definitely time for bed." I'm actually thrilled to see her react like a normal child who's been told they have to go to bed, not only because it means our communication is improving, but also because things haven't been normal for her lately. Still, we both need sleep.

I move to activate the bed button again when I notice something about the toy — or rather the lack of something. I run a finger across the empty handle. "Holly, where did your help button go?" I ask, pointing to the handle.

She bites her lip and stares at her lap.

"Did you lose it?" I ask the question mostly to myself as I scan the immediate area, trying to remember back to when I last noticed the sound button attached to the toy. Hopefully, it's in the house somewhere. I stopped using the remote fob after Holly figured out how the buttons work, and I can't remember what I did with it.

It could be pretty much anywhere down here, or maybe even in the car. I decide I'll find it in the morning. Maybe I can try to make a game out of it with her. I'm about to press the bed button when Holly releases a tiny sigh and lifts her head. She slides a hand into her pajama pants pocket.

"*Help!*"

The muffled sound drifts from under the table, and I laugh. "Well, there it is," I say and hold a hand out. "Do you want to hand it to me, and I'll attach it to your board?"

Holly shakes her head. "*Help!*"

"Okay. You can keep it in your pocket if you want to." I hope she doesn't keep pressing the button all night to make me react, so she doesn't have to go to sleep.

I push the bed button again. This time, Holly lets out a small sigh and slides off the chair, resigned to her restful fate.

"Don't worry. We'll have plenty more fun tomorrow," I say, though of course she doesn't understand.

We move through the house and up the stairs side by side. By the time we reach the girls' bedroom, I can practically feel my body sinking into that cool, pillowy mattress.

If nothing else, I think I'll get some solid sleep tonight.

CHAPTER 36

When I wake up like a normal person, knowing where I am and in full control of my body, it almost feels wrong. It's not the middle of the night. I haven't heard any sounds. And I can move whenever I want to.

I don't want to yet.

I'm not sure if I feel fully rested, but I'm less tired than I have been in days. The light framing the windows beyond the sheer curtains isn't direct — it feels early, but not too early. I hear birdsong and the occasional wash of distant vehicles on the main road a few blocks from here. It's comforting. The world is going about its business, starting a new day.

That's what I need. A new start, a chance to reset.

I still have a few days before I need to pick up working in any serious way. And though this time off was never meant to be a vacation, I decide that today, at least, I'm going to relax. I won't try to play armchair detective or tie myself into knots over every mistake I've ever made in my life. I won't be afraid of being in the world.

I've already wasted five years hiding.

A leisurely breakfast sounds like just the thing to kick off a day of renewal. Pancakes, eggs, bacon, the works. We've also got our lunch date with Clara to look forward to. If the weather holds up, we can spend the rest of the afternoon at the playground. Holly and I both had a blast in the water park last time.

I smile and stretch, then roll over toward the bunks across the room, a little surprised I haven't heard Holly stirring yet. But then, she was exhausted last night, too. At first, I can't make her out under the bunched blanket.

Then I realize it's because she's not under it.

My pleasant, sleepy feeling drains in a snap, and I sit up for a better view. She's definitely not in the bed. Instant panic flares in me, but I push it down and force myself to be rational. She probably needed the bathroom, or she got thirsty. She knows how to get herself a glass of water. She could've even gone downstairs — maybe I didn't hear her wake up, and she went to find a snack or play with the tablet.

Except she's the only thing missing from the bed. Her stuffed cat and her light toy are still there, and she's never left them behind. Not even to use the bathroom.

My heart jackknifes into my throat. I grab my phone from the bedside table and glance at the time as I hurry from the room. It's around eight in the morning. Holly was practically asleep already when I got her into bed last night, and I wasn't far behind her. I've been sleeping for almost twelve hours.

Even though the upstairs bathroom door is open and the room is dark, I check there first. Of course, it's empty. I try once more to make myself calm down and believe I'll find her sitting on the couch watching cartoons, or at the kitchen table with all the food she could reach, but I *know* something is wrong.

She's not here. I knew it the instant I saw her abandoned stuffed animal.

Still, I check everything as thoroughly as I can. I look in the boys' bedroom, my room, even the master bedroom that I have yet to clean up from when the police tossed it. I call out her name several times, despite knowing she can't hear me.

I'm shaking by the time I rush downstairs. She's not in the living room. Not in the downstairs bathroom or the dining room. Not in the kitchen—

No. No, no, no.

The back door is wide open.

"Holly!" I rush outside, into the back yard. It looks unchanged from its state after the police finished with it. Fluttering crime scene tape, the shed's red-spattered remains scattered across the space. One of the Adirondack chairs turned over. The mounds of dirt around the hole they pulled Evie from.

I rush to the patio and look under the upright chair, not really expecting her to be there. She's not. From there, I pivot to the hole and scramble up the nearest dirt pile. Damp clumps of earth, roots, and stones cascade away from my feet. I reach the top and peer down.

No little girl, alive or dead.

Shivering, I start to turn and slide down when something catches my eye along the corner of the chain-link fence, the section that's remained hidden behind the shed until now. Some of the wire looks popped and frayed along the edges.

I make my way to the ground and circle the mounds, my dread increasing with each step closer to the fence. It's cut from the frame, all the way up the support post and across the top rail for around four feet.

Scrapes and grooves arc outward across the ground from the cut section. As if someone's been peeling this section back like a door to let themselves in and out of the yard.

And there are footprints in the disturbed ground on the other side.

* * *

Detective Wyetta returns to the kitchen from the back yard, where one of the officers called him outside a few minutes ago. The look on his face dashes my hopes that they've found something.

"Anything helpful?" I ask anyway.

He shakes his head and takes the seat across from me. "It actually may be the opposite of helpful," he says. "Zach — Officer Lockwood — noticed something about the fence where it's been damaged. The tips of the wires are rusty. Which means . . . well, that it's probably been cut open like that for years."

Fresh chills invade me. Someone's had a way in and out of the yard for a long time, and they've definitely used it lately. Were they using it before? Is that how they got to Evie — and maybe even my father?

Detective Wyetta showed up within minutes of me calling 911 to report Holly missing, and the officers who are processing things outside weren't far behind. Alina is not among them. I'm not sure how to feel about that. Mostly, I'm trying to believe her shift ended before all this and she has nothing to do with what's happening. That she's asleep and oblivious.

I thought about texting her. I did call Drew, right after the police, and he's on his way here now.

I've already gone through the initial questioning with the detective. When did I last see Holly, what was she wearing, what happened when I noticed she was missing. The questions were apparently standard, some kind of form interview, a checklist for frantic parents whose children aren't where they're supposed to be that almost seems designed to make them feel worse.

I couldn't even answer some of the basic information he'd asked for. Name? Holly, but that's only what I call her, and she doesn't even know that's my name for her. Last name? No idea. Birth date? Not a clue. Age? Probably five, but I can't even be sure about that. I had to guess at her height and weight.

The process left me hollow and heavy. I'm not her mother, no matter how much I've been acting like it, how much I want to be. She's been in my life for less than a week. I know so little about her, especially since we can't communicate beyond a few basic concepts that can be represented with simple pictures or gestures.

None of that stops me from *feeling* like her mother. From being desperate to get her back, ready to tear whoever took her limb from limb if I have to.

But I can't help thinking my non-parental status is going to hurt me here.

What if they don't try as hard to find her because I'm not actually her mother? What if they can't because I don't know enough about her to point them in the right direction?

What if they decide I'm unfit to foster her because she vanished under my care — and if they find her, they don't give her back?

When they find her, I tell myself. *When. They* have *to find her. I* have to find her.

Wyetta opens the small notebook he's been writing things down in. "We've got patrols out going door-to-door, asking if anyone's seen anything, and we're issuing an Amber alert," he tells me, pen poised above the paper. "Now. You said you're sure the back door was locked, correct?"

"Positive." After the ladder incident, I've been double-checking the doors every night. I clearly remember checking it last night, right after I talked to Clara. "Both doors were locked."

"Okay." He writes something down, then looks at me with no expression. "So, there are no signs of forced entry," he says. "Your front door has a deadbolt, but the back is only a twist lock. It's in the unlock position now. Did you turn it at all this morning?"

"What? No, I didn't." My vision is swimming, and a hard pulse beats in my temples. "I *know* it was locked last night."

"Okay. And does anyone else have keys to this house?"

"Of course not."

The detective's lips firm briefly. "All right," he says, and stares at the notebook for a moment, tapping the end of the pen against the open page. "So it's possible that Holly unlocked the door and left the house on her own."

"No!" I shake my head vehemently, not caring if it seems like I'm protesting too hard. "No, she wouldn't do that. Why would she do that?"

"Maybe she decided to look for her parents?"

He says it gently, a suggestion rather than a question. That doesn't stop the anger from flaring through me in bright, blinding lines. "She wouldn't do that," I insist again. "She feels safe here. Cared for."

There's another uncomfortable pause. "Holly is deaf, is that correct?" he asks. "And she doesn't know sign language. You said you use pictures to talk to her."

"That's right."

Detective Wyetta clears his throat. "So . . . how do you know how she feels?"

The throbbing in my head becomes a roar. Somehow, I resist the urge to spring to my feet and scream at him, to demand that he stop being an idiot and start looking for whoever took Holly. Because someone *had* to take her.

"She is five years old," I say as evenly as possible, though I'm not confident of even that. "What five-year-old would leave a place where she's warm, fed, and loved to wander off in the middle of the night?"

He's struggling not to lose his patience. "Maybe one who can't tell you that she wants to find her parents," he says. "Who might think she knows the way home but can't communicate that, either."

Nausea clogs my throat. I can't bear to admit that he could have a point, but wasn't I just thinking something along those lines? That even though I care for her more than I thought possible after such a short time, I still know almost nothing about her?

No. He's wrong. She *didn't* leave willingly.

"Even if she wanted to try finding her way home alone, she wouldn't have left without her things," I tell him. "Her light toy, the one we use to talk. And especially her stuffed cat. She had that with her when I found her, and she never goes anywhere without it. Not even to the bathroom. It's still upstairs in her bed."

At least he looks like he's considering it. But before he can say anything, the doorbell rings.

I'm on my feet and racing for the front door before the chiming stops. *Please say they've found her. Please, please, please.* Part of me knows that since the detective is still here and presumably in charge of the case, they would've told him they found her instead of coming to my door. But I can't stop the wild bloom of hope.

It's Drew, with his clipboard and name badge and a stricken expression.

At that moment, the reality of everything crashes down on me, and I burst into tears.

I'm barely aware of Drew rushing to embrace me, his clipboard clattering on the stoop. I don't know how long we stand there while I gasp until I can't breathe, or when he managed to guide me to the couch and sit beside me, his arms never leaving me as my shoulders heave uncontrollably.

"We'll find her," he keeps saying in a broken voice. "I promise we'll find her."

He can't promise that. She's gone as abruptly as she arrived, and as much as I thought I'd figured out about the world-shattering events that keep happening, one after another like a line of malicious dominoes, I never came close to discovering anything about the little girl tangled in the holly bushes.

She could be anywhere, with anyone. Or with no one.

And I can't think of a single way to start finding her.

CHAPTER 37

My parents' house feels emptier than it ever has.

I can't remember a time when I've been alone here. It's always been a home bustling with life and love, even before the first foster kids came to stay. This quiet, this *nothing*, is not only the absence of occupants. It's an oppressive weight, a malevolently active subtraction. The presence of a void.

The police have done all they can here, they tell me. Wyetta strongly encouraged me to stay here and wait, as if he believes Holly will magically reappear the same way she vanished. Drew stayed for a while after they left, explaining everything DSS will be doing to help the police look for her. But even he reiterated that my best course of action is to do nothing.

There's no way I can do nothing. The booming silence of everything I've lost surrounds me here, pushing in until I fear the walls will collapse under the pressure and the roof will drop onto me. Which, if it happened, might not even matter.

I am so very, very alone.

I know Drew would have stayed with me if he could, but I'd rather he was out there using the channels they've already established for situations like this. I texted Blake, but he hasn't answered me. I even sent a message to Alina — though if I was wrong about my suspicions, she'll probably never speak to me again. I did apologize to her, but I know a 'sorry' text isn't going to cut it. I might've even made things worse.

I seriously considered asking Clara to come over, but then I would have to explain everything about how Holly ended up with me, what we've been through, and why I'm so distraught that I can't see straight. I don't think I can get through that. It would be awkward for both of us, and she's already grieving the loss of my father.

Instead, I texted her and said I wasn't feeling well, and apologized that I wouldn't be able to make it for coffee. She's already answered to say she hopes I feel better soon, and do I want to reschedule? I didn't reply, though. I can't think about random coffee dates now.

Unable to sit still any longer, I stand and pace the living room. The Hearth Wall keeps flashing into my peripheral vision with its decades-spanning photos and handprints, from Michelle DiMarco to Holly Gray, and suddenly, I can't stand the sight of it.

Rather than give in to a primal urge to take a sledgehammer to the painful reminder of everything that's gone from my life, I head upstairs with renewed determination. Maybe there's something I missed, or the police missed, that will bring Holly back to me.

I start in the girls' bedroom. Tear everything from Holly's bunk, including the sheet, as if I'll find a ransom note or Holly herself hiding against the mattress. Investigate the windows like they'll tell me if someone opened one, climbed in, and took her. Get on my hands and knees on the floor and run my fingers through the carpet as if the kidnapper dropped some clue to their identification where I can conveniently find it, like an earring or their driver's license.

To my lack of surprise, I find nothing.

I start working my way through the upstairs rooms. Boys' bedroom, bathroom, my old room, until only the master bedroom remains. I still don't want to go in there, and I'm sure that's the last place I'll find any hint of what happened to Holly. But I will be thorough.

The wave of pain I expect to feel when I open the door to my parents' bedroom, where I'll never find either of them again, is lessened by the mess. This room was always neat as a pin, so it's hard to associate the clothes erupting from open dresser drawers and piled on the bed, the boxes from the closet lined up and rifled through, with Mom and Dad.

My heart still pinches, though. And along with it comes a sense of hopelessness. Even if there's anything to find in here, it will take me hours to sort through.

Yet I find my feet carrying me past the threshold, my arm lifting to flip the light on. I wind my way through boxes and piles, my gaze picking out snapshots of the past. Mom's photo albums. Dad's softball trophies. A collection of various school awards, mostly mine, since my parents tried to make sure any of the kids who left kept their memories with them.

Matching nightstands flank the king-sized bed. My mother's, on the side closest to the door, is bare now. She used to keep a lamp, a few books, and a box of tissues on it with a first-aid kit tucked into the drawer for middle-of-the-night emergencies.

Dad's lamp and alarm clock still remain on his nightstand, on the side closest to the window. If he kept anything in his drawer, I never knew what. There was never a reason to go all the way to his side of the bed. Mom was always right there and prepared for anything. She'd been the one to get up and handle things in the wee hours because Dad had to be at work so early.

Then, I realize something else about Dad's nightstand. It's the only drawer in the room that's still closed.

The police looked everywhere else. Why not there?

With a faint frown, I walk around the bed and up to the nightstand. The drawer slides open easily. Inside is a rubber-banded stack of envelopes that seem to be bills, a small, lidless box with an assortment of tie clips, and a . . . can of Hormel chili?

The sight of it sparks a memory. One of Dad's birthdays, when I was in high school. Him opening a gift from Drew and looking as confused as I feel right now at receiving a can of chili, which he didn't even like. Drew, the master of practical jokes, laughing as he explained that it was actually a can of secrets.

A hidey-hole, like those fake rocks people use for their spare keys.

I smile and pick up the can. It's not as heavy as a real one would be, but you'd be hard-pressed to tell it was fake if it was on a shelf with a bunch of other canned goods. I shake it, expecting to find it empty. But there's a faint flutter and scrape from inside. Like paper shifting. Maybe Dad tucked some pocket money into it?

The can opens from the bottom. I flip it over, twist the plastic plug, and pull it away.

It's not cash.

At first, I'm not sure what I'm looking at. A few loose sheets of paper folded into quarters rest inside the can, unfurled enough to touch the sides. I fish them out, and my breath catches.

They're half-sheets, the exact cream-colored shade as the notes Naomi and I both received. And there are messages computer-printed on them.

Hi, Joe! I hope you're not thinking of trying to report me or send me back. Because if you do, I will tell Audrey what you did. And I will tell her that I didn't want you to do it.

"What the hell?" I blurt to the empty room.
The next one is even more cryptic and ominous.

Hi, Joe! Thanks so much for the talk we had. I can tell that you're upset, but I think you'll see things my way over time. You just have to be more open. I really don't want to tell Audrey, but I have to make sure you don't do anything stupid until you come around. So just watch what happens to Naomi and understand that's another thing I can implicate you with.

My God, what is this? *Who* is this? Of course there's no name, no date, no details other than first names. They're clearly threatening my father. And the part about Naomi suggests this is the person who spread her photo around.

That person almost has to be Alina. Does that mean she wrote these notes?

There's only one more — and it's the worst of the three.

Hi, Joe! How sad for you. Evie ran away, and then Audrey died! Are you ready to see things my way now? Because if you're not, there's a surprise in Audrey's garden for you. A fresh planting! Believe me when I say that if you talk to anyone about the new crop, they'll only find what YOU did. Don't worry, though. They probably won't find out.

Unless I tell them.

My hands tremble so hard that I almost rip the notes. Hurriedly, I stuff them back in the fake can and replace the bottom. The implications of these are so horrific that I can't even begin to think about them. I need to bring this to Detective Wyetta.

I need to find Alina.

Before I can take a step away from the nightstand, my phone chimes. I yank it out, praying for news about Holly. But it's a Facebook notification. I'm about to dismiss it, since I don't give a damn about anything social-media-related right now, when I recognize the sender.

Droo Zoo.

Oh, God. It's Drew. Does he have proof? Can I get the police on my side?

I open the message. As I'm reading it, another message pings through, then another.

Hey, Kat, Sorry about the FB message. I would've texted, but I somehow managed to lose my phone. Wanted to let you know that you don't have to worry about Alina. That assault and battery charge? She beat the hell out of a guy who was trying to rape a drunk woman. Got charged because the guy had money and a good lawyer.

And the 'prostitute' thing was her going on a crusade, trying to bust predators. Found out from one of the cops she works with, a guy named Bennie Wade. Apparently, that's why she's a cop now. He busted one of her meetups and, instead of arresting her, said she'd be better off becoming a cop so she could do this legally.

He also told me about the planted evidence thing. After she arrested a drug dealer who I guess was her foster father, he's the one who said she planted the meth because she 'knew his house.' The suspension was a formality because they have to investigate complaints, but she did everything by the book.

Hope that helps. I'm drowning at my desk, doing whatever I can to find Holly. We WILL find her (and hopefully my phone, too!). Talk to you soon.

The mix of relief, shame, and gut-wrenching fear that floods me makes my knees wobble. Alina didn't do anything . . . but that means I was a complete asshole to her for no reason. And worse, I'm back to having absolutely no idea who *is* responsible.

The only thing I do know is that I need to see Detective Wyetta right now.

CHAPTER 38

The detective is not impressed by my proof.

I ended up sitting in the waiting room of the police station for over an hour because the detective was out questioning people with the other officers. When he returned, he seemed irritated that I'd shown up. Especially when I insisted on talking to him in private.

"You really should be at your house," he'd said to me the instant he shut the door to his office. "I know this is hard, but you have to let us do our jobs."

I'd swallowed a few scathing retorts and managed to explain why I was there, then handed him the notes. Now, he's staring at the last one like he's a waiter who's just received a 'tip' of a million-dollar bill stating that Jesus is the only wealth he needs.

"I'm sorry, Ms. Gray, but these aren't sufficient evidence of anything," he finally says, as he puts them down on his desk.

I gape at him. "Seriously?"

"Seriously." He taps the top note, the one about threatening to tell my mother something. "Even if they were signed and dated, it doesn't matter what they may or may not be inferring. It only matters what they actually say, which is nothing. Insinuation is not proof, especially in a court of law."

"A court of law? I'm trying to find Holly!"

His brow raises. "What, exactly, do these have to do with Holly? They're about your father. And I hate to say it, but the murder investigation is not looking good for him."

"What?"

"I don't want it to be him. You know that," he says. "But there's evidence, Ms. Gray. I can't reveal what, but it's pretty damn strong."

My pulse spikes. "That's what the note says, though. This person made sure there was evidence. They framed him."

"Come on. Anyone could have written those notes. You could have. *Joe* could have." There's a flicker in his eyes, and I realized at some point, he's changed his mind. He thinks Dad murdered a fourteen-year-old girl, and he's furious about it.

"He moved the shed over the body," Wyetta says through gritted teeth. "That's not a potential angle of investigation. That is a *fact*. Why would he do that if he was innocent?"

Because he still had more to lose, I think but don't tell him.

His shoulders slump, and he tucks the notes back in the fake chili can and hands it to me. "Please, go home," he says. "I swear I'll update you the second we find out anything at all about Holly. Let's focus on her right now, okay?"

The set of his jaw tells me nothing is going to change his mind about this. At least, not today. And I know how to pick my battles.

"Thank you," I tell him as I stand with the can in hand. "I'd really appreciate you keeping me in the loop."

He nods. "We're going to find her."

Drew told me the same thing. But I know about that first critical twenty-four hours and how quickly they can pass. We're not even sure how long she's been gone. It could've happened at any point during the twelve hours I was asleep, oblivious to the crime taking place in the room with me.

I will never forgive myself if anything happens to her because I was too tired to hear it.

I head out of the police station and start around the building, which they share with the fire department. There's only a small lot around the back where the entrance leads, and most

223

people who park there are going to the city clerk's office — also in the same building. So I'm parked in the larger front lot.

My thoughts are pinging and churning, searching for any connection I might have missed. I can't shake the feeling that it's all related, even Holly. Maybe her appearance *and* her abduction. Like whoever is doing this left her with me for the sole purpose of taking her away.

I've been looking at all this with a lens that's filtered through my father, but what if it's not about him?

I'm so lost in my own head that I don't see the car parked beside mine or the figure standing next to it until I'm pulling my keys out to unlock the car, and a voice says, "Why didn't you just call me?"

It's so unexpected, the sound of a voice and the identity of its owner, that I startle and drop my keys on the pavement. "Shit!" A hand goes involuntarily to my chest, and I feel my heart racing against my ribs as I bend to pick them up, then force myself to meet Alina's gaze.

She still looks hurt, but there's a sparkle of amusement in her eyes.

"I'm going to guess you're not sorry about that," I say lamely.

"Nope."

"Well . . . I am." I bite my lip. I can't bring myself to get into the weeds of why I acted the way I did, or admit that I had Drew investigate her — God, she's going to hate me for that — but I have to say something. "I was an idiot and an asshole. You *should* be mad, and I don't blame you if you want me to stay away from you—"

Alina cuts me off with an enormous, crushing hug. "Don't you *dare* stay away from me, Kit-Kat," she says. "We're sisters. Nothing else matters."

For the second time that day, I fall into huge, noisy sobs.

When I finally calm down enough to breathe, we pull back, and Alina swipes at her face. "Seriously, just call me next time. I didn't get your text right away because I was sleeping. Do they have any leads at all on Holly? And . . . why are you carrying a can of chili?" she finishes with a puzzled glance at my hand.

I'm relieved to have someone to talk to about this who'll actually see it for what it is.

I explain everything that's happened and show her the notes. As she reads them, her expression keeps crumpling until tears are streaming down her face. "Who would do this?" she half-whispers in a rasping tone. "They killed Evie and tried to frame Daddy Joe? And what's this about Naomi?"

I'm not sure I want to get into that, but I reason that she already knows about the photo. Unfortunately, telling her means I have to explain why *I* know about it.

I give her the quick-and-dirty version, including why Naomi thought it was me all this time. She's as horrified as I was. "Plus, Naomi showed me the note somebody left in her mailbox, claiming Dad was the one who'd passed the picture around," I say. "And it looked exactly like those notes. Same paper, same printing."

"Jesus." Alina shudders. "You showed these to Wyetta, right? What did he say about it?"

My features draw into an involuntary scowl. "He said they're not evidence and maybe I'm the one who wrote them."

"What an idiot." Alina's thunderous expression matches mine. She looks over her shoulder at the police station like she's trying to smack the detective upside the head through the walls. "Okay, here's what's happening," she says. "I'm taking these inside, and I'm going to pull prints off them. Won't do any good if they aren't in the system, but it's a shot."

I suck in a breath. "Won't you get in trouble for that?"

"Nah. The captain loves me." She grins. "You head home like Detective Whyever said. Soon as I get the results from this, I'll call you. And while I'm at it, I'll see if they have anything on Holly's case they're not telling you."

"Oh, God. Thank you so much." I don't think twice about hugging her, and it feels like the first good thing that's happened today.

So I'll go home. For now. But I'm not giving up.

If the police don't find Holly, I will.

CHAPTER 39

Things feel so much worse after the sun goes down, and there's still nothing.

Drew and Alina keep checking in on me. They're both still working on their ends of things, and I'm so grateful for their help and concern that I could cry . . . and have done so. But I'm getting antsy again, alone in this big house.

I'm close to getting in my car and driving the whole city, block by block, looking for her.

I've gone through all the upstairs rooms again. I started to tear things apart downstairs, too, but I got frustrated and gave up halfway through. Now, I'm standing in the living room, staring at Holly's picture on the Hearth Wall as if I can will her to step through it, into my arms.

If I get her back, I'm never letting her go. Even if her parents turn up and try to take her. I'll fight for her.

I'll find her.

The moment I decide to head out and conduct my own search, no matter what the police say, my phone dings. Everything in me jumps and convulses at the sound like it has every time the thing's gone off today. I am Pavlov's dog, drooling for scraps of information instead of food.

It's a text from Drew. I stab it open and read:

I'm home, found my phone. I've been cracking every resource I've got. Can you stop over? I'll text you my address. I'm not sure, but I think I found something that could help. It's about your daughter.

I'm stuffing my feet into my sneakers before I finish reading. I'll take anything at all that might help — and I'm relieved that he wants me to go to him. I'm losing my shit here on my own.

On my way.

I send the text as I'm walking out the door, not bothering to lock it behind me. I'm not familiar with the street in the address Drew gave me, but that's what GPS is for. I tap it into Google Maps as I head for the car. It shows up as about four miles away on a road that splits off from Broadway out by the Walmart. Almost in Granby Center. The boonies of Fulton.

After I'm in the car and buckled, I mount the phone on the dash and hit *start* on the driving directions. I'm backing out of the driveway when it rings through the Bluetooth. Alina's name materializes on the screen.

I tap it to answer: "Hey," I greet her, swinging the car onto the road. "Drew might've found something."

"Oh my God, that's great! What did he find?"

"I don't know yet," I admit. "I'm headed to his place now."

"Damn. I really wish I could get out of work tonight." I hear her drumming her fingers on a hard surface. "Well, I've got news too, but I'm not sure how much good it's going to do."

"Anything could help," I tell her, forcing myself not to floor the gas pedal down a residential street.

"Yeah, but so far this just makes everything make less sense." She huffs out a breath. "I actually got a hit on a fingerprint from those notes," she says. "For a Michelle DiMarco."

Mickey?

I'm so stunned and confused that I can't even sputter a response.

"Kat?"

"Yeah. Shit." I slam on the brakes, realizing that I almost blew through a stop sign. "I don't understand," I say. "Mickey never met Naomi or Evie. She was long gone before either of them came to stay with us."

"Wait. Mickey Dee? From the Facebook group?"

"Yeah. That's Michelle."

Alina is quiet for a moment. Finally, she says, "Well, it just can't be right, that's all. Maybe it was a bad print, or . . . I don't know. She touched the paper at some point, then somebody else used it to write threatening notes."

I feel like I'm losing my mind. Every time something new pops up, it's like one step forward and ten steps back. "Maybe," I say, just so Alina knows I'm still here.

At that moment, I spot Naomi's house. Her SUV is in the driveway, and a few lights are on downstairs.

She had a piece of that paper, too.

Detective Wyetta flashes into my mind. His clenched jaw, the spark of anger in his eyes. *Maybe you wrote the note yourself.*

I didn't. But maybe Naomi did. If she got the paper from the house somewhere, it could've already had Mickey's fingerprints on it.

Was she playing me? Did she come over to talk just to throw me off her scent?

Did she put that photo of her in the linen closet, trying to make my father look like a child molester? Trying to make me believe he could've ever done something like that?

"Alina." I keep going past Naomi's house to the end of the road. "You're going to think I'm insane, but is there any way you can come up with a reason to question Naomi?"

She hesitates as I make the turn onto Broadway. "Probably," she responds carefully. "But why?"

"Because . . . you know that picture you helped her take?" I'd skipped this part in my explanation because Alina is still a cop, and I didn't want to put her in a position where she'd know I removed evidence from the scene.

"Yeah?" she says, even more slowly.

"I told you I found it, but I didn't say where." I sigh. "It was in Dad's candy box, in the linen closet. With a note addressed to me, saying I didn't know my father at all."

"Fuck. So you think Naomi was trying to frame Daddy Joe?" she says. "But what about the other note, the one threatening her?"

"Like the detective said, maybe she wrote it herself."

"Damn it. Okay, yeah. I'll get to her as soon as I can," she tells me. "And you let me know what Drew found, all right?"

"I definitely will." I'd confront Naomi myself if I wasn't terrified she'd somehow manage to deny it, then get away with Holly. If that's what happened. This needs to go through official channels. "Thank you so much," I say to Alina.

"Any time."

The call ends, and I try to clear my head and focus on the road. Only a few more miles, and hopefully, I'll be one step closer to finding Holly.

To bringing her home.

CHAPTER 40

Drew's house is a red split-level with an attached garage set back from the road, nestled among trees. The homes on this street are much farther apart than in the city blocks. It feels more country here — fewer cars, fewer streetlights. More stars.

I pull in and stop in front of the closed garage door, in a pool of light from twin lampposts that mark the beginning of a paved walkway leading from the driveway to the door. There's no entryway light on, and the front windows are dark, but a few lights are on deeper in the house.

After turning off the engine, I grab my phone and fire off a text to Drew: *Here!* I get out and start up the walkway, figuring he'll probably meet me at the entrance. But as I draw closer to the house, I feel like something is off. Something about the front door.

It's open. Not flung wide, only a crack, but the sight chills my spine.

I try to believe he left the door open as an invitation for me to come on in, but I can't quite convince myself.

Then, as my foot hits the concrete block in front of the entrance, a low shape slinks through the crack and darts past me.

I let out a startled gasp and spin to look.

It's a calico cat, with green eyes and markings almost exactly like Holly's stuffed toy.

That has to be a coincidence. Doesn't it?

"Drew?" I call into the darkness beyond the door. There's no doorbell, and knocking will just swing it open more. "Are you okay?"

I don't hear anything in there.

Frowning, I unlock my phone and dial Drew's number, then hold it to my ear. It starts ringing. There's no corresponding sound from inside the house, but again, that doesn't mean much. He could have it on vibrate or silent. Or he could be too far from the door for me to hear it.

But what if something happened to him?

I don't like anything about this.

"Drew! I'm coming inside."

I ease past the door, still listening to the ringing in my ear and straining to hear a corresponding sound. The entryway hooks to the right and opens into a dark living room. Faint light from a hallway at the far end, leading deeper into the house, leaks around the shapes of furniture and television.

As I head toward the light, the ringing stops. "Drew?" I dial the number again. "Say something if you hear me, please."

I think I hear a faint sound from the direction of the hallway. A creak, like someone shifting on a mattress.

"Are you back there?" I pick up the pace, listening for the corresponding ring or buzz of another phone. I reach the hallway and find four doors, two on either side. The closest door on the right is open onto a darkened bathroom. The one across from it is closed. Farther down, there's a closed door on the bathroom side and an open door with light spilling through on the left. He must be in there.

I rush down the hall. Now I hear buzzing that matches the rings. "Drew, I'm coming!" I stuff my phone in my pocket without bothering to hang up. When I reach the lighted doorway, I'm halfway into a step across the threshold when my brain recognizes what my eyes are seeing.

The jolt that slams through my body is like an electric shock, so fierce that I feel it in my back teeth. A high-pitched whine fills my ears.

That's not Drew.

Neither of them is Drew.

But there's a phone with them on the bed they're sitting on, flashing in time to the vibration in my pocket.

I don't understand any of this. How is this happening?

"Holly," I whisper.

She sees me and starts to get up, but the other person on the bed with her grabs her arm, and she freezes. A whimper crawls from her throat.

"Her name is Shiloh," Lynette says in a flat, toneless voice. "And she's *my* daughter. Mine and . . . Tyler's."

What?

Holly — Shiloh — tries again to get up. Lynette holds her down, not hard, but firmly enough that she can't go anywhere. They're sitting cross-legged, turned toward each other, but right now they're looking at me.

And I can see the resemblance. Not in hair or eye color, but in the shapes of their faces. That delicate-boned, heart-shaped face that broke me out of believing she was Marisol.

"How . . ."

Before I can formulate any of the thousand questions stuck in my throat, Shiloh makes another sound. Lynette reaches out and lays a finger on her lips. When the little girl looks at her, she makes a series of hand gestures.

And Shiloh signs something back.

It's not standard ASL. They're *communicating*. In some made-up sign language.

And they both seem terrified.

"Why are you in Drew's house?" I finally manage to say. "With Drew's phone?"

Lynette drags in a trembling breath. "It's not Drew's house," she says in that same flat tone, then drops her gaze to the bed. "She made me follow him. Made me steal it."

I blink. "She?"

"I'm sorry," Lynette whispers.

A deafening *bang* goes off in my head. The searing pain that accompanies it only lasts for a few seconds before darkness erases me.

CHAPTER 41

The Journal

I can't believe I went through with it.

I can't believe *she* did.

She didn't even tell me what she was planning to do to the bio kid. I thought she was going after the mom. I had no idea she'd take it that far.

I mean, the dad deserved it, but the kid?

She was only five!

It's been so awful here. The mom is practically in a walking coma, and the house feels . . . haunted. There's only the two of us, but it might as well be just me.

She said if I did it, she'd take me back and love me like a parent is supposed to, but she's not doing that. She's abandoning me. Again.

Why? She got what she wanted. I started to feel it not even three days after that night, that horrible night when she came to the house and told me everything was going to be okay after she *murdered* the little one. I didn't even need to take the mom's credit card and go to the drugstore to find out.

I'm pregnant. With *his* child.

She says I have to keep staying here. She says I'm the only way he'll get convicted and go to jail so she can get away with what she did. She says after that, she'll come for me and we can finally be a family.

But I don't know if I want to be *her* family anymore. I think she might have been lying about some things. Maybe everything. I think the mom really did like me, possibly even love me. And now, she can't love anyone.

Mama Kat is broken, just like *she* wanted.

The worst part is that I know she's not done. It wasn't enough that she killed her daughter. She's going to take *everything* from her.

For the first time, I wonder how much she'll take from me in the process.

How much she'll take from my child.

I should've killed my mother when I had the chance . . . because there's no stopping her now.

CHAPTER 42

My daughter is screaming.

Not Marisol. Lynette.

It's so dark, and I can't move. Can't breathe. Can't speak.
Am I awake?

". . . does it matter if I told her? I did what you said!"

Lynette's voice is breaking, and she's breathing hard. I have to help her. But I can't get to her, can I? I'm in this . . . blackness, this oubliette. She needs me, and I'm hundreds of miles away.

There's a sharp, fleshy crack, and a thud that shakes the darkness.

She's not far away. She's right outside the dark, but I'm stuck inside it. My heart lurches into overdrive, slamming in my ears.

"It matters because I told you not to say anything," another voice says. "I told you to stay away and leave all this to me, and you *went to her house*."

I know that voice. Don't I? I can't tell, because the panic is spiking, locking me further into my limbs.

I need to calm down. I need to save my daughter.

Five things you can see.

Dark. Black. Nothing. Shadows.

Light. The thinnest streak, somewhere beyond my frozen body.

A door.

"Are you done throwing a fit now?"

That voice. It's not possible.

Four things you can feel.

My head is throbbing. My hair is sodden where it hurts. My face is wet.

My soul is cold.

Three things you can hear.

"Give her back. I did what you said. *Give me my daughter back!*"

I hear Lynette.

"I will. If you behave until this is over."

I hear . . . someone else.

Lynette desperately tries to stifle her sobs. "Mother, *please*. She's so scared."

I hear . . . something that snaps my mind.

Two things you can smell.

The stench of betrayal years in the making. My imminent death.

One thing you can taste.

Blood.

My body shivers into loose helplessness. I'm lying on the floor in what I think is a closet. My hands are in front of me, bound together with what feels like duct tape, but my feet are free. Lynette is out there, beyond the closed door, and I have to get to her.

Though my motor control is restored, everything in me aches like a rotten tooth. I grit my teeth, plant my bound hands on the floor, and try to shove up as quietly as possible — but I move too fast. Lose my balance. I drop down with a jerk that smacks the back of my bleeding head into the wall behind me, and a cry escapes my lips.

Footsteps approach my prison. There's a click, and the door swings open. The face that leers down at me splits into a blood-curdling grin.

"Hey, little sister. Remember me?" she says in a maniacal sing-song. "Mickey's back!"

CHAPTER 43

That's not Mickey.

That's *Clara*.

Except it's Mickey. She doesn't look anything like her Facebook photos, but I realize with a start that they must have been fake, too. Just like Evie's. Herself, her husband, her kids. The level of deception she's engaged in knocks the breath from me.

Of course I'd fallen for it, because I never would've recognized her after all this time. Especially since she was eighteen the last time I saw her. And because Clara's a blonde, not a brunette. Plus, her eyes are blue.

Only they're not now. They're brown.

Those are Mickey's eyes.

My father was dating *Mickey DiMarco*.

She killed him. I'm sure of it now. I'm sure of so many things she's done. There's only one thing I don't know, and I think she's about to tell me. I believe she's going to unload all sorts of batshit crazy revelations for my benefit and her . . . daughter's.

Then, she'll send me to join my father.

I can't let her do that. I have to save Lynette. And Shiloh.

239

So for now, I'll listen.

Clara, who's actually Mickey, hauled me out of the closet and sat me on a wooden chair. The movement made me woozy. I'm not sure how much blood I've lost, but I think it's not a small amount. In the light, I confirmed that it's duct tape binding my hands. Now, my feet are also taped to the chair legs.

Lynette is sitting on the edge of the bed, her folded hands squeezed between her knees, eyes wide and frantic. There's a darkening bruise on her cheek where Mickey hit her.

And there's no sign of Shiloh.

"So . . . hair dye and colored contacts?" I croak.

"Very good. You're not an idiot, after all." Mickey slants me a wicked smile. "A spare set of blue eyes comes in handy. And blonde hair. Isn't that right, Lynnie?"

"Mother. Don't," Lynette pleads.

"Especially when certain men have a type. Blonde hair . . . and he likes 'em young. *God*, Tyler was so easy!" Mickey laughs. "All she had to do was play a little dress-up, and he decides she's not really his daughter, so it doesn't count."

"I didn't want to sleep with him!" Lynette cries out. "He was such a creep, and he tried to—"

"Shut the *fuck* up," Mickey snarls, whirling around with her hand raised.

Lynette draws back with a whimper.

"One more word, and you know what's going to happen." She spends another minute glaring at her daughter before she turns back to me. "So, yes. She sleeps with your husband, I smother your precious bio-brat, he goes to jail for it, yadda-yadda-yadda. What a small world, right?"

I don't know how I manage not to react to that, but something tells me it's imperative that I stay calm. Even if I'm seething and screaming inside.

"Very small," I intone, already trying to loosen the tape around my wrists and ankles without her noticing. "Like Tyler's dick."

Mickey throws back her head and cackles. "You know, I kinda liked you back then. You were a funny kid. Almost a shame to kill you now, really."

A sharp sob wrenches from Lynette, but she doesn't say a word.

I have to keep my cool. Keep her talking. "Lynette is my sister, then," I say. "Right? And Hol — Shiloh, she's my niece."

"Hence the resemblance." Mickey nods. "Oh, don't worry. Our daddy didn't rape me or anything like that. He just . . . couldn't resist."

"You slept with him."

"*He* slept with *me*!" A manic light enters her eyes. "He loved me. He's the first person who really did, and I wanted to show him that I loved him, too. I showed him *plenty* of love. It was . . . magical." She stares off into the distance, and her smile falls into a snarl. "But then he called me a *mistake*," she spits. "He tried to give me away to somebody else! I made sure he couldn't, though. I made sure he'd come around and realize we belonged together."

I can't hide my shudder. She's even crazier than I thought.

But Mickey doesn't seem to notice, because she keeps going. "He just needed a little help to get there," she says. "A little more freedom. He wouldn't take it for himself, so I gave it to him. First, I freed him from Evie — she was taking way too much of his attention." She faces me fully, and her brown eyes glitter with mad pride. "Then . . . I freed him from Audrey."

"You killed my mother?" I blurt before I can stop myself.

"Let's say I helped her die," she says, rubbing her hands together. "The way I helped Joe leave this world, so he wouldn't have to see what we were doing to *you*."

Oh, God, this madwoman murdered both my parents. I'm going to be sick.

"You went to the news station. The day he died," I manage. "Bryon said he had a visitor . . ."

"Of course. His devoted girlfriend, bringing him a *special* cup of coffee." For an instant, she actually looks sad. "It didn't have to end that way. I tried to tell him that we were finally free to be together, like I knew he wanted. The coffee was just in case he wanted to do something . . . stupid."

The dark look that infuses her face tells me everything I need to know about my father. Maybe he did make a mistake with her all those years ago, but he *knew* it was a mistake. He knew Mickey was insane.

He just didn't know she was also 'Clara.' Unless . . .

Suddenly, I understood what must have happened that morning between my dad and Mickey.

"He'd found out. And he was going to talk to Lynette, wasn't he?" I blurt, unable to push back the rage. "She was his *daughter*, and he wanted her to know the truth. He *knew* what she went through, and he would've been heartbroken that he never had the chance to be in her life—"

"He had *no right* to my daughter!" she screams. "He was supposed to love me. But he would have turned her against me. Picked *her* over me. I couldn't let him do that, so I told him we would work it out. Then I gave him the coffee." That flash of sadness returns, so brief that I'm not sure it's really there. "I knew there would be no repercussions, either. That's the beauty of being a nurse." She leans toward my face. "I can *make* natural deaths happen."

That definitely sounds like an immediate threat.

Keep her talking, Kat.

"You know, Mickey, I really don't want to be . . . but I'm impressed," I say. "You played everyone, for years. You convinced me you were Evie, made up a whole fake life for 'Mickey,' and got me to tell you everything you'd need to spin all this out. And you executed that with *perfect* timing." I pause for a breath, catching the preening expression on Mickey's face. "But . . . how did you manipulate things so I'd end up fostering Lynette?"

She laughs. "I found a stupid man who'd do anything to get his dick wet."

"Myron Drummond," I whisper. Lynette's father — or so I thought. The one who went to jail for abusing Lynette, especially after she claimed he'd murdered her mother.

242

"That's the one!" A sly smile stretches Mickey's lips. "See, I knew right away, after that magical night we spent together, that your father would take some . . . convincing to be with me. So I did my homework and started hooking up with the dumbest, ugliest guy I could find. Told him that *he* was the father, and he bought it.

"I shacked up with him after I aged out. He was a nobody, fallen through the cracks, and I slipped down there with him. Changed my looks and my name, went to school under the new one, got my nursing degree. The hardest part was getting him to move to Syracuse after you went there with Tyler, so I'd be in the right county. But I did it."

I look past her to Lynette, who's staring at me with silent tears streaming down her cheeks.

"And then . . ." Mickey follows my gaze, and her expression turns cruel. "Why don't you tell her what happened, Lynnie?"

Lynette shivers and swallows hard. "Mother said she had to hurt me. For the . . . good of the plan," she says. She's back to that flat, toneless voice. "She said when I was at the hospital, I had to say Myron did it. That he hurt me, and hurt my mom, and that I thought he killed her. She said they would believe me and not him, because I was the child. And they did."

"I kept track of the foster parents in the county," Mickey says, picking up the story. "I timed it so you were the only one with availability in the area when Lynnie got taken away, and voila! You were your sister's mother."

As she talks, Lynette's features harden. Suddenly, she leaps to her feet. "You told me Kat didn't want me anymore!" she screams. "You said she hated me because I wasn't really hers, and she gave me back, like Grandpa tried to do with you. She had my adoption papers! *She's* the one who wanted me. Not you. And *I want my daughter, RIGHT NOW!*"

With that, she lunges.

And so do I.

CHAPTER 44

Mickey doesn't see me move. She's busy punching Lynette in the stomach, doubling her over. Going for her throat.

The whole time she's been waxing insane on the awful things she's done, the people she's killed, I've been moving my legs, wiggling my ankles. Working the hastily wrapped duct tape loose.

When I stand with the biggest jerk forward I can manage, one foot yanks free.

That'll have to be good enough.

"*Get your hands off my daughter,*" I growl.

Mickey straightens and whirls toward me.

And I swing my bound hands into her face like a club.

"Lynette, *run!*" I scream.

But I don't wait to see if she does it.

Mickey shakes her head and leaps at me. I stumble aside. The back of my shin barks the chair, and I tip over, dragging it with me. The good thing is that my other foot rips out of the tape.

The bad news is that Mickey lands on me.

She puts a hand on my breastbone and pushes herself up. Her greater weight creates a sickening pressure, and I'm terrified it's going to snap. I twist and buck, kicking my feet until one connects with something.

The pressure eases enough for me to shove her with my bound hands. I crab-crawl back before she can slam into me again. Somehow, I manage to get on my feet.

Mickey vaults upright and sneers. "Really? I know I fed you all those stories as 'Evie,' but they came from the truth. I do work in a retirement home. I spend hours lifting fat old people. And you think your scrawny, video-editing ass is going to take me down?"

"No," I gasp. "I think this chair is going to take you down."

She may be stronger, but I'm faster. I grab the chair and spin it around toward her with all the strength I can muster.

It smashes into her side, and she collapses with a cry.

I glance around wildly. Lynette's gone from the room. *Thank God.* Maybe Mickey will end up killing me, but at least Lynette is safe. And she'll find Shiloh. They'll both be safe.

Wait. Where's Mickey?

Something hard drives into my spine. It feels like I've been hit by a car. I snap forward, and my stomach rams against the top bar of the chair back.

My breath whooshes out, and my vision grays.

When it clears, I'm on the floor, and Mickey is looming over me. With a baseball bat.

No. It's a softball bat.

My father's.

"I suppose I don't *have* to take my time with you," Mickey sneers. "All I need is for you to die."

She raises the bat over her head with both hands.

There's a tremendous blast, and I wonder why the blow didn't hurt at all. Maybe you can't feel a traumatic brain injury because your brain stops working before it can transmit the pain.

Then, a thud.

Mickey's face is next to mine, her expression frozen in shock, the side of her head covered in paint like the shed.

No. That's not paint. It's blood.

What —?

"Kat!" Footsteps pound the floor, and Lynette's tear-streaked, panicked face swims into view as she leans over me.

There's a gun in her hand.

"Oh, God. I'm sorry. I'm so, so, sorry." She glances down at the gun, then tosses it away with a small cry and starts pawing at the tape around my hands. "I stopped her this time. I never could before, but . . . I stopped her." She can barely get the words out between her sobs.

"You did, honey," I say. "Thank you."

"I couldn't let her . . ." She has the end of the tape now, and she's pulling it, unwinding it rapidly, loop by loop. "She said you left me, and Grandpa didn't want me, but she lied. About all of it. She made me do it. You have to believe me."

"I do. I believe you."

She gets to the last of the tape and yanks it off. I know it should hurt, but I barely feel it rip at my skin. The wooziness isn't stopping.

There's so much blood in here. Is that all mine?

Lynette backs up and holds her hands out. I take them, and she helps me climb to my feet. "Shiloh," she pants. "I have to find her. She's here, somewhere. Mother never left the house."

"Okay. Let's go."

We cling to each other and move out of the room, maneuvering around Mickey's body. When we get out into the hall, Lynette pauses and stamps her foot hard on the floor. Once. Twice. Then, she waits.

"What . . . ?"

I'm too tired to finish the sentence, but Lynette knows what I'm asking. "If she's close enough, she'll feel the vibrations, and she'll bang something twice. If she can." Her features darken. "Mother might have tied her up. She does that sometimes to punish me."

If I had the capacity to feel any worse, I would've hated Mickey even more.

"Okay," Lynette says after a beat. "We'll try the rooms."

We stop in each room along the hall. Lynette stomps the floor twice, then rushes around, looking in all the places that are big enough to stash a little girl. Then we check the living room. When we move on to the kitchen, I gasp out, "Wait. I . . . need to rest. For just a minute."

Lynette helps me into a bench seat at a breakfast nook by the window. "You okay? I'm going to look in here."

"Yes. Look."

I'm not as okay as I want to be. I have to get someone out here. Police. Ambulance. My phone was in my pocket, but it's gone now.

Thump. Thump.

Lynette stomps in the middle of the kitchen floor and waits, then moves across the room, toward the cabinets. *Thump. Thump.* After another pause, she starts looking in the lower cabinets.

"*Help!*"

The sound is so faint, I almost don't hear it over the opening and closing cabinets. But it's there. I just can't tell where it's coming from.

Thump. Thump.

"*Help!*"

"Lynette . . ." My voice is a papery rasp. I clear my throat and try again. "Lynette!"

She whirls to face me. "What? Do you see her?"

"Come over here."

She rushes across the room. Her gaze darts around the breakfast nook, looking under the table, opening the broom closet behind me.

"Stop. Try again, over here," I tell her.

She returns to my side and stomps her foot. *Thump. Thump.* "*Help!*"

Lynette jerks back in surprise. "That wasn't you. How . . ."

"It's a sound button. I gave it to her," I say. "It was in her pocket."

"Shiloh!" She drops to her knees beside the bench across the table and knocks twice on the side.

"*Help!*"

"She's in here. Oh, baby, I'm coming." Lynette yanks the cushion off the bench seat. Underneath is a hinged wooden top. She pushes it up and gasps, then bends into the storage compartment and lifts Shiloh out carefully. Her wrists and ankles are taped together, and there's another piece of tape across her mouth.

The sound button dangles from her hand, looped over her pinky.

"Mama's got you," Lynette croons as she sits Shiloh on the table and starts delicately removing the tape. "You're safe now. You're safe forever."

Though I'm on the verge of passing out, a smile lifts my lips. They're *both* safe now. Sisters, daughters . . . *family*. Family is what matters.

And then I decide I must be hallucinating, because I hear sirens.

My brow furrows. "Did you . . ."

. . . *call them?* I try to finish. But the words never leave my mouth.

CHAPTER 45

"Didn't I tell you to call me next time?"

That's the first thing I hear when I open my eyes to far too much light.

My vision takes a few minutes to adjust. Eventually, the bright blur resolves into Alina standing by a window, grinning at me. Then I notice the metal rail, the IV stand, the vital signs monitor. I'm in the hospital, and I'm alive. But my head still hurts like hell.

"Did they give me a happy button?" I mutter. "I could really use one."

Alina laughs. "See? I knew you didn't have brain damage."

My brain definitely feels damaged.

I groan. "Don't get me wrong, I'm glad you found me, but . . . how did you find me?"

"Naomi, actually," she says.

"Wait. Naomi *Young*?"

"That's the one." Alina smiles and wanders closer to the bed, looking me over as if she's worried I might start bleeding to death in front of her. "I went to question her like you asked. She was pissed at first, but when I started explaining why I was asking and how somebody was trying to frame Joe, she wanted to help. So I told her everything I could, even about you thinking Daddy Joe was murdered."

"He was," I tell her.

"Yeah, I know that *now*." She smirks. "Anyway, I said Bryon told you he had a mystery visitor the morning he died, and Naomi knew who it was. She was at the studio, sitting by a window in a back room and doing new hire paperwork, and she saw them talking. She says, 'Yeah, it was his girlfriend. Clara.'" Alina pulls her head back and makes her eyes wide, pantomiming shock. "So I went to Clara's house, and . . . there you all were. Even though you said you were going to Drew's. Imagine my surprise."

"Uh-huh." I twist a smile at her. "Turns out, that was not Drew's house."

"No shit."

I grunt as I try to straighten in the bed. "And that was not Clara, either."

"I know." Alina's features sober. "Lynette told me everything."

A ripple of worry passes over me. "It was self-defense," I rush out. "Lynette didn't do anything wrong. It was all Mickey. I mean, Clara . . ."

"It's okay. All I did was tell her the truth."

My heart leaps as I turn toward the voice from the door of the room. Lynette walks in, holding Shiloh's hand. The little girl beams at me and breaks into a run, trying to tug her mother along.

When they reach the bedside opposite Alina, Lynette nods down at her daughter. My niece. "She wants to give you a hug. Is that okay?"

My smile is almost as wide as Shiloh's. "I will *always* take a hug."

Lynette lifts her onto the bed. I hold my arms out, and Shiloh falls into them.

This is everything.

This is home.

CHAPTER 46

One month later

As psychotic as she turned out to be, I actually have Mickey DiMarco to thank for at least one good thing in my life. My bastard of an ex-husband is back in jail where he belongs — and there won't be any overturning this sentence.

Because Lynette knew where in the Syracuse house he'd hidden the nude photos he took of her. And it turned out hers weren't the only ones there.

He had a *collection* of underage nudes.

Even without those, he would've gone down. Lynette was seventeen when he slept with her, when he got her pregnant. She had documented proof from the clinic where she received care during the pregnancy.

That fact, along with the child porn and the willing testimony of the sex workers he'd abused after his release, was enough to get him two consecutive life sentences without the possibility of parole.

What's more, Lynette and Shiloh have moved into my parents' house with me. I'm selling the Syracuse place, and Shiloh is going to start attending the best deaf school in the area this fall. We've all been through enough hell to last those two lifetimes Tyler is serving.

Now, we're ready to get to the good stuff.

The three of us crowd onto the couch in front of my laptop. We have three guests on the Zoom call, chatting away as the big moment draws near.

"Is he there yet?" Alina asks.

I snort. "Do you see him?"

"Hey." Drew waves on the screen from behind the wheel of his car.

"Yep. I see him."

"Then he's not here yet."

Naomi chuckles. "You're not supposed to Zoom and drive, bro."

"Hey, I'm hands-free."

"Does that mean the call, or your driving?" Naomi quips.

That gets a laugh. I'm glad she was able to join the call. She's technically at work right now, but we managed to arrange everything so this is happening on her lunch break.

Lynette signs something to Shiloh, who thinks about it, then signs back so quickly that Lynette signs asking her to slow down. This time, it's ASL. The three of us are learning it together — and of course, Shiloh is picking it up far faster than us slow adults.

"Uncle Drew, Shiloh wants to know if the next time you come, you can bring a kitten," Lynette translates for him.

Drew barks a laugh. "What's wrong with the one right behind you?"

Princess Peach — Peaches for short — twists her head deeper into the back of the couch, as if she knows Drew is talking about her. The green-eyed calico cat who scared the crap out of me at Mickey's ranch house is actually Lynette's, and she had Shiloh's stuffed replica custom-made to be as close as possible. Now that we're all together, the toy is only Shiloh's second favorite thing in the world, because Peaches is her first.

Lynette signs Drew's reply, and Shiloh signs back.

"She says it's not fair if she gets a friend and Peaches doesn't," Lynette announces.

Laughs and happy sighs chorus from the laptop speakers.

"Okay, folks. Pulling onto your road now, Kat," Drew says. "Are we ready?"

"Hell, yeah!" Alina fist-pumps.

"So dramatic." Naomi chuckles. "I love it."

"I see your driveway," Drew says. "Signing off."

He leaves the meeting, and the squares shuffle themselves into a split screen.

"It's time!" Lynette, Shiloh, and I get up. The two of them head for the front door, hand in hand, and I pick up the laptop and follow. Lynette opens the door, and we stand back with enough room for our new arrivals to enter. I hold the laptop in front of me with the screen facing out so everyone can see them, and vice versa.

Outside, car doors open and shut. Footsteps approach the walk. Drew comes into view first, then the much shorter person with him.

They climb the steps. When they reach the stoop, everybody choruses at once.

"Welcome home, Sebastian!"

The little boy gasps, and a sun-bright smile bursts onto his face. "Wow! All this is for me? Do I really get to live *here*?"

"Yes!" I kneel to his level, holding the laptop. Sebastian is seven years old. He lost his parents when he was four, and he's been living with a larger foster family who recently returned him because he was 'too rambunctious.' When I told Drew I planned to stay in Fulton and pick up where my parents left off, he immediately recommended starting with this little guy.

And Sebastian's whole family is excited to meet him.

"This is Aunt Alina and Aunt Naomi," I tell him, pointing to each of them on the screen in turn. "You'll meet them in person this weekend at the party."

"Hi!" Sebastian gives the screen an enthusiastic wave, and they all greet him back. He hops from foot to foot, then looks from me to Lynette. "And you guys are my moms?"

"We sure are," Lynette says before I can respond.

"Wow. Hi!" He pats my knee, then shakes Lynette's hand. Finally, he turns to Shiloh. "I have a baby sister!" he cries.

Without hesitation, he throws his arms around her. And Shiloh hugs him right back.

"Dang it, will you guys put those onions away?" Naomi's voice says from the laptop.

The lump in my throat almost prevents me from laughing.

We usher everyone into the house and wrap up the Zoom call while Sebastian zips around the living room, pointing things out and exclaiming over everything. Drew comes up next to me with a grin. "Reminds you of somebody you know, right?" he says.

"He sure does, Sunshine."

He waggles his eyebrows. "I think I'll call him Drew Junior."

Sebastian really is a lot like little Drew. I hate that the little boy's previous family labeled him 'too rambunctious' when he's so exuberant and cheerful, and I hope they didn't treat him badly. But he's safe here. That sparkling spirit will never be crushed.

"Ooh!" Sebastian exclaims, practically screeching to a halt in front of the Hearth Wall. "You guys get to paint on the walls here?"

I laugh and head toward him. "Sort of. You see all those pictures? That's our family."

There's one missing now, though. I took down Mickey's page and painted over her handprint. After all the harm she caused, the terrible things she did, she doesn't deserve that place anymore.

But there will be plenty more to fill it out.

"Oh. Okay." Sebastian's expression dims slightly. "I, uh . . . I like your family."

I crouch in front of him. "It's *our* family. That means you, too," I tell him. "Would you like to add your picture to the wall? You can even paint on it."

"Yes!" He flings his arms around my neck. "It's *our* family."

I smile. "Always."

THE END

ACKNOWLEDGMENTS

Every person is more than themselves. They're also the collection of their interactions and relationships with other people. And every writer, whether they admit it or not, is influenced by those relationships and interactions that accumulate throughout their lives.

Which means if I listed every single person I'm grateful for here, I'd end up writing an extra book on top of what you just read.

Therefore, allow me to spare you my life's story by sticking to a few of them to start with. Rest assured, there will be many more books, with many more acknowledgments — so if I miss you this time around, I'll catch you next time.

I'm incredibly lucky to be part of a huge, sprawling, crazy family who would require a book by themselves to thank. You all know I love you. I'm especially thankful to my husband and son, who have put up with all my quirks and late nights, mad bursts of inspiration and unhinged bouts of frustration and self-doubt, for many years; my mom and dad, who raised us all to be flexible, accepting, and above all, to never give up; my sisters, who know all my secrets and haven't disowned me yet; and my Therapy Friday crew, who keep proving that any topic of conversation can be fascinating with the right . . . *enhancements*, and that the red dice are not lucky at all.

I'd also like to thank my friends, both IRL (few and far between that they are) and online. Special thanks to Bonnie Scherr for inadvertently reminding me, several years back, that I am in fact a Real Writer™, even when I don't feel like one; to Emmy Ellis for inspiring me to write the kind of books I love without feeling guilty about it; and to Marjorie Teoh for loving everything I write, even if maybe she doesn't love *everything* but would never, ever say that.

Thank you so much to the Joffe Books team for enjoying my books enough to bring me on board. In particular, I'd like to thank Steph Carey for seeing merit in my work and for helping me hone this plot to the sharpest possible edge with her brilliant suggestions, as well as Kate Lyall Grant, who has been fantastic in seeing the book through its final stages and helping me transition after Steph accepted a new opportunity elsewhere.

Finally, my eternal gratitude to you, reader. Whether this is the first book of mine you've read or the twentieth (yes, I've written at least that many!), I'm so glad you spent some of your time with my stories. I hope you found something to root for, something unexpected, and something that made you think. Those are the loftiest goals a writer can hope for.

All my best . . . and until next time,
Sonya Bateman

THE JOFFE BOOKS STORY

We began in 2014 when Jasper agreed to publish his mum's much-rejected romance novel and it became a bestseller.

Since then we've grown into the largest independent publisher in the UK. We're extremely proud to publish some of the very best writers in the world, including Joy Ellis, Faith Martin, Caro Ramsay, Helen Forrester, Simon Brett and Robert Goddard. Everyone at Joffe Books loves reading and we never forget that it all begins with the magic of an author telling a story.

We are proud to publish talented first-time authors, as well as established writers whose books we love introducing to a new generation of readers.

We won Trade Publisher of the Year at the Independent Publishing Awards in 2023. We have been shortlisted for Independent Publisher of the Year at the British Book Awards for the last four years, and were shortlisted for the Diversity and Inclusivity Award at the 2022 Independent Publishing Awards. In 2023 we were shortlisted for Publisher of the Year at the RNA Industry Awards.

We built this company with your help, and we love to hear from you, so please email us about absolutely anything bookish at feedback@joffebooks.com.

If you want to receive free books every Friday and hear about all our new releases, join our mailing list: www.joffebooks.com/contact

And when you tell your friends about us, just remember: it's pronounced Joffe as in coffee or toffee!